D0941951

Our 13ᵗʰ Divorce

A Novel

Matthew Deshe Cashion

Livingston Press
The University of West Alabama

ISBN 13: 978-1-60489-184-3, hardcover
ISBN 13: 978-1-60489-185-0, trade paper
ISBN: 1-60489-184-X hardcover
ISBN: 1-60489-185-8 trade paper
Library of Congress Control Number 2016958354
Printed on acid-free paper
by Publishers Graphics
Printed in the United States of America

Hardcover binding by: Heckman Bindery
Typesetting and page layout: Amanda Nolin, Joe Taylor, Teresa Boykin,
and Sarah Coffey
Proofreading: Joe Taylor, Ciara Denson, Heather Jett, Hannah Evans,
Jessica Gonzalez, Jessie Hagler, Patricia Taylor
Cover design: Amanda Nolin

I'm grateful to the following readers, supporters, and sympathizers,
one of whom I'll thank repeatedly: Heather Jett. Thanks too to Georgia Burgess
Erwin, John Cashion, Myrna & Clayton Jett, The Burgess Family Founda-
tion for Prodigal Sons, Joseph & Joan Bathanti, Bradley Butterfield, Virginia
Crank, Susan Crutchfield. Heather Jett. The Terrell and Jean Beck Sanctuary
for Wayward Southerners, Patrick M. Gilsenan, David Krump, Jill McCorkle,
Roxanne Newton, Otis Redding, Jerry D. Saviano, William Stobb, Sir Robert
L. Treu, Brian Turner, Steve Yarbrough, Kenneth P. Welborn. Heather Jett.
And a note: for readers who may speculate whether some version of
any of the fictional characters you'll meet henceforth is based upon a living
soul, I'd offer this: your imagination has been engaged. Every sentence, even
the weather, is fiction. Honest.

Livingston Press is part of The University of West Alabama,
and thereby has non-profit status.
Donations are tax-deductible:
brothers and sisters, we need 'em.

first edition
6 5 4 3 3 2 1

for John Fred Cashion

my hero,

(1940-2016)

Our 13th Divorce

"History may not repeat itself, but it sure does rhyme."

—*attributed to Mark Twain*

Chapter 1
Jude

The headlights bouncing down my gravel road belonged to a battered old truck pulling a U-Haul trailer, so I knew at once that it was him—my first love and my first heartbreak, father of my only child, king of the bad-luck blues—and I knew he was desperate now, thirty years after I divorced him, for a place to stay. I wanted to drop my garden hose and run inside and turn off all the lights. I was in no shape for the sob story I knew he'd be eager to unload. My three dogs didn't want him either. They lifted their snouts and cocked their ears toward the road, ready to rise and repel, which I was ready to let them do.

His truck was a clue, but the U-Haul was the clincher. Certain objects get attached to people, and moving equipment has been hooked to Buddy Owen since 1957, when (as his first sob story goes) he dropped out of high school, stole his uncle's hearse and drove to Hollywood to become a movie star. A week later, he joined the Army. I had no interest in listening to his latest story. I was fifty-six years old, and I was making progress, finally, on salvaging my own life.

He stopped at the end of my driveway, forty yards away, and even in the near-darkness, I could see him leaning over his steering wheel as if collecting the courage to come ahead. The dogs growled in his direction. I imagined him clinging to some hope that I'd be sympathetic. I could see him betting that I'd live up to the nickname my mother had given me long ago: Jude, after the patron saint of lost causes, helper of the hopeless.

Harold, our thirty-two year-old child, had told me just two days ago that Buddy was nearly suicidal: he was jobless, his fifth wife had kicked him out of her North Carolina home, his health was worsening. And now I saw that Harold had been preparing me for this very moment, when his father would show up after driving eight hours to south Georgia on the same day (some coincidence) that Harold emptied the backyard "condo" and drove his own U-Haul to Atlanta for his first teaching job.

I watered a hydrangea and did not look toward his idling truck. Did he think he was lost? And that was the thought that made my sympathies betray me. I decided then—before I told him no and gently turned him away—that I would take the high road and offer him a mercy hug. The soft and forgiving dusk was partly to blame. I would take pity and stay strong and still say no. Following the hug, I'd look him in the eye, say *hello, so sorry you're homeless, good luck, so long*. I had no intention of letting him ruin the peaceful place I'd waited so long to have to myself. He deserved worse, but I knew where the high road was.

I watered a bougainvillea and looked his way. Once his wheels rolled over the oyster-shell driveway, the dogs jumped and charged and barked as if the Devil himself were coming. Sister Alice barked high, Saint Jerome barked low, and Father Cletus yelped, a trio of ugly notes that shattered what had, until now, been a beautiful evening. I watered my peach tree and resolved to remain peaceful.

But he came too fast and drove too far, which made me spray the side of his truck.

"You're on my grass," I yelled.

He turned off his rumbling engine and stared through his window, a drop of water on his chin. I yelled for the dogs to hush, and they did, of course, though Sister Alice continued to show her teeth. He looked old. He was unshaved a week, unshowered a couple days at least, fatter, white hair, thicker glasses, dollar-store frames, puffy bags beneath the eyes. I'd last seen him ten years ago, after Harold's college graduation in Asheville, and it depressed me even then to see how all his disappointments had caught up with him and collected inside his tired eyes. Now, he looked worse. He looked like he'd spent the last six years sleeping in a lawn chair.

"*Well*," he said. "I expected worse."

"I suppose you're just passing through," I said.

"I'm headed to Palm Beach. I figured I'd retire there."

I laughed at this, a little too loudly, I'm afraid.

When he opened his door, a beer can fell out. When he bent for it, his dentures fell from his shirt pocket to the ground. He bent and groaned, picked up the can and his teeth, bumped his head on the door's arm rest, and said, "Goddamnit" just as calmly as if he suffered a head injury every night about this time. He threw the can on his seat, popped his teeth into his mouth, smiled and spread his arms like some old-time comedian at the end of a bad joke.

"Well?" he said. "How 'bout a hug for your favorite ex-husband?"

I no longer wanted to hug him. But I took pity. I dropped my hose and stepped into the smell of beer and dirt and sweat. I'd forgotten his 6'-5" height, which meant my nose went a little too close to his armpit. His shirt was soaked. When he let go, I took a long step back, stared at my hands and wiped them on my shorts.

He said, "My air conditioner died about 40,000 miles ago."

We looked each other over. We looked for damage behind the eyes, we looked to see how much of the past was present, and we looked to see if anything new was living there. When he asked me for a place to stay, I would tell him no. I didn't want him living out his final years in my back yard.

He stared over the top of his glasses, studying *me* for signs of aging, no doubt, judging my appearance now, after a day of mowing and burning brush. My arms, face and legs were streaked with windblown ashes I'd smudged like charcoal while fighting off mosquitoes. I wore the same work clothes I'd worn since 1976—a t-shirt featuring the peanut-shaped smile of Jimmy Carter beneath the slogan, "The Grin Will Win," and a pair of paint-speckled shorts Harold outgrew when he was nine. My straw hat, string beneath the chin, was a sweat-stained hand-me-down from my father, and my short hair swelled from every side. I made no apologies and offered no excuses. It felt good to no longer care about such things in the presence of any man.

"You're looking better than ever," he said.

I shook my head at his first lie.

He looked at the ground, took a breath, looked back at me. He said, "I was wondering if you might happen to know where a homeless man could find some shelter for just one night."

I looked him in the eye. I said, "Not around here I don't." I paused to let it sink in. I did not look away.

He leaned against the front of his truck and looked over the back yard toward the marsh.

He said, "I was just hoping to camp out somewhere for a night. Maybe I could pitch a tent. Or sleep with the dogs or something. Then I'd be up and gone before anybody even knew I was here."

"No," I said. "Sorry."

I looked at the studio apartment Harold vacated that morning. Buddy looked there, too. My second husband helped me convert it from a dirt floor shed, big as a single-wide garage. We poured and leveled concrete, used a backhoe to dig a septic tank, plumbed, wired, insulated, ran a gas line, hung sheetrock and paneling, added two windows. My third husband helped me build a porch big enough for a chair. We hung a screen door and a wooden door and nailed a new layer of tin over the old tin roof. My fourth husband helped me install a wall-unit gas heater and a window-unit air conditioner. We boxed off a closet, carved a small bookcase into one wall, added a linen closet in the bathroom, put down second-hand carpet, nailed strips of finish around the edges, caulked every pinhole, installed a used stove, refrigerator, water heater. Sprayed for termites. Called it "The Condo."

Harold never knew this, but I built it with him in mind, thinking he'd one day need a place to return to. While he went through college I rented it (very cheaply) to my drug-addicted niece after her first divorce, then to a one-legged AM disc jockey after his divorce, then to a woman in her fifties after her divorce. Then, sure enough, Harold lived there for a year after he dropped out of his Ph.D program and came back home. I had no intention of letting Buddy Owen demolish it.

He said, "I don't mean to be a burden. I'll find something." He scratched the stubble on his chin and stared at the ground. He sounded sincere. He didn't want to be a burden.

I said, "You got nowhere else to go?"

He looked back toward the road. He said, "I'll find something."

I paused. I cursed myself. I said, "Just for one night?"

"So help me, God."

So it was happening. The lost cause was winning; the helper of the hopeless was helping. Still, I refused to be taken advantage of. I told him the truth about the condo's condition and offered no amenities.

"Harold took the bed," I told him.

"I slept on the ground in the Army. I can sleep on the floor."

"There are roaches and maybe rats and snakes, since Harold wasn't the best housekeeper, one of many things he may have learned from you."

"I probably wouldn't notice."

"You're out of propane," I said. "Which means no hot water."

"Does the refrigerator work?"

"It stinks like hell and it's full of fungus."

"I just need a place to store my insulin. That's all I need."

"It should work for one night—one night and maybe half the morning."

"You don't know how much this means to me."

I shrugged, afraid he was headed toward a long and depressing story about another dead marriage, which I had no interest, just then, in hearing. I wondered how long it would take me to get to sleep. Too often lately, while courting sleep, the men in my life intruded. I saw, for example, my fifth husband (Buddy's own brother, no less) a man sick with paranoia, who played with his handguns in his North Carolina basement, wearing his holster over his underwear, pulling a gun on himself while he faced the mirror. I'd see Charlie Clarkson, a man I loved but did not marry, who died from cancer, skin peeling off in my hands while I bathed him. I'd see my fourth husband, J.D., crying endlessly over his dead mother, isolated in the houseboat on the Altamaha River he lived in before he lived with me. I'd see my third husband, Lewis Foster, the son of farmers who never forgave me my single indiscretion, and then I'd see my second husband, Johnny Tate, who loved Harold, at least, and then I'd see Buddy Owen, a reckless man I once loved madly who loved to drink too much, and then I'd see the room I rented from his mother in Asheville where I'd gone after leaving my own mother because I was going to be different from her and live a life full of adventures. Then I'd see a picture of a picture—Buddy, wearing an ill-fitted suit (baptism/1967) holding Harold in the crook of his arm, his other hand spread across his back, watching his son and not the camera, looking for all the world like he might fool everyone and grow into being a good father.

I said, "If you need a shower, you can borrow mine tomorrow on your way out."

"I appreciate it," he said. "It's been a rough year. You just don't know."

I knew. Tomorrow, we might talk, or we might not. For now, I'd be a friend. I could do that much for one night and half a day. He stared at the ground.

"Are you hungry?" I said.

"You have no idea."

I told him to wait, then went inside. When I came back, he was rubbing Saint Jerome's belly. I handed him a spoon, a paper towel, and a container of Brunswick stew, left from a recent batch my mother made.

He said, "You've saved my life. If I don't die in the night, I'll wake up stronger."

"Don't get carried away," I told him. "It's just one night."

Four months later, the dogs still barked at him. I'd added another dachshund and another stray—five dogs total, and they were barking now, at noon, which meant Buddy was strolling across the yard toward my kitchen door, carrying his first cup of coffee and the classifieds. His voice got louder as he climbed the porch steps and spoke to Sister Agnes, the landfill mutt with the soulful eyes who had been sleeping lately on Buddy's porch.

It was Christmas Eve. I was not in the best mood, just now, for his daily intrusion. I was hungry, my back hurt from being crouched at my desk since seven a.m., and I did *not* want to discuss the topic that had kept me from sleeping: Harold was coming later tonight with his fiancée, his first serious girlfriend, a therapist who grew up in New York City, who was bringing her chihuahua.

I'd been crouched at my desk since seven a.m. because I'd been trying to organize another funeral dinner (as Chair of the St. Sebastian Bereavement Committee) while balancing the end-of-month, end-of-quarter, and end-of-year books for Bruce Hill, owner of Hill's Heating and Air Conditioning, now $30,000 in debt. Six and a half years ago, when Bruce's mother died, I felt sorry for him and accepted his marriage proposal. We'd been engaged ever since. Harold, on the other hand, was rushing into his first marriage. They'd been dating only a few months, and their wedding was set for June. Clearly, he hadn't learned enough by watching his father's failures, or one or two of my own.

The best part of my day, the first hour, was long gone. At daybreak, I had checked the river, as I did each morning, and saw the sun rising on a tide so high that water lay in the far edge of the yard. Soft light splashed around the trees and the moss hung toward the water like strips of fur. I looked for passing dolphins or alligators, as I did each morning, and I looked again, briefly, at the spot where, twenty-five years ago, Harold, then seven, found his five year-old cousin's drowned body. Is that the thing that made him so fragile? I'm sure it didn't help. I checked my parents' porch light to make sure they'd survived their sleep. And I looked at my sister Carol's house, then my sister Mary's house, and counted us lucky, again, for having grown up with five hundred acres around us, down to twelve now, though the pine trees shielded us from the subdivision on the other side. I knew Harold would want to raise his children here, but I worried his fiancée favored the concrete, the skyscrapers, the pollution, and the noise of New York. And I feared she would win any argument with Harold, who hated any hint of conflict. He'd spent so much of his life trying to avoid it that he stayed on the verge of a breakdown. His voice had even trembled over the phone when he'd asked whether Libby could please bring her little dog, who would need newspapers spread on the kitchen floor because she was too delicate to be outside among other dogs. I worried over what would happen to him when it didn't work out with her. I feared his father's genes would talk him into drinking himself to death or jumping off a bridge.

And here was Harold's father now, stepping through my kitchen door like a burglar gearing up to ask a question.

"Anybody naked?" he yelled.

I didn't answer him.

"Can I borrow your phone?" he asked.

Again, I didn't answer. My right hand drummed numbers on an adding machine while my left hand lifted invoices. A stranger with a discerning eye might see I once had a talent for piano. The discerning stranger with some intuition might infer that I could have been a concert pianist if only a few key moments of my early life had played out differently—if I hadn't married too young, for example, to the non-discerning man with the dead memory who was marching now across my living room.

He plopped into the recliner, whipped out the footrest and released a sigh he'd been holding for fifty years. It was more of a moan, with a sigh singing backup, his body recovering from the hike he'd begun in the back yard. I'd heard a similar sigh from Harold on the phone just this morning, and I ordered him to cease that habit immediately. Buddy set his coffee cup on the table and stared at CNN, where two men in suits argued over the Y2K computer-induced economic apocalypse they both agreed would arrive January 1.

"Please use a coaster," I said.

He did. In his lap, he dropped his classifieds, two paragraphs circled in red ink.

"Merry Christmas," he told me. With alarming sincerity, it seemed.

"Will you be staying long?" This, my quiet joke he never seemed to get.

The men in suits raised their voices simultaneously. One said, "You're crazy. You don't know your history." The other said, "*I'm* crazy? You think *I'm* crazy? *You're* crazy."

Buddy said, "Where's the remote control?"

"None of your business."

"I'm having trouble hearing you," he said.

"I need to concentrate on this for a moment, please."

"Fine," he said. "I'll go to the bathroom." He released the footrest and lurched his way to the kitchen, sighing like a child, clomping his size 16 Florsheims (with tassels) across the tile. He pulled down my Jacksonville paper from the top of my refrigerator and carried it down the hall into my bathroom.

My thoughts returned to Harold, who was too young for marriage. Thirty-two, yes, but still too young. No matter how long he lived, he'd be too young. He'd been a late starter and a slow learner, not uttering his first word ("bye") until he was four. When he turned three, I took him to a specialist who checked his hearing and set some toys in front of him, but Harold just spent a half-hour staring out the window. On the way home, he cried. When he was six, just after I divorced Johnny Tate, he sank into a deeper silence, so I took him to another therapist. He spent a half-hour staring at the ceiling. On the way home, in the longest sentence of his young life, where he very suddenly appeared like an old philosopher, he said, "I don't understand the point of talking because we all end up alone anyway." I tried desperately to keep him talking, but nothing worked. I tried to make him less fragile, but maybe I tried too hard. Where I failed the most, I'm sure, was waiting too long to divorce his father (a full year after Harold's birth), and then, later, letting Harold spend time with him in the summers, where he learned too much.

Buddy moaned from the bathroom, then sighed, then flushed.

Some afternoons I saw Buddy sitting beside the river in a kitchen chair, leaning forward like a fisherman without a pole, St. Agnes beside him, staring at the same invisible cork. I kept my eyes on him when he sat like that, convinced he was ready to throw himself in the river at the same spot where Harold's cousin drowned. I imagined him nursing his history and fearing for his future, and I imagined Harold doing the same wherever he was sitting. They both worried too much, but Buddy did it with his back to you. It was worse to see the worry in Harold's face—the brow-wrinkle that grew deeper between his eyes, which grew darker as he kept worrying.

Buddy came whistling back down the hall, plopped into the recliner again, whipped out the foot rest, and launched a yawn-moan combo that stretched into reverberating waves, like a geriatric Tarzan calling across the continent.

"Jesus H. *Christ*," I said.

"What's wrong?" He looked around the room, suddenly alarmed.

"Didn't your phone get reconnected?" I said.

"I can't make long distance calls. And I like for people to hear your adding machine in the background. It makes it sound like I'm in an office and you're crunching my sales numbers."

I didn't answer. I convinced myself, again, that Harold had learned more from me than he'd learned from Buddy. One thing I tried to teach him, was that he shouldn't be scared of living alone. In fact, as soon as Buddy barged in, I'd reminded myself how much I liked living alone, free of the obligation to hash out the day's itinerary—decisions about breakfast, errands, bills, lunch, house work, yard work, dinner, television viewing, sleep. Harold hated to be alone, which I feared would be his downfall. I planned to talk to him about it at the first opportunity, if I could get him away from Libby long enough.

From my recliner, Buddy coughed and hacked and moaned while CNN replayed footage of an Iowa family stocking its bomb shelter with beans, board games, and Bibles. I said, "Please be on your best behavior tomorrow for the Christmas party. Harold will be nervous, and she will be nervous, and—"

"I know," Buddy said. "He called me last night. He's kind of anxious about—"

"He called *you?*"

"He's anxious about bringing her here and about getting married, and—"

"And he called *you?* Dear God, what did you tell him?"

"I just tried to listen. I think he'd been drinking, and he was kind of whispering. He has this foolish idea that he's cursed, like he inherited some kind of divorce gene, but I told him that was silly. I told him—"

"It's not *completely* silly."

"I told him we'd have a long talk when he got here. I'll set him straight."

I laughed, then tried to stop.

"What's so funny?"

I couldn't stop laughing. And I realized, if Buddy wasn't around, I might miss him. Most days we got along like siblings who no longer needed to point out their scars. We each knew we'd collected enough regret and sorrow for several lifetimes, so we did not (except for occasional slips on *his* part) need to bring up history or cast aspersions. We were surviving our mistakes. On our best days, in fact, we relied on each other like war buddies who spoke different languages.

I stopped laughing. Then started again. I added numbers, tore and stapled tape, laughed, stopped laughing, then laughed again.

He said, "I know as much about being married as you do. You've been married five times, I've been married five times—there's a lot of wisdom in this room."

"Four times."

"No, I've been married five times."

"Me. *I've* been married four times. I don't count the first one because it was your fault."

"It wasn't *all* my fault," he said.

"Yes it was. Which is one of many reasons you should give Harold no advice."

"Maybe so. Maybe you're right."

"I know I'm right."

"I just said you were right. I'm the least qualified person I know to give advice. What advice do *you* plan to give him?"

"To ignore the advice you give him. Because it's no contest that the bad things Harold learned over the years, he learned from you."

"Who said anything about a contest?"

"I said it's *no* contest."

"You think he never learned anything bad from watching you make a mistake or five?"

"Do you really want to argue over who screwed him up the most?"

When I said this, I thought: now there's a question (though the answer to me was obvious) that could be the subject of my memoir, if I ever wrote one.

"What about when you married my asshole brother for a few weeks and—"

"Harold left *me* every summer in fine condition and *you* returned him in worse condition, chipped teeth, bruises, bad haircuts, unstable mental states. He should wait until he's forty to get married so he can outgrow the sins of the father and the apple can roll far from the tree and all that sort of thing."

"I'm not sure I should get all the credit for screwing him up."

I was sure. But I took the high road and refused to belabor the point.

A CNN expert reported that Y2K fears had seized the holiday spirit in Topeka, where stores were running short on food and water.

Buddy said, "Does his future ex-wife have money?"

"I guess so. She was his therapist, then they started dating."

"He went to a therapist? Why did he go to a therapist?"

"To address all the problems he developed in the summers he spent with you, learning God knows what. Would you like to use the phone now?"

"I sure would," he said. But he didn't move.

Four hours ago, I'd felt peaceful. I'd watered all my plants, first indoor, then out—ninety-seven of them, according to Buddy, who took the trouble once to conduct a plant census, wondering why any sane person would need so many plants. Once outside, in the mild December air, I fed my dogs and took pleasure in their company while they trailed along beside me. What I discovered, even before I got married the first time, was that dogs are the best company. Inside again, I spread Mom's peach preserves over her leftover biscuits, took the biscuits to my desk and started calling my Bereavement Committee members to see who could take food to the Griffin family, whose father had died of a stroke. Now, I was ready to be alone again.

But here was Buddy, flapping his classifieds and dialing a number and clearing his throat, a terrible racket that made me want to leave the room.

He said, "Frank? My name is Buddy Owen, and I'm calling to let you know that I'm ready to start work *today*."

His voice sounded like a coat of paint trying to disguise a disaster— the exaggerated inflections and the loud optimism he'd learned long ago from Dale Carnegie and his influential friends. The obvious secret here was to repeat Frank's name as often as possible.

"I'm doing *super*, Frank. I hope you are. Let me tell you right away: death is what I know, Frank. I embalmed my first body when I was fifteen years old, Frank. Lived in the funeral home my uncle owned in Asheville. Drove the ambulance too, Frank, back before the government started over-regulating the death industry. We had a '55 Cadillac that could outrun the word of God."

He'd been trying to get a job selling final expense insurance to people close to the casket. Coming next, I knew, was a report on the number of funerals he'd attended.

"Frank, I figure I've attended over one thousand funerals. I've dug some graves too, Frank, I'll tell you that. I'm not afraid to get my hands dirty."

After five more minutes, Buddy agreed with Frank that they might not be the best match since Frank required travel and Buddy said he was too old to return to a life of living out of motel rooms. He wished Frank the best with his business, hung up and drew a red X through a circled ad.

I said, "Has it ever occurred to you that you've been making that same call since 1963?"

"It occurs to me every day about this time, thank you."

"You're welcome," I said, sincerely, thinking it takes an honest and well-meaning friend to offer an objective observation about another's history, which a good friend should appreciate.

I said, "Maybe you'd have better luck if you were honest. You've dug your share of graves? Really?"

"I didn't mean literally."

"You'd have better luck," I said again, "if you were honest."

"Every rejection makes me stronger."

I looked to see how strong he was. In a deep frown passed down by a grandfather, a father, and several uncles, he poked his bottom lip out, though *under* his upper lip, so that both lips formed a sickly pucker and sharp lines fell around the edges of his hollow chin. This was the face I saw too many times when we were married and he was slouched beneath a low-watt lamp, holding a whiskey glass on his stomach while he listened to Johnny Cash, his mouth caved in because his teeth were soaking. He'd lost his teeth in his early twenties when he crashed the Cadillac-ambulance he'd been driving. He'd been racing another ambulance down a mountain road in Asheville and flew through a curve and into a brick building, where he was pronounced dead. He floated above the scene for a few seconds, he swears, looking down on his broken bones and bloody mouth before plummeting back into his body. The first time he told me this story he said the crash had made him stronger.

Once, last summer, when Harold's frown reminded me of his father's frown, I slapped his face (gently) and told him never to frown like that again.

Now, Buddy said, "Can I make one more call?"

"By all means. I'd hate to be rude."

"There's no need to be—"

"Far be it from me to be anything but the most gracious hostess, constantly concerned with your well-being."

"You don't have to be—"

"Could I get you anything?"

"No. Maybe just—"

"A Spanish omelet? Some poached salmon?"

"Could you make your adding machine noise again?"

"Of course," I said. So I did, *allegro agitato.*

He dialed another number, frowning, until someone answered and he boomed: "Good morning, Gayle, *this* is Buddy Owen, and I'm calling on this beautiful morning to speak with Mr. Randall Phillips." He looked at the ceiling and frowned. He said, "I'd be *delighted* to hold." When Gayle came back to tell him Mr. Phillips wasn't in, Buddy left my number and said, "Gayle, I hope you have a super-duper Christmas." Then he drew an X through the circled ad.

I said, "Did I hear you leave this number?"

"Is that okay?"

"It's *not* okay. I am not your secretary, and this is not your house."

"How can I pay rent if I don't have a job?"

"You had a job. You've had hundreds of jobs. Try keeping one."

"You keep up that tone, and I'll have to leave."

I laughed again so he'd feel better. I knew, at fifty-nine, with a failed life behind him, and worse health ahead, that it got harder for him to keep going. Without the VA clinic in Savannah keeping him stocked in insulin and antidepressants, and without me giving him a place to live, he'd likely be a dead man.

CNN showed footage of empty malls and closed retail outlets in Detroit, an "out of business" sign plastered across the window of a well-known clothing store, a headless mannequin with her palms facing up, as if to say, *I don't know.*

Buddy said, "Maybe the trip will change his mind. You can learn a lot by being trapped in the car with someone for a few hundred miles."

"Too bad we never went anywhere," I said. "Although, we went far enough for me to learn that you were a terrible driver."

"I learned to drive from Junior Johnson when I was twelve."

"Are you through with the phone?"

"Couple years later I was driving in the Joie Chitwood Auto Thrill Show, which was how I got that part in *Thunder Road*, playing alongside Robert Mitchum, 19 and 57."

"Please pass the phone."

"Next thing you know, I had a scene with Grace Kelly in *The Swan*, filmed at the Biltmore estate." The phone rang while he held it.

"Don't answer that," I said.

"Hello, hello, hello!" he sang like a circus star. "Hello?"

When I snatched the phone, he rolled his eyes like a little boy, which made me think, again, of Harold.

It was Margaret, my Bereavement Committee secretary. I said, "That was my asshole ex-husband. The first one. Peanut Griffin died, and I need beans." I lit a new cigarette.

14

"I know, Margaret. Death rarely knocks at a convenient time. Can I count on you?" I blew smoke back out. "Beans would be great, thank you." I hung up, sighed, smoked.

Buddy said, "Don't get me anything for Christmas."

"Okay."

"It's the saddest time of year for me. And you have no tree up, no music going, no chestnuts roasting. It's not going to be very festive for Harold and his therapist. Gives me the blues."

"Maybe you'd find it happier at your house."

"No. I get the blues there too."

I understood. I knew he was worried about Harold. He was worried that Harold would spend his life searching in vain for the same things Buddy had spent his life searching for: lasting love, money, meaningful work, self-respect. I'm sure he worried, as I worried, about Harold marrying his first real girlfriend. And if that relationship failed, he worried, as I worried, that it would take Harold a very long time to recover. We both worried that he'd lose a decade to drink, another to regret, another to shame and guilt. I worried that eventually Harold would lose his job and end up living in my back yard, replacing his father, who would probably die out there, leaving me his corpse to discover one fine morning.

And I worried that Harold also worried about these things. I feared his worries were getting worse. He already hated teaching. And he was turning too quickly toward some woman who claimed she could save him. I had little faith in her. I pictured her as a prima donna big-city pretentious type who had never once gotten dirt beneath her nails and had never spoken kindly to anyone who had. But I would open my home to her and give her a fighting chance. For Harold. CNN went from images of a tsunami in Japan to a smiling supermodel-anchor to a commercial for adult undergarments.

Buddy said, "Need anything from the drug store?"

"Stool softener and Preparation H."

"I have that at my house. Need anything from Winn Dixie?"

"I'd like my own stool softener and my own Preparation H, please. There's also a grocery list on the refrigerator. For your reward, I'll make a pot of chili and give you half a bowl."

"Should I just mention your name at the register, or do they still take cash?"

I picked up three twenties from the right side of my desk, wrote myself an IOU, and handed him the cash.

I said, "What's for lunch?"

"I'll get a little handout from my girlfriend at the deli. She loves me."

"Bring me a half-pound of thickly-sliced turkey. Hurry, I'm hungry."

"Do you ever think we should get remarried? To each other, I mean. We could be like Liz Taylor and what's-his-name."

"Are you still here?"

"I'll let you think about it while I'm gone."

I was proud of myself for not being too hard on him. If I'd wanted to be cruel, I would've reminded him that in 1969 I'd taken two-year-old Harold away from North Carolina and home to Georgia because I believed his healthy future depended on Buddy's absence. I wanted him to grow up under the watchful eye of women, a grandmother/godmother on one side, two aunts on the other side, me in the middle. And it *was* good—Harold learned from women how to be a man. He was never burdened with the belief (taught by men) that women are too mysterious. He attended the same school I attended with my sisters, St. Sebastian, where the nuns taught him the basic tenets of good behavior. It was *I* who taught him his firm handshake. It was *I* who taught him not to go around with his mouth hanging open. It was *I* who taught him to stand up straight, to look people in the eye, to smile when all else failed.

But I didn't belabor the point with Buddy Owen. I didn't say that Harold's future wife would thank *me* for raising him so well. I didn't say that his home had always been with me. I didn't say that my home was the sanctuary he was bound to and could never leave. I didn't need to say those things. I knew where the high road was, and Harold did too—it's something else I taught him.

Chapter 2
Harold

December 24, 1999

Libby, my fiancée, held tightly to Penelope, her chihuahua, who shivered in her lap while I crept through the center of Atlanta's eight-lanes of rush-hour traffic toward my mother's house, three hundred miles away. Libby suffered intense interstate phobia, so I wanted to do whatever I could to make her more comfortable. She believed every driver was drunk, blind, suicidal, murderous, *and* stupid, and I did not disagree. She'd taken a Valium last night while packing, another at breakfast so she could get through the day without excessive dread, and then another a half-hour ago, just after she clicked her seatbelt. If the Valium helped, I couldn't tell, which made me feel bad for her. I admired the courage she showed simply by getting in the car and agreeing to go.

My top speed was fifteen miles per hour, but every time I reached it, I had to hit the brakes again. Every time I stopped, Libby sighed. When Libby sighed, Penelope squirmed. When Penelope squirmed, I tightened my grip on the wheel. My hands were sweating.

I said, "I love you."

"Please," she said. "Be careful."

"Okay," I said. I put more space between my car and the car ahead so Libby would feel safer. I stroked Penelope's ear. I turned on the radio news, thinking the noise might distract her, but an authoritative male spoke too dramatically of the chaos we would face at the turn of the new year, when global financial systems would go kaput because of a computer glitch.

"At least we'll have each other," I said.

"This traffic," she said. "Are people evacuating?"

"This is the daily evacuation. It helps if you close your eyes. That's what I do."

But she didn't laugh. And she didn't close her eyes. She turned off the radio, which was an action I should've taken sooner. I wanted to move three lanes to my right, so I'd be in the outside lane, the slow lane, where

Libby would feel safest because no cars would be on her right. Once there, I would go as slowly as I could for as long as I needed to make her more comfortable. I looked over my right shoulder to check my blind spots.

Libby slapped her door. I thought we'd wrecked without my knowing it.

"Shit," I said. And then, "Sorry. That just kind of scared me is all. Are you okay?"

"That truck's blinker came on," she said.

"I saw it. But at our current rate of speed, which is five miles per hour, it's fairly unlikely that we will suffer a fatality." Then I apologized again. I said, "I'm sorry if my tone was sharp just then. This traffic makes me anxious too. It's enough to drive us off the edge, so to speak."

"I can't help it," Libby said.

"I know. It's okay."

"I'll take another pill."

"Give me one too," I said, but she didn't laugh.

She sighed. Penelope squirmed. My hands sweated. I tightened my two-handed ten and two grip on the wheel and stayed in the center lane, boxed in by loud and slow-moving trucks.

"We're making steady progress," I said. "Two hundred ninety-nine and a half miles to go. Maybe some Brahms would help. Would you like to hear some Brahms?"

She sighed again. Penelope squirmed. I tightened my grip. I looked over my right shoulder at the wall of tractor-trailers.

I found Libby, three months ago, in the yellow pages. I picked the first available counselor with the quickest opening because I needed a prescription that would prevent me from breaking into an anxiety-ridden sweat every time I walked toward a classroom to face the students who insisted on facing me. I was no good at teaching, and I did not like it, but I didn't know any other job I could try to get away with performing. Libby told me then that she was not a psychiatrist "per se" and could not write prescriptions. Furthermore, she said she didn't believe prescriptions should be used for conditions one could manage by applying more natural methods.

She'd said, "I prefer the talking cure."

"How long does that take?" I answered. And she laughed a musical laugh that made me want to keep talking.

I looked over my right shoulder again to see if I could get over. She sighed. I tightened my grip.

I knew her background, so I tried to sympathize. She'd grown up in New York City with parents who had each had a parent killed in a car crash, then Libby's older brother, (he was 13; she was 10) was struck and killed by a drunk driver who ran over a sidewalk and pinned him to a building. She developed agyrophobia (fear of crossing roads), and her parents clung to her more fiercely. They understood they'd been marked as victims, and they planned their lives carefully to avoid further trauma. To get to Atlanta for her first job, after a series of phone interviews, she took two Valium to board the plane, then another Valium for the taxi ride to the furnished apartment she'd rented (with her parents' help) within walking distance to her new position among a staff of counselors connected to an HMO. When she told me these stories, it endeared her to me. I saw us both as vulnerable underdogs who would help each other survive a difficult and dangerous life. She was determined to help me, which I appreciated, so I wanted to help her now, in the car, by easing her travel-related anxiety. What I feared was reacting badly to her bad reactions, which could cause a chain reaction of escalated exchanges that ended badly.

I looked over my shoulder. There was no opening. She sighed. Penelope squirmed.

I'd prepared for the trip by drinking a bottle of wine the previous night, thinking a hangover would dull my rapid-firing neurons enough to ensure calm reactions. I wanted to remain patient. I wanted to avoid all tension altogether while I drove her to meet my parents.

I looked over my shoulder again, looking for an opening to perform a graceful lane-change. She sighed and Penelope squirmed. I commanded every muscle in my body to go limp—one of the relaxation strategies Libby herself had guided me through as a way for me to stand in front of my students without sweating. Usually, the first ball of sweat popped through my forehead while I was calling roll, often by the M's. I'd pretend I had an itch so I could wipe it, but a second sweat-ball soon followed the first, which meant a waterfall was on the way.

The students' glazed eyes were the same eyes I'd seen when I taught in graduate school, just before I dropped out, which is when I promised myself I would never teach again. But I'd been desperate to leave the condo/shed behind my mother's house that I'd inhabited for a year while I bartended at a smoke-infested swamp of a blue-collar dive, and when I applied for a position at a technical college in Atlanta (having completed "at least 36 hours of graduate coursework"), I got a call the next day from the department chair, Richard Jenkins, who said he was desperate for "an emergency hire" to replace a teacher who had abruptly quit for reasons he could not, for legal reasons, just then get into. A week later, one day before the first day of classes, I drove a U-Haul to a studio apartment on the northern side of Atlanta, unpacked, and went from listening to drunks (and being drunk myself much of the time) to standing blank-faced in front of students who expected me to say important things. I sweated. In the Women's Studies course I'd been asked to take over, I sweated on the way to class. I wore dark clothes, wiped my forehead on my sleeves, claimed to have the flu, dismissed classes early.

I stumbled through my first semester, taking comfort in the knowledge that I would quit at the end of the year. Every night, while I wasn't sleeping, I replayed every tortured second of every class—moments when I froze in the middle of sentences and couldn't remember what I'd wanted to say or what I'd already said, and other moments when I knew exactly what I wanted to say but the proper words lived a long way off. Or I'd recall a moment when I managed to complete a fluid sentence of some substance, but I'd dwell on how I delivered it in monotone while facing the chalkboard.

One student evaluation went like this: *I think maybe Mr. O has a gland problem. Or Lupus. He looks pretty pale. He could also stand to shed thirty pounds, which might help his sweating condition. I'm a nursing major, so this class is a compleat waste of time for me accept I get to diagnose Mr. O on a daily bases. He should get a work-up.*

At the end of my first semester, Richard Jenkins, a thick-bearded perpetually-exhausted Vietnam vet with cigarette breath, brought me into his office, pointed to a chair. He pulled a liquor bottle from his bottom drawer, poured a shot into a paper cup and passed it to me. He said, "Listen, Harold. We need to get your evaluation scores up. My bosses can't read, but they look at numbers and they look to see whose numbers are average and whose numbers are below average. If we can get you fairly close to average, you'll be okay."

He took a sip from his cup and I took a sip from mine. He slouched a little further in his seat, looked out his window, then back to me. He said, "The key to teaching is to accept it as a lost cause. Learn the art of losing; it isn't hard to master. That's from Elizabeth Bishop. The poet. You like baseball? Think of yourself as part of a very bad team—you might win a few, but you're going to lose most, and you're going to suffer through some long seasons that will make you wonder why you shouldn't shoot yourself in the heart, but after the short offseason, when you nurse your injuries by drinking too much and find yourself grown older and slower, you can come back on opening day and say to yourself, 'Maybe this year, we won't lose as many as we lost last year.' How's that?"

He refilled our cups and gave me a lecture on the history of the Cubs since 1908, when they'd last won the Series. I appreciated it.

Mr. O. just sits there the whole time and lets the know-it-all goody two-shoes run off at the mouth about their boyfriend problems like he just wants to leave so he can get back to playing with his stamp collection or whatever. He looks like he could use a girlfriend.

The lectures in my head, which I kept to myself, went like this: "I'm not qualified to tell you anything. I understand how much you hate being trapped in this white-bricked room while the sun is shining. If we could watch cartoons, it'd be more worthwhile. Maybe I'll design a course in cartoon-watching. Until then, I apologize in advance for the punishment I'm required to inflict upon you, grade-wise, when you fail to remember what I'm going to do a poor job teaching you. You have my sympathy." While I thought these things, the students slouched and yawned. Richard Jenkins said, "Maybe you're not inflating grades enough. Try that."

I faced my students with the certainty that my fraudulence was obvious. *Sometimes its hard to even hear Mr O when he's talking and I sit in the front row. He probably should borrow whatever meds my crazy math teacher Ms. Osborne is taking. Talk about crazy? That woman's crazy. Is Ms. O single? Mr. O and Ms. O ought to get together, make some baby O's. Something.*

After just one month, I turned to the yellow pages, found Libby, and went to her. I liked her short red hair and narrow glasses. I imagined her as a wild woman eager to shed her professional demeanor. I pictured her naked, with her glasses on, framed degrees hanging over her bed, violins coming from lavender-scented speakers. When I told her, after my first half-hour, that I couldn't afford the talking cure, she said, "Let's meet when I get off. We'll call this a consultation, end your official therapy, then have a date."

"A date," I said. It sounded like a foreign word. When I quit tending bar, I stopped drinking and took a vow of solitude, prepared to punish myself for having slept with three married women—all of whom initiated it after they talked of being lonely—something I would have discussed with Libby if she hadn't terminated my therapy. And during my brief vow of solitude, I'd been healthy. I visited my apartment complex treadmill three times a week, usually at 9 p.m., when the room was empty. Then I'd go home and shower and lie on the couch in a deep and relaxing silence I promised myself I'd never ruin by succumbing to desire, that evil thing.

Then a therapist asked *me* for a date. I tried to think of another word for "no." Something desperate lurked in her hazel eyes, even then, and it scared me. I imagined she hadn't had a date for a very long time, which made me think she had problems worse than mine. This reminded me of the only advice my father gave me, which was this: don't get into bed with anyone whose problems are worse than yours. Then again, I thought, she probably knew the pain of loneliness, which meant she might be grateful for my company for the next fifty years and be easy to please and never desire another thing. Then I imagined our lives after fifty years and worried that she'd die first and leave me lonely. It was best to nip that sorrow in the bud by saying *no* right now. Thank you, but *no*.

"Okay," I said. "A date."

We met on a bench a few blocks from her office, in Centennial Park. It was a hot and bright afternoon, and she wore sunglasses too big for her head, like someone famous hiding from her public. She smiled, looked around the paved paths at mothers pushing baby strollers. The park had been created for the '96 Olympics, and in July, a terrorist's bomb killed two people (though one death was from a heart attack) and injured a hundred others.

I said, "Were you here for the Olympics? The bomb? That was scary, wasn't it?"

She turned to face me, propped a foot on the bench, chin on her knee. And she started talking. While she talked, my mind wandered. I made a note to myself that I should ask her whether great listening skills could be learned. I wondered, while she continued talking, whether being a bad listener was a symptom of the pernicious selfishness that would cause me forever to be alone. Fearing her eyes would distract me more, I watched her lips. Her words came rapidly, without pause, more words per minute than the fastest typist could ever type, and the sentences piled upon themselves with such manic force that I pictured a fast-forwarded movie of blurry railroad workers laying tracks from east to west. I pictured a 9-volt battery beneath her tongue. I heard fragments of John Bonham's drum solo, "Moby Dick." She'd been talking a long time, it seemed, without me making out too many words. I blinked and tried again to listen.

"And I'm *so* homesick," she said. "Do you mind? I feel like disclosing. All day I hear people disclose and I have to sit there and act interested. Now it's my turn, damn it." Then she laughed. "The truth is, I cry every night when I get home to my dog and I cry again in the mornings before I go in, and there are some mornings—I feel vulnerable revealing this—but there are some mornings when I simply can't get out of bed, so I call my father, and he orders me to get up and get going. I'm also starting to feel, for the first time in my life, some profound anxieties associated with aging. I'm thirty-three, and I *might* want children, but probably just one because of all the global problems related to overpopulation. Would you like to have dinner?"

I looked down the path in front of us and saw that it was clear. I saw a version of myself jump from the bench and sprint away, leaving Libby to stare open-mouthed at my vanishing back. What she needed was a well-conditioned boyfriend who could listen at great length while she detailed the minutia of her problems as they waxed and waned. Which meant, in no time at all, she'd accuse me of not listening. Which I would deny. Then I'd repeat what she'd said, but I'd get it wrong, and she'd say, "See. You only care about yourself." And I'd have to wonder, for the first time ever, whether this was true. Which would mean she'd be helping me. I'd been alone too long. I needed help from someone who could help me get to know myself. And we had this in common: I too had trouble getting out of bed some mornings. But wasn't that an unhealthy thing to have in common? Or would this produce a higher rate of sex? I needed to be alone to think about it. Maybe I'd solicit my parents' opinions. What I knew I wanted most fiercely that very second was to rush home and eat a slaw dog in front of a baseball game so I could spill mustard on my shirt without a witness pointing to the obvious.

"Dinner," I said. "Dinner would be nice."

She talked while she led the way, turning every few seconds to make eye contact. I saw that she walked with a little limp, but I hoped she hadn't noticed that I'd noticed. I tried to listen. She said, "I hate the heat of Atlanta and I miss the cold of New York, and I hate the provincial attitudes of some people, and I miss the progressive attitudes of my New York friends, and I miss the New York streets where sometimes I feel safer because I know not to trust anyone; whereas, here in the good ol' South, you might be seduced more easily into believing that folks are trustworthy, though I hope you know I don't approve of such wide-sweeping generalizations as the ones I've just made."

One leg was shorter than the other it seemed. When she stepped on her left foot, we were the same height, but when she stepped on her right foot, her head rose above mine. And how did I know, right then, that if I wasn't careful, we would end up married?

"I want to go home," she said. "I miss my family."

I liked this about her. I wanted to go home too, very often, which meant we probably shared the sensitive parts of the soul that had to do with connecting one's spirit to a particular place whose ground and air know you intimately, immediately.

She said, "My parents are still affectionate after forty years of marriage—the perfect model for a long-lasting relationship that keeps renewing itself, you know, even after the terrible trauma they went through early on—the kind of trauma that most couples don't survive, which was the death of a child, my older brother in this case. Are your parents still married?"

We were at the restaurant door now, which I entered first so I could demonstrate my progressive attitude, learned from an essay in chapter 9 of my Women's Studies textbook that suggested opening doors for women reinforces the traditional power structure that puts men in permission-granting positions. In this case, I was doubly progressive because I didn't presume that her slight limp made her helpless. I barged through the door, then looked at Libby to see if she'd been impressed. She looked confused. She widened her eyes and lifted her eyebrows, which made me want to back up and try re-entering.

She said, "I just asked if your parents were still married."

"Oh no. No, they've each been divorced five times. Booth or table?"

Libby led us to a corner booth. She narrowed her eyes and smiled. She said, "You must have some juicy issues." I felt a sweatball forming between my eyes. I looked at the door, plotting my escape. I'd already said more than I'd intended. When she went to the bathroom I would run. Then never visit this side of town again.

She said, "Have you had trouble managing the grief in your life?"

"The grief?"

"My brother's death inspired me to become a therapist so I could help people manage grief. I think we endure relentless heartbreak and spend our lives looking for ways to either medicate or to kill ourselves. It's difficult, isn't it?" She tilted her head and stared at me.

"Yes," I said. "It *is* difficult, sometimes."

While we ate, she detailed the day her brother died, the funeral, the difficult days afterward, the months and years of *healing*, and her eyes watered while she talked of how old he'd be now and what he'd be doing, and how they could have helped each other at different times of their lives, like when she moved to Atlanta, maybe he would have moved with her, just to help her adapt to a strange new place.

She said, "Has anyone close to you ever died?"

"My cousin drowned in the river in front of my house when she was five and I was seven. I was the one who found her, but I've never really talked about it and no one's really mentioned it since then." I looked at the door again.

"Classical repression," Libby said. "That's the worst grief-management style. All the pain lives in the subconscious, but it constantly manifests itself in self-sabotaging ways. Every time we *ingest* pain, we must secrete it."

I couldn't finish my shrimp vindaloo. Libby's eyes were too intense, and they were constantly locked on mine, trying to prod around behind them and uncover things I had ingested but not secreted. I wiped my sweating face with my napkin and blamed the spicy food. I promised myself I would never see her again.

The following night, we met on the same bench, then walked to a Thai restaurant. She asked about my teaching day, whether I had sweated. When she narrowed her eyes and waited for my answer, I got nervous. When she stared at me above her wine glass, a ball of sweat popped through my left armpit.

"Did you grow up in a non-disclosing environment?"

I picked at my red curry. "Not much."

"What?"

"I didn't sweat too much today."

"Are your parents disclosers?"

"My parents?"

"Did they—particularly your father—provide consistent emotional access and create an environment that valued language?"

"You mean am I standing at the back of the historically long line of deeply repressed nonverbal men uncomfortable discussing matters of intimacy?" This was straight from my Women's Studies textbook, Chapter 1, which addressed common perceptions and stereotypes related to gender.

"Yes."

"I'd rather not discuss it."

She didn't laugh. "How did you keep from sweating today?"

"Put them in groups."

"Collaboration comes more naturally to women, of course, so it's a wonderfully appropriate teaching apparatus for men."

"Some days I show movies."

"Pretty soon you'll be lecturing loudly with the passion of classical orators."

"Some days, they color."

"That's wonderful."

"I was kidding." I scratched my stomach.

"You just made a stain on your shirt."

I watched her stare at the stain. I swore I'd never see her again.

Two weeks later, I moved in. A week before, she had played her violin for me—a Bach piece that convinced me she knew the dark soul's deepest truth about the superiority of music over language, and I saw her as the instrument capable of sharing and receiving this truth, so I felt what I imagined love must feel like because there was no language to account for it.

She invited me to split her rent, providing I agreed to the following terms, which she typed out and had me sign:

1. Penelope will sleep between us.
2. You will keep our only bathroom spotless.
3. You will not exceed two alcoholic beverages per night.
4. You will prepare (or purchase) a sugar-free, flour-free, and gluten-free vegetarian dinner with one serving of fruit four times a week.
5. You will shower daily, including weekends and holidays, and you will attend daily to all other hygiene-related rituals (e.g. brushing, flossing, toe-nail trimming).
6. You will walk Penelope every weekday when you get home (I'll walk her on weekends).
7. You will stop watching sports. They emphasize wrong-headed ideas of competition and masculinity.
8. On nights when you'd like to initiate acts of intimacy, you will do so prior to 9 p.m.
9. You will maintain a separate checking account, but you will provide me, on the first day of each month, individual checks for the amounts listed on the attached document.
10. If you should like to articulate your position on a disagreeable issue, you will type out the rationale behind your position, and you will email the document to me as an attachment (double-spaced, 12 pt font, Times New Roman) between 8-11 a.m., Mondays through Fridays, allowing me sufficient time to prepare a response, which I will deliver orally, over dinner (see #4), while you listen without interrupting.
11. You will develop your listening skills.
12. You will never lie.
13. If I should ever, in a moment of weakness, drop my guard and trust you to drive me somewhere, you will be respectful of my travel-related phobia (beyond my control) and you will proceed, always, with utmost caution.

I trusted her uneven legs. I loved her violin. So I learned to cook with tofu, made broccoli lasagna, continued not to drink, swore off sports, scrubbed the toilet and tub, wrote checks at the beginning of each month, and walked Penelope, which meant carrying her across intersections and picking her up if another dog appeared within fifty yards, whispering all the while in a soft baby-voice that everything was going to be just fine.

In early November, following a brief bit of unsatisfying sex, she said, "Let's get married."

I stared at the dark ceiling. My pores prepared the floodgates. I opened my mouth and closed it and opened it again. I said, "Wouldn't that be a lot of trouble?"

"What are you really afraid of, Harold Owen? Tell the truth."

I made a passionate speech about the "institution" being a tradition worth killing off, paraphrasing from Chapter 14 of my Women's Studies textbook, a perspective that saw no need, in the century to come, to enter a relationship under legal mandates mixed from church and state.

I paraphrased: "In the new century, the sacrament of matrimony may as well be given the sacrament of last rites."

"Of course you're afraid," Libby said. "I know your history. Which is exactly why you *should* get married. You should confront your biggest fear by facing it. Those afraid of flying should get on planes. Those afraid of making speeches should make speeches. Those afraid of being alone should be alone awhile. That used to be my biggest fear, but I conquered it long ago. I'm not afraid of being alone. I'm not. I can *be* alone. *You* are afraid of repeating your parents' failures. But you must transcend the people and the place that spawned you. You are not your parents. You are you and I am me and we are here together."

"I am the eggman."

"You need to assert your individual power and claim your destiny."

"I am the walrus."

"You're afraid of becoming a real adult, which means surrendering a significant amount of selfishness. You're a scared little boy."

"Coo-coo-cachoo."

"You need me to help you see these things."

"Experts experts—"

"And I need to be needed, valued, and respected, though that doesn't make me needy. I'm *not* needy. Do you think I'm needy? I am *not* needy. I also believe in a formal and symbolic statement of commitment expressed in front of witnesses. And I will never leave you, Harold Owen. All your life you've had people leave you, but I won't leave."

"Pigs from a gun, see how they run."

"Our wedding will be small and intimate. Family and friends. And my clients. I need my clients to be there. They need to see me as a healthy model. And it's good for business."

"See how they run."

She kissed me goodnight and rolled over. I stared at the dark ceiling. In my head, the Beatles sang; Yellow bits of custard dripping from a dead dog's eye.

The next day, I called my mother. She said, "Oh, Harold. Don't be a wuss. If you have big doubts, take action. I had big doubts about each of my marriages, but I thought things would magically work themselves out if I applied enough willpower. But they don't magically work out. You have to decide how much imperfection you're willing to live with, then lower your expectations. And you know how people say, 'You can always get divorced?' That's the wrong thing to say. It's like saying you can get a massage after you've had a head-on collision and broken your neck. Which is true, of course, but once you need one massage, you'll be desperate for a massage every day of your life. I'll tell you something else. If you're afraid this is the only woman who will come along and show you any interest, you're wrong. But the best advice I can offer is for you *not* to call your father for advice. Promise me you won't ask your father for advice."

I promised and hung up. I called my father.

He said, "Hell-fire, Harold. Next to your mother, I'm the least-qualified person I know on the subject. But since you asked, I'd say don't worry *now*, it'll get worse later. And I'd say never get into bed with anyone who has worse problems than you. And don't be afraid to walk away. The customer who can walk away is always in control. But hell, if you can't walk away, you can always get divorced. You wreck one car, you get another car, right? Are you writing this down?"

On the Saturday afternoon following Thanksgiving, Libby entered the kitchen, kissed me, and calmly delivered the traditional ultimatum. She said, "Marry me or move out."

I walked away. I said I was taking Penelope for a walk, but three blocks later I realized I was carrying the leash and had forgotten the dog. I went to the back booth of a bar, drank six beers, listened to the country music some sad sack of shit kept playing on the jukebox, wiped my eyes when George Jones said they placed a wreath upon his door. Alone inside this bar of sad and lonely people, a decision struck me like a blow. I would break up with Libby because she had helped me mature enough for the woman I'd meet next, who would never have to remind me how far I'd come. Then I said this out loud: *she has helped me mature.* I rushed to the nearest jewelry store, bought an engagement ring on credit (taking the pretty clerk's word on the beauty of the ring) and quickly walked home.

I sat beside her on the couch, pulled out the ring, picked up her right hand and slipped the ring on her index finger.

She pulled her right hand back and gave me her left. She said, "Have you been drinking?"

"Would you do me the marry of pleasuring me?"

She stared at the ring. She stared at me.

She said, "June 21st. We'll get married on the summer solstice. Or on the closest Saturday to it."

"June of 2001?" I said. "As in nineteen months from now?"

She pulled the ring off, held it out to me and turned away.

"June as in seven months!" My voice was strong, as if to say, *I am not afraid.*

She put the ring on and kissed me. Penelope licked my arm.

The next day, I called my mother to announce June 21st.

"June of 2001?" she said. "As in nineteen months from now?"

"No."

"Oh, Harold. Well, that's what engagements are for. You'll be sure in seven months. Just don't be a wuss, Harold. If you think you're stuck in a bad situation, take action so you won't be stuck for long. Life is too short to spend any amount of it unhappy. Think of your father."

I thought of my father. She was right. I would not be a wuss. If I needed to take action, I would become the kind of man who would not be afraid to take action.

In the car now, Libby bent to check her mirror. She stiffened her legs, pushed her head against the back of the seat and held tightly to Penelope, who continued shaking.

"I need to say," she said. "I'm feeling a bit uncomfortable with how close we keep coming to the car in front of us."

"You *need* to say that?" And there it was. My failure to react properly to

Libby's reaction to the stressor of traffic. "Sorry," I said. "I'm trying very hard to take your discomfort into account here, believe it or not."

"I know," she said. "I'm sorry."

"Not much longer now. Just two hundred and ninety-eight miles to go." My tone carried a sharper edge than I'd intended, clearly a reaction to the tension locked in the car with us.

"Sarcasm is for children," she said, and stroked Penelope's ear.

I inhaled and held my breath to the count of eight, then exhaled to the count of eight, just as Libby had instructed me to do so I'd feel calmer while walking toward the classrooms I feared entering. And just now, I felt relaxed enough to communicate to Libby the rationale behind my driving strategies.

"The thing is," I said. "I'm more concerned with the car behind us, which I don't believe you're in very good position to see just now."

"But the car behind us is beyond our control."

"Precisely," I pointed out, finger raised. "The closer I come to the car in front of us, the more room I allow for the person behind us to stop before hitting us, which is an action I can't control." I braked again, abruptly, and she slapped the side of her door again, more violently.

"*Control*," she said. "Interesting word, that."

Picturing a peaceful place was doubly effective at stress reduction, Libby once assured me, especially while inhaling to a count of eight. The place I pictured now was the river behind my mother's house at high tide, a salt breeze filling my nostrils, herons and egrets swooning above the marsh in morning light.

"There's simply nothing we can do about this," Libby said.

I looked at her.

"Don't look at me. Keep your eyes on the road."

"We're not moving."

"I think we'll move again very soon."

I pictured water and greenery. I pictured six dogs running between my mother's house and my grandparents' house. Then I focused on comforting Libby. I wanted to help her the way she'd helped me some mornings when I felt such dread that I asked her to call in sick for me. She always talked me out of bed and into the shower and out the door, assuring me I was smarter than my community-college students. Now, in turn, I wanted to make her feel safe. It wasn't too much to ask. I appreciated the courage she showed by agreeing to ride three hundred miles to meet my parents and to attend the big Christmas Day dinner party to be hosted by my grandparents, where she'd be on display in front of all my aunts and uncles and cousins.

I wanted to turn around. The night before, deep into my bottle of wine, I'd realized that Libby and my mother would dislike each other. Jude would see Libby as a pampered big-city rich girl with delicate sensibilities, unable to relate to the working class. And Libby had already voiced her opinion: my parents were deeply flawed for having ten marriages and ten divorces between them, and they were disturbed for living on the same property thirty years after their divorce, surrounded by Jude's parents and sisters on "a co-dependent family commune." She said she'd wanted to study them so she could help me learn about myself. She said I didn't have to inherit their habits. She said the sins of the father needn't visit the son if I didn't want them to. With her help, she said, the apple could roll from the tree. She'd said all this in bed one night just before falling asleep, leaving me to stare at the ceiling, stomach bubbling with fear, Penelope's chin on my arm.

I accelerated quickly to fill the fifteen feet between us and the bumper ahead. Then braked sharply. Libby slapped her door.

"I'm getting nauseated," she said.

"My father taught me to drive when I was fourteen. He took me to a racetrack in North Wilkesboro, North Carolina, and turned me loose while he talked to the track manager, Enoch Staley, who's still a legend there."

"That sounds rather juvenile."

"I was fourteen."

"*And* unsupervised. You could have been killed."

"It was an El Camino—a half-car half-truck hybrid with no aerody-namics—now discontinued and destined to be a classic. I only reached 45 miles per hour on the backstretches."

"It sounds like classical thrill-seeking."

I detected a small opening to my right, accelerated and swerved quick-ly to fill it, then braked, spilling Penelope to the floorboard.

"Asshole," Libby said. She scooped up Penelope and kissed her head.

"Sorry. I had to do that." I petted Penelope. She was shaking.

"Is this lane more to your liking?"

I wanted to get to the outside lane for her. The wall of cars around us made her nervous, and the aggressive drivers (mostly men, I will freely admit) cared nothing about being considerate to fellow travelers. In the past year on this very interstate, one driver had shot another driver, though I knew better than to introduce this now as a subject of conversation.

I said, "My father taught me to drive down mountains. The key is to *accelerate* through curves to get through them more quickly, then coast down the mountain in a straight line without touching the brakes. If you brake while going down the mountain, it means you're a bad driver."

"That's the stupidest thing I've ever heard. But it explains a lot."

I'd been terrified while Buddy drove down mountains so casually, a feeling I should have shared just then, had I been man enough to do so. Now, I accelerated to get ahead of a tractor-trailer and Libby slapped her door, which spilled Penelope from her lap again.

"What is wrong with you?" She picked up Penelope, then whispered in her ear.

"Sorry," I said.

A yellow Hummer with tinted windows stopped even with me, on Libby's side, bass thumping loud enough to rattle our windows. Libby locked her door. I raised my voice.

"Plus," I said, "the fact that I was once a drummer makes me a good driver. Rhythm and reflex are the most essential skills in driving."

"Stop talking."

"Being a basketball fan also helps. Sometimes while I'm driving I imagine that I'm playing basketball. When I'm cruising down a six-or eight-lane interstate I feel like a point guard who sees the entire court at once, intuiting motion before it occurs. Magic Johnson is probably the best driver in the world. It takes great vision to be a good driver."

Libby looked over her right shoulder. The sports analogy was useless. She found all forms of sport a trivial and primitive activity. Drumming (distinct from percussion), she also found barbaric. Her only hobby was classical music, but never as background. When she listened to classical music, she sat in a room with her eyes closed so she could concentrate, which I started doing too—it's one of many things I'm happy to have learned from her, something I should have made a point of telling her.

I wanted to get over just one more lane. I sped up, then stopped. I said, "You know, some data suggests that—on the whole, and with exceptions—there are dramatic differences in the ways men and women perceive things spatially. Women tend to see objects much closer than they are." I braked sharply again, and Libby slapped her door again.

"How many near-sighted and sexist old men did it take to come up with that bullshit? And even if it were true, wouldn't it take a highly evolved male to account for the innate differences while driving, so the female, if riding, would be less fearful? *If* that were true?"

I looked over my shoulder at the Hummer, perceived a small space between the Hummer and the RV ahead of it.

"Possibly." I sped up to see if I could swerve into the space, but the space closed, so I braked again.

"Let me out, please."

"I think it all depends upon the ability of the individual to adapt to stressful stimuli."

"Please. I'll call a cab to take me home."

"Adaptation is what it's all about," I said.

"This is never going to work." She held Penelope with her left hand while cocking her right hand above her thigh, ready to slap the door. "And do *not* ever again speak to me like I'm one of your fucking students who believes whatever comes out of your sweating head."

Fair enough, I thought. I said, "Would you like your sleeping mask now?" A week ago, she'd bought herself a sleeping mask to wear while traveling, believing reduced exposure to stressful stimuli would promote relaxation.

"What I would like," she said, "is for you to take the mask and cram it up your ass."

I stopped abruptly, so close to the car in front that I couldn't see the bumper. Libby slapped her door.

"Listen," I said. "If you don't believe that I care enough about you to do everything in my power to avoid hurting you in an accident, then maybe you could believe that I care enough about myself to avoid being crushed or killed or paralyzed. With that in mind, I'd rather not have this conversation for the rest of our lives about my driving and your fears. I mean—would you like me to snap my fingers and make all traffic disappear forever?"

"Yes, please."

"I'm afraid we'll be surrounded by cars for the rest of our lives. There will be cars in front of us and cars behind us and cars beside us, and I don't know what else to do but learn to cope with this fact."

"You could learn to be more careful."

I counted to eight, though I did so, apparently, while grinding my teeth.

"Typical adolescent reaction," she said. "Very childish."

I accelerated to get ahead of the Hummer, swerved quickly to fill the shrinking space, then braked sharply. Libby held more tightly to Penelope, though both their heads sprung forward. Libby's head bounced back against the headrest.

"We made it," I said. "This lane will be better."

"I'm never going anywhere with you ever again, you fucking asshole."

I accelerated to the shoulder, came to a head-springing halt, and shifted into park. With both hands, I pushed the center of the wheel, straightening my arms to amplify the volume of the horn, which sounded for a count of eight. Penelope tried jumping to the backseat, but Libby caught her and held her tightly.

"You're insane," Libby said.

I unbuckled my seatbelt, flung myself from the car and ran around to Libby's door, which she'd locked long ago. I said, "Maybe you should drive!"

Libby lifted her middle finger.

I struck the glass with the heel of my hand. Then I saw the spider web of splintering cracks. I grabbed my stinging hand and through the cracked glass saw Libby's horrified face. She pulled Penelope close and stared straight ahead, her face broken into prisms like a Picasso portrait. I felt regret and shame so intense that I put my back to the car, slid to the ground, and faced a thin row of pine trees. It was nearly dark, and all the noise from the slow-moving traffic grew amplified and frightening—the explosion of air brakes, bomb-like horns, the soft hurricane of so many whirring engines moving so much weight more slowly than an advancing army. An eighteen-wheeler shook the ground and rattled my tailbone. I reached into my pocket for the phone I'd bought in case Libby ever needed me.

She was probably already dialing 911 to report her abusive boyfriend. In which case, I would wait patiently for them to take me away. I would impress her with how calmly I surrendered. And just now, as a first step toward reconciliation, I would suggest a separation. She answered her phone without saying anything.

I said, "Sorry about that."

She made a sobbing sound, then paused.

"I'll take you home and go alone."

She sniffled. "You're a fucking ape."

"It appears so. I'm very sorry."

"You really need some help."

"Yes. It seems I do."

"You have some dangerous anger issues."

"I know. I'm sorry."

"Your tantrum is typical of a five-year-old."

"Yes, I guess so."

"You're the one who needs pills."

"I know." I started a Hail Mary, which was what my mother advised in times of stress.

"I think," she said, "that you should go alone."

"Listen," I said, then paused. I thought, yes, of course, this was the exact spot where I should follow through with the decisive and necessary action of calling it off for good. We should cut our losses, move on, spare each other all the pain to come. Here was the escape hatch I'd searched for while staring at the ceiling during so many sleepless nights.

"Maybe I should," I said. "Go alone, that is."

"Bastard."

"But you just said—"

"Take me to the next exit. I'll get a cab."

She insisted I drop her at the closest gas station. She refused to talk. I knew to offer any word at all would be unwise. Any word at all would be combustible. When we got to the gas station, I turned off the car, folded my hands in my lap and stared at them. I cleared my throat. She got out, cradled Penelope in one arm and slammed her door with the other.

I got out too, hands buried in my pockets.

"Listen," I said.

"Shut up. You never get to speak to me again. Open the trunk." Her voice was loud enough to make two people entering the store turn their heads and stare.

I opened the trunk.

She held Penelope with one arm and lifted the Christmas presents intended for my parents and grandparents—presents she had bought and carefully wrapped, complete with bows and tags—and dropped them on the ground. She pulled out two suitcases and a makeup bag, struggling with the weight. I reached to help.

"Don't touch my things," she said.

I picked up the presents and placed them gently back into the trunk.

She pulled her bags, one by one to the corner beside the payphones, then flipped through the yellow pages of a phonebook, looking either for cab companies or cops, I wasn't sure.

I stood beside her, hands still pocketed. I hung my head and talked softly.

"Listen," I said.

"Go away." She dialed a number on her cell phone.

"What can I do?"

"I'd like a taxi," she said into the phone.

"I have to say something," I said.

"Hold on," she said. And then to me: "Where are we?"

"Exit 44, I-285 South. But—"

She repeated this into the phone, then said *thank you* so politely I did a double take. She folded her phone into her pocket, leaned against the building and kissed Penelope's head.

I said, "I don't know."

She looked toward the road, focusing on a spot where she believed the taxi would appear. I looked there too. It was dark now on the interstate, and I still had a long way to go. I looked at Libby. She turned away and lifted her chin. It reminded me of the pose she'd struck when she gave back her engagement ring before taking it some seconds later.

I said, "Listen."

She looked at me with cold eyes and didn't blink.

"Don't go," I said.

She squinted.

"I'll do anything you ask," I said.

She stroked Penelope's head and stared at me and didn't blink.

"I'm sorry."

She blinked.

I said, "I'm not that person back there. I'm very ashamed of myself."

She stroked Penelope's ear, looked at the sky and back to me. She said, "Here's what you will do if I agree to go with you: you will go to therapy *and* anger management counseling, *and* you will write out weekly reports detailing your progress in both areas, which you will read aloud to me every Friday night."

"That sounds fair," I said.

"And you will stop scaring me with your driving."

"I agree. It's insensitive and childish."

She returned to the passenger seat, leaving me to return her bags to the trunk.

She took another pill, and I drove.

Around Macon she leaned her head against the window and started snoring. I drove the speed limit, even with her asleep. I drove carefully, so she could rest. Every time I hit a bump, I looked to see if she'd woken. I wanted music, but I knew music would wake her, so I settled on silence. I fantasized about the singer whose company I'd most enjoy while driving deeper into the woods toward home. Maybe Gram Parsons singing "We'll Sweep Out the Ashes in the Morning," with Emmylou singing along like a fallen angel pleading for forgiveness. And then everything by Otis Redding, starting with "Lover's Prayer," and then "A Little Tenderness," which I would make my mantra. If I was alone—which I was glad not to be—I'd listen to Vic Chesnutt, whose voice would beg me to stop around Savannah for a six pack, half of which I'd drink while driving the final hour home, sinking further into the lowland, Vic's voice taking me all the way to the front porch, where I'd sit with the dogs lying around me and stare beyond the moss-draped pecan trees toward the dark river, where I'd drink my final three beers in silence, worrying about my future.

She snored softly all the way down I-95, and she snored as I crossed the Altamaha River into my home county. I was glad she was with me. I would be proud to introduce her to my family. And I looked forward to the feeling I'd get for seeming successful in their eyes because a successful woman had

38

agreed to marry *me*. And because I had, so far, been able to keep a decent job. These were the things, I thought, that would keep me from becoming my father. Even though he was a smart and ambitious man, he'd always suffered bad luck when it came to love and work. He would blame himself for being unlucky, and he would say it's silly to believe bad luck can be genetic, but this didn't stop me from remaining afraid that I too would someday end up jobless and alone.

When I pulled into my mother's driveway, it was ten-thirty. The pecan trees were dressed in Spanish moss so thick they looked like great-grandmothers wearing grey dresses, a sight I found comforting, which Libby might find strange. She woke now, to the sound of barking dogs. They circled the car, showing their teeth. She held tightly to Penelope, who started shaking.

"Hold on," I said. "I'll settle them down."

I got out and dropped to my knees to be closer to them. They wagged their tails and licked my face. I waved for Libby to get out, but she didn't move. The air was mild and the ground was the most comfortable ground on earth. The moon lit a little patch of marsh, a salt-breeze struck my nose, and the air itself seemed to know my name. I waved again for Libby to get out. Again, she shook her head. I pushed my nose into Father Cletus's dirty coat, closed my eyes, and heard my father come whistling through the darkness. I knew he was marching toward Libby's door so he could open it for her, administer a grand hug, welcome her to the family and *insist* that she walk straight to his "condo" for a celebratory glass of wine.

Chapter 3
Harold

1986

Libby was not, as my mother might believe, my first serious girlfriend. My first serious girlfriend was Sandra Delgado, who approached me at my high school locker in April of my senior year, strip of pink hair hanging toward her chin, earring in the center of her lower lip, black eyeliner layered at the bottoms of her eyes. She said, "We live in the same neighborhood. Can you give me a ride home?"

So I shrugged. I didn't want her thinking it was the first time a girl had asked me to give her a ride home.

She said, "You play drums, right? I hear them every afternoon."

I closed my locker and leaned against it, suddenly aware that the shape and structure of my entire future had just presented itself as a clear portrait of happiness.

"You should learn some new songs," she said.

She invited me into her empty house and then into her bedroom. Her walls held posters of The Sex Pistols, The Kinks, The Clash, The Ramones, Patti Smith. I sat on her bed while she played "God Save the Queen." She said, "Learn *this* song."

Two days later, I took her to my house and played it for her.

Jude had bought my drum set four years earlier, right after I broke my left leg trying out for the freshmen football team, something I did so I could make the kinds of friends who attracted the kinds of girls who would like me for the company I kept. I was 5'-6", but 160 pounds, and maybe because I wore my fear on my face, the coaches chuckled to each other and put me at noseguard. On the first play of the first day's practice (three days before school started), my foot got wedged beneath a sideways-moving pile. Bones popped. I screamed until the pile cleared, then I cried and moaned while a coach carried me to the locker room, where he lit a cigar and I called my mother, who came at once.

I scuttled down halls on wooden crutches too big for me (pulled from my grandfather's shed), hopping on one thrift-shop Dingo boot, acne-infested face pointed down, patches of my cheeks peeled away from anti-acne medication side effects, big-framed glasses slipping down my nose, cowlicks sprouting while my hair recovered from the crew cut Buddy's ninety-year-old barber administered during my August visit.

For four years, I hid inside the pockets of grooves I'd played the day before and would play again that afternoon, measuring time with my own soft and secret pulse until the final bell, when I rushed home and (after twice hitting a one-hit pipe packed with marijuana) played along to Moon and Bonham, using sticks heavy as hammers. I orchestrated solos, colors splashing my brainpan, sweat flying from my face. I learned the intricate fills and odd time signatures of Peart and the nuances of Copeland, mixing rim shots with sixteenth notes on the high-hat. With money from fast-food jobs (which is how I spent my weekend nights), I added cymbals, toms, cowbells, percussion blocks, crowding the living room so much that Jude never entered it. I bought *Modern Drummer* magazines and read them during classes—learned from Krupa, Rich, Roach. I used heel-down bass for jazz and heel-up bass for rock, worked through flam and flam-tap fills, practiced every paradiddle, counted beats until I didn't need to count, taught myself to read music, overworked my left hand to keep it even with the right, embraced the tension between notes, frequently read the phrase "keeping time," which I accepted as my life-calling.

Sandra was the only person, besides Jude, who saw my athleticism behind the kit. And thirty seconds into "God Save the Queen," she stepped out of her skirt and pulled her shirt over her head. I lost time. She waved for me to follow her down the hall to my bedroom. I knocked over my high-hat hurrying after her.

It was over in sixty seconds. I knew this because the playing time for "God Save the Queen" was 3:25, and after sex the song played for another minute before reaching the final refrain of *no future in England's dreamland, no future, no future, no future.*

Sandra said, "Don't worry, we have time to practice."

I burst into song. I sang, "Ti-i-ime. Is on my side," the Stones' version, from *Still Life*.

"Yes it is," she said.

I said, "Let's get married."

She said, "I have to go now."

Three days before graduation, Jude's boyfriend, J.D., stood with his foot on the back bumper of his truck, drinking a beer. When I stepped out to say Jude would be another minute, he told me to grab a beer from his cooler and to pass him another while I was at it. I put my foot on the other corner of the bumper and propped a forearm on the tailgate, like J.D. We sipped our beers and stared toward the marsh. The air was crisp and alive and one squirrel chased another around the trunk of a nearby pecan tree, claws scratching the bark like a drum solo on rims.

J.D. normally wore a cap, but today, without one, his bald head made him look old and honest. Wrinkles sprawled from the sides of his narrow eyes and a single deep line fell down each of his cheeks. He'd hurt his back twenty years ago, Jude said, lifting bags of concrete, so all his movements were slow.

He said, "Harold, I'm going to marry your mother." He burped, then spat.

I wanted to say, *I don't approve*. I wanted to say, *bad idea*. I wanted to run into the house and call Sandra Delgado at once so I could share this upsetting news.

J.D. said, "I've married four women I shouldn't have, but this time I'm getting it right. The only thing that matters in this short life is finding someone you want to say good morning to and goodnight to until you die."

I wanted to tell Sandra that it felt like J.D. was proposing to *me*.

"As long as I'm around," he said, "I'll help you any way I can." He lowered his left foot from his bumper, made a noise like he'd been hurt, then raised his right foot.

I gulped my beer and didn't look at him. I wanted to say, *please don't help me*.

"What's your plan after you graduate, son?"

I didn't know whether I could plan on graduating. I needed an 88 on my Geometry final, so I planned on cheating—writing key equations on a slip of paper I planned to pull from my pocket. If that plan worked and if I graduated, I had no plan except to say good morning and good night to Sandra Delgado until I died. I planned to avoid further classrooms, and I planned to keep hanging up on the military recruiter who kept promising I would attract lots of girls if I played drums in the Marine marching band.

J.D. said, "Come work for me. You'll learn construction, which means you'll never be without a job. It'll toughen you up some too, put some muscle on those scrawny arms."

A woodpecker banged out a full measure of sixteenth notes, then stopped. I didn't want to work. I wanted to bang on the drum all day.

"There's two kinds of men in this world, son: hard-working men and men who step on their own dicks."

I looked at my crotch, then my foot. Sandra would love this part.

"Men who step on their own dicks make their own bad luck. They're lazy fuckups who look for shortcuts. You ought to decide right now what kind of man you'll be."

It was 5:20. I didn't know why I needed to decide right then.

J.D. sipped his beer. "I'm not going to say anything bad about your father because I've never met him, but I'm guessing he's the kind of man who might step on his own dick."

I wanted to tell J.D. he'd just stepped into a contradiction, but I sipped my beer and looked toward the kitchen window to see if Jude was coming.

"You should make sure you don't follow in his footsteps. You work for me a little while, you won't step on your own dick. You might be too tired to lift it, but you won't step on it."

I laughed, imagining Sandra's reaction to this.

J.D. said, "I haven't seen my own son in ten years. I wonder where I went wrong. If he walked down this road right now, I'd tell him that I'd help him any way I could. A man who turns his back on his family ain't no good. Johnny Cash said that."

I wanted to turn my back and step inside. I finished my beer.

"Get you another one."

I got another one. The woodpecker banged out four trills with half note rests between.

J.D. said, "I want to give you something." He lowered his foot from the bumper, grimaced, walked to the cab, pulled a rifle from behind the seat, and brought it back to me.

It was heavier than I thought it should be. I knew the gun was supposed to win me over, but I wouldn't let it. I didn't want a gun.

"It's just a little bolt-action single-shot .22. Good for squirrels and rats. Woodpeckers. I'll have to bring you some bullets."

I didn't want bullets. I didn't want to shoot any animals, but I didn't say so.

"I want to give you something else," J.D. said. He pulled his keys from his pocket, removed two of them from the ring and handed them to me. He said, "After you graduate, you should show your girlfriend a good time."

One key started the boat I would take from the Everett City dock of the Altamaha River out past the third bend to the ninth houseboat on the left, moored with cables fifty feet from shore, a place J.D. assured me that women loved. He looked at me as if to say it was no small gift. "You need rubbers?" He pulled out his wallet, opened it, removed three linked condoms and held them out.

I put my beer on the bumper, moved the gun from my left to right hand and reached for the condoms.

"The best way to step on your dick is to become a daddy too soon. Trust me on that."

I buried the condoms in my front jeans pocket, then picked up my beer.

"I won't make it to your graduation. I can't sit still that long on account of my back, but I'll put a cooler of beer in your trunk that you can take to the houseboat. You get six or eight beers in you, you can frig all night. Keep your woman satisfied and she'll keep coming back. If it goes off too early, rest and reload."

Jude stepped out then, came down the steps, stared at me, and then at J.D., and asked just what the hell we were shooting.

J.D. said, "Hello, beautiful." He kissed her on the lips. "It's just a little starter gun for Harold to get some target practice with. He doesn't have any bullets yet."

She said, "A gun's fine if you don't have bullets."

I said, "Can I have a beer for the road?"

"Just what every man needs," Jude said. "Guns and beer."

J.D. said, "One beer won't hurt him." He winked at me.

Jude said, "One beer's okay, as long as you agree not to like it too much."

I took my gun and beer inside and immediately called Sandra. I said,

"Come over?"

"No time," she said.

I paused. The silence lasted too long.

She said, "I have to do some things. I'll see you later."

I opened the windows and played my drums as loudly as I could, serenading Sandra with a drum solo I called "Sandra's Song." I played with my heaviest sticks—Vic Firth's 2B hickory w/tear-drop tip—so I could clearly articulate every nuance of every sound, including the rim shots and cymbal bells, which meant she would know the precise shapes, sizes, textures, and colors of all the many things bouncing inside my heart just then that spoke of my love for her.

I hadn't been good at cheating, but the Geometry teacher passed me anyway. After the graduation ceremony, I took Sandra to the houseboat. We each drank a beer while I paddled the boat down the dark river. We had sex on the houseboat roof (which didn't take long), dove naked from the roof into the river, floated beneath the dark and moonless sky, then I drank another beer, and we had sex on the houseboat deck (which didn't take long), then I drank another and we went for another swim, and I drank two more in quick succession, then returned to the roof for the longest-lasting sex of my short sex-life, which required monumental endurance to finish, and afterward, swamped in the sound of crickets, bullfrogs, and owls, we stared at the sky. I imagined cutting the cables to the houseboat and drifting out to sea with Sandra, where we could float our lives away.

I said, "Now, can we get married?"

She laughed. She said, "I'm leaving very soon. Going to Virginia to live with my father, where I'll be going to college next fall. If you think you *must* get married, please wait until you're forty after you've been in therapy for five years. In fact, you should marry a therapist."

"I can't go on without you."

She pressed a finger across my lips.

I said, "Pwease thon't go."

I determined it was midnight. In my memory, I recorded the crickets' angry chorus and the bullfrogs' deep lament. I stored the image of the lower tips of Spanish moss touching the still water. I slept on the houseboat roof with Sandra Delgado and took her home the next morning. In her driveway, she kissed me. She put a palm on my cheek. She said, "Forget me, Harold."

I said, "I'll call you later."

The next day, I walked to her house. No one answered the doorbell. I sat on her porch for an hour, then walked home. I felt like writing a song for the drums—to play until my clothes were soaked in sweat and my arms were too heavy to lift, but I couldn't summon the energy.

In June, I dismantled my drums to make room for J.D.'s recliner. I went to work on his construction crew, waking at six a.m. when he'd barge into my room and say, "Slam your dick in a dresser drawer, son, and let's beat it."

I turned over wheelbarrows of wet cement, repeatedly hammered my thumb, blistered my hands while carrying cinderblocks in hundred-degree heat, fell off scaffolding, tripped over scrap lumber. At day's end, my forty-year-old co-workers bought me quarts of beer, passed me joints, and warned me against marriage. They complained about wives and kids, confessed that the rest of their lives looked just like today and the best they could hope for was a continuous supply of dope and beer, more fishing time, and maybe a little on the side from time to time.

I fell asleep each night at the kitchen table and J.D. fell asleep in his recliner.

At the end of July, I went to Jude. I said, "I'm leaving."

I told her I was going to live with my father. He'd opened his own business and he'd married a college professor. I wanted to be more like him and less like J.D. I wanted him to teach me how to be the kind of businessman who attracted beautiful women.

Jude cried. She cried while I loaded my drums. She cried while I packed my clothes.

She said, "Next thing you know, you'll be bringing your fiancée home for me to meet." She took a deep breath and sighed. She said, "Don't let your father teach you about women, Harold. If you want to bring the right fiancée home for me to meet one day, don't let him teach you too much about anything."

I assured her that I would not let my father teach me anything.

The next morning, Jude stood in the yard with J.D.'s arm around her, her hand covering her mouth while I backed out of the driveway. I waved, then collided with J.D.'s truck.

J.D. said, "Goddamn, son. You can't even get out the driveway?"

We looked over the damage. I'd knocked out a taillight against J.D.'s bumper. Jude said I should stay an extra day so they could fix it, but J.D. said it wouldn't slow me down once I hit the interstate, then Buddy could fix it for me in North Carolina. I knew better than to mention my worn brakes.

"Give it another shot," J.D. said.

"Be careful," Jude said.

I gave it another shot. I waved and pulled away and looked in my rearview mirror. J.D. had one arm around Jude's shoulder while she covered her face with both hands, terrified of the life I was headed toward.

After the eight-hour drive, I pulled into the empty parking lot of the convenience store my father owned and walked inside, expecting a big welcome, but the place was vacant. Bells rattled against the glass, but no one noticed. I waited for someone to pop around a corner or rise from behind a shelf, but no one did. Jocko, a mute parrot, filled a cage that hung over the cash register. Buddy had paid $1,000 for him, thinking he would eventually greet customers, that word would spread to people in surrounding counties who would make special trips to see "the bird," and tourists would pull off the Blue Ridge Parkway and talk to the bird while they bought over-priced apples and jams.

I stared at Jocko. I said, "Welcome to Grand Central Station." Jocko pooped. Then looked away.

I imagined a robber had shot everyone, so I looked inside the cooler. Empty beer cans were scattered among full cases, but there were no bodies. Then I remembered my father's office and imagined corpses stacked there. Nine years earlier, my grandfather, whom I never knew, had been murdered in Boone by some random passers-by who pulled him from his house. Murders were common around there. People were always asking each other if they'd known the person whose body was found in a lake or in the woods or in a trunk, then people talked about the dead person and the dead person's family. Among the well-hidden pockets in the mountains were people who were smart about keeping themselves undetected as criminals. Many of them shopped, on credit, at my father's store.

The phone started ringing, so I went behind the counter to answer it.

A woman said, "Who's this?"

"Harold."

"Oh, Christ." It was Buddy's fourth wife, Dr. Linda. She sounded like something bad had happened or was about to.

"Where's your father?"

"I'm not sure."

"Did he tell you to say that?"

"What?"

"You have a lot to learn, don't you?" Then she hung up.

I weaved through the wooden barrels of iced beer, past the pinball machines, and out the back door which opened into a single stall garage, where Roger Barker, the mechanic, was instructed to sell people *spare* batteries, belts, and blades.

Buddy's office was also Roger's office—a windowless room stuck in the front corner of the garage. And this is where I found my father, in the midst of a poker game with men I'd known from previous summers. It was the beginning of a betting round, so I was mostly ignored, though Buddy did manage to say, "Here comes my luck."

Roger sat on a stool beside Buddy, who sat behind the desk, and on the other side of Buddy sat his accountant, Gordon, a one-legged three-hundred-pound community college dropout everyone called Lightfoot because he'd lost a leg ten years earlier when a drunk driver collided with the bicycle Gordon used because he'd lost his own license from driving drunk.

Across from Lightfoot sat Jake, whom everyone called Sarah, because he owned Aunt Sarah's Pancake House, located behind Buddy's store. In another month it would burn to ashes, chief suspect being Sarah himself, who was deep in debt and would not be found for questioning, not even by his wife or child.

Roger said, "I'll check."

I said, "I thought everyone had been shot."

"You can get your check on Friday," Buddy said. "It'll cost you a dollar now."

"Because no one's at the counter," I said.

Lightfoot said, "A dollar plus one."

"And one more," Sarah said, "which makes it three to you, greaseball."

"And no one's in the store," I said.

Roger shook his head and threw in three dollars.

Lightfoot said, "Why do all my aces have grease on them, Roger?"

"So I thought everyone had been shot," I said.

Buddy tossed in two dollars and Lightfoot threw in one.

Roger laughed and threw down three kings over two sevens. Then he called everyone a dumbass for buying into his check.

Buddy removed a liquor bottle from a desk drawer and poured into a plastic cup. Last summer, he'd waited until five o'clock to start his daily drinking. He'd said at five he could reward himself at the end of the work-day, even if he woke up at eleven, proceeded slowly through showering and shaving, started breakfast at Sarah's by one, then ambled into his own store by two, large coffee in hand to dismantle his hangover.

He lifted his cup to me. He said, "Viva lost wages, sonny-boy."

Sarah said, "Hello, good luck."

Roger said, "Hey, Junior."

Lightfoot said, "Can I borrow twenty dollars?"

Buddy said, "Don't get my son involved with your gambling problem. I'll loan you twenty today against twenty-five on payday."

I said, "No one's watching the store."

Buddy lifted a blue deposit bag from beside his chair, unzipped it, pulled out a twenty, and handed it to Lightfoot. "You'll make a note of that, right?"

"That's my job," Lightfoot said. "I never forget a figure."

"You never forget the *right* figure. But I wish you'd remember one thing. I wish you'd remember to stand a little closer to the goddamned washrag. Sitting between you and Roger is like living in a goddamned dumpster. I have to smoke just to cover up the smell. Son, go tell Garvey to give you a pack of Kool Filter Kings in the box."

"Well," I said, then everyone turned to me, which made me lose my tongue. Suddenly, I'd become a natural-born stutterer.

"Well what?" Buddy said.

"Garvey's not—Garvey's not—Garvey's not here. I've been—"

"That sorry sack of shit," Buddy said.

"Good help's hard to find," Roger said.

"So's good work," Lightfoot said.

Buddy started shuffling. "You should've said something."

"I heard him say something," Roger said.

"Me too," Lightfoot said.

Buddy said, "Harold, go watch the register while we play one more hand. Just make the right change, be nice, and don't fuck up anything."

"But he's *your* son," Sarah said.

"First, bring me those cigarettes," Buddy said.

"And a bag of chips," Lightfoot said.

"I'll take a beer," Roger said.

I went and came back, arms full.

"In the *box*," Buddy said. "Nobody listens."

I went and came back and left again.

I stood behind the counter, studied the empty parking lot, the well-traveled road, the full parking lot of the convenience store across the street. Within thirty minutes, two people came in to give me a dime for a newspaper, but that was all. They'd seen the portable marquee pointing from the roadside that advertised local newspapers, available elsewhere for a quarter, priced here at ten cents. The idea was to lure people into the store, where they'd fill their hands with inflated cigarettes and drinks. Many people entered, asking how Buddy could offer papers so cheaply.

"We make up for it in volume," Buddy told them, every time as if for the first time.

Then they'd leave, laughing, one hand empty.

At 4:30, a girl about my age plopped a six pack of beer on the counter. Her jean-shorts were very short and one strap of her halter top had fallen across her shoulder. She smiled. She was clearly underage, but I wanted to help her because I knew how it felt to badly want beer without being able to buy it, and I thought she'd like me for helping her and this would be the start of a summer romance that would make me forget Sandra Delgado. I also wanted to help my father, who needed her money. When I counted back her change, she winked. She walked out, looked once over her shoulder and offered me a sly smile, as if to say, *yes, I'll help you forget Sandra Delgado.*

At five o'clock, Garvey came in, ready to start his three to eleven shift.

He said, "Whaya say, Junior?" as if he'd seen me just yesterday. Garvey, my father's first cousin, didn't need to ask where he was. He took down a pack of cigarettes from the overhead rack and opened them while he leaned against the counter, worried eyes pointed toward the road.

He said, "Did your daddy remember I was going to be late today on account of taking my boy to the heart doctor?"

"I don't know. He's—"

"I told him yesterday, then I called Clyde this morning, but I don't know if either fucking one of them was fucking sober enough to understand me. My boy's got a bad heart valve."

"Shit," I said. "Sorry to hear that."

"They don't fucking listen. What you'll come to learn about this fucking life, son, is that nobody fucking listens worth a good goddamn."

Clyde, uncle to Garvey and Buddy, worked the seven to three shift, relieving Bruce, Clyde's grandson, who read porn magazines on the graveyard shift. Clyde was eighty, but he couldn't drink at home, where his wife brooded over him, so he preferred to keep working, where he could drink more freely.

"Junior?" Garvey said. "Watch the fucking counter a minute while I stock the fucking cooler, which I see Clyde was too goddamn busy to do."

When Garvey left, Jocko screeched. I opened his door to pet him, and he flew straight out and collided with the front door. He slid to the ground and lay comatose. I looked toward the cooler to see if Garvey had seen, but he was sitting on a crate, drinking a beer. When I scooped up Jocko, he came back to life. He flapped his wings hard enough to make me squeeze him. When he bit my finger, I flung him against the glass. I picked him up and tightened my grip, one hand slipping up around his neck while I walked him back to the cage and tossed him in. I wiped my hands on my jeans and faced the parking lot.

Garvey came out and burped. He said, "Well, that's done."

"Yes, it is," I said.

In the coming weeks, customers mistook Jocko for a piece of merchandise.

"How much for the bird?" they'd ask.

"Make me an offer," Buddy would say. But no one ever did.

Garvey lit a new cigarette and stared out the window. I removed some quarters from the register and took them to a pinball machine. When I pulled the plunger, the phone rang.

Garvey said, "He's in his office, Dr. Linda, but I'll go tell the idiot to get home to his pretty wife like any sane man would've done a long time ago." Garvey hung up, but he didn't move. He said, "Junior? When you fuck up and get married, don't fucking marry somebody with fucking letters behind her name, okay? You hear me?"

"Okay," I said, and pulled the plunger again.

An hour later, Buddy strolled through the back door from the garage, ducking beneath the door frame. Roger followed, stopping at the pinball machine, cigarette drooping from his mouth, plastic cup full of beer. He reached under the machine and flipped the power off and back on, then deposited two quarters, handed me his cigarette and beer, then pulled the plunger. I took a drag, then a sip. A sip, then a drag.

"Hey," he said. "Get your own."

Buddy carried his cup and his blue deposit bag toward Jocko's cage.

"Welcome to Grand Central Station," Buddy told Jocko. "Garvey's an *asshole.*" Jocko said nothing. "That's a thousand-dollar bird. I wonder if he'd taste like it."

Buddy stared at passing traffic. Garvey leaned against the counter, seemingly armed with a response he'd use as soon as Buddy offered a bossy comment about keeping track of time.

Instead, Buddy said, "How's Sam?"

"They're talking about taking him to Duke fucking hospital for fucking open heart surgery."

"He'll be fine," Buddy said. But he didn't sound convincing. They stared at passing cars. Buddy said, "Let me know if you need some time off."

"I'll need some time off."

"Talk to Clyde."

"That's what I thought," Garvey said. "Your current wife called. I told her you were gambling and couldn't be disturbed."

"I'm sure you did. I'm going to the bank and then home."

"Bank's closed," Garvey said. "You ought to steal you one of those fucking cheap-ass watches hanging right there. I did." He lifted his hand to show him.

Garvey had a point. When I asked my father why he never wore a watch, he said, "Hell-fire, the time is the easiest thing in the world to find out."

Buddy walked around the counter, told Garvey to look the other way, then hid his deposit bag, which included all the money collected over four days, including the weekend, in the bottom of the trashcan, covering it with paper.

When the phone rang again, Buddy yelled for me to follow him, so we walked out in a hurry, waving to Garvey, Buddy's long legs leaving me behind.

I wondered then if Buddy had thought to tell Dr. Linda I was coming. She had no children of her own, and didn't seem to want any. Buddy had met her when he'd enrolled in an Introduction to Business course at the community college when he was thirty-three. He said he'd wanted to go to college to be a good example to his son. And apparently, he'd impressed Dr. Linda, Ph.D., who was in her second year of college-level teaching, a divorcée, who found in Buddy someone whose natural charisma seemed a perfect fit for his ambitions in business. But once they married, he concluded all her knowledge came from books and was therefore useless.

While we sped down the back roads to Dr. Linda's, I remembered the worn brakes I'd first worried about when leaving the south Georgia flatlands, which I hadn't told my mother about because she would insist I delay my exit until the brakes were fixed, and I told myself that I'd get Roger to take a look as soon as I coasted into the North Carolina mountains. I could still stop when I pressed real hard and when I dropped the automatic transmission into L2, which helped slow me with a sudden jolt. And I kept one eye on the emergency brake so my hand would know where to go should any emergency crop up.

But I'd forgotten about the brakes until I was back in the car, speeding to keep up with my father, who was going faster than I wanted him to. Around corners, I lost him for a few seconds before he came into view again. There were no stop signs or red lights, and Buddy accelerated through the curves. It was a test. He wanted to see if I could keep up on mountain roads. I feared failing the test, and I feared being left behind. We were going too fast for me to spot a single landmark, which was why I didn't remember that at the very bottom of the steepest hill we were now speeding down was the driveway belonging to Dr. Linda, which Buddy very suddenly swerved into, braking harshly with the briefest skid on the far right side of the driveway, leaving me room to the left should I happen to hit the driveway at all, which I did, foolishly, instead of staying straight into the upward slant of the next hill to slow down (which would've meant I'd failed). I stomped on the brake pedal that smacked now against the floorboard, but the driveway was shorter than I remembered, twenty feet long maybe, leaving no time at all for the mismanagement of a single second, so I jerked the gear shift down, looking for a gear lower than L2, and I stomped the brake with no second to spare for an eye to lower itself to the spot where the left hand should reach at a time like this to pull an emergency brake, just as the eye's mind had rehearsed, which made me, for a full second, hate myself for having failed the test and for all the failings prior to this that made this failing possible and for all the failings this would lead to when I wished for nothing but my father to be beside me as my sole confidante and only sympathizer. But with the driveway disappearing and Dr. Linda's house approaching, there appeared the glimmer of hope every gambler spots from the bottom of every pit: I decided I'd bounce off the brick column that separated the two closed garage doors, inside the left of which was Dr. Linda's new Cadillac, license plate spelling, "Erned It."

The bricks gave way, of course. I thought they'd repel me, but they didn't. The bricks broke through my front windshield, forming a head-sized hole where water now poured, pipes breaking more easily than bricks, as it happens. Dr. Linda's Cadillac was totaled. So was her garage, which caused great embarrassment for days to come as neighbors craned their necks to view the odd sight of a car buried in rubble, just the back end (with a broken tail light) sticking out. My car was also totaled, but no one seemed concerned about that.

At two a.m. Buddy kicked my bed and told me we were leaving. Hours earlier, I'd heard him and Dr. Linda arguing. This was long after Dr. Linda had run out the front door, fearful that a bomb had struck. They argued long after she'd said, "Like father, like son." They argued long after Buddy had called a friend to survey the damage and give an estimate for repairs, long after the friend shined his flashlight into the rubble to say, "It's not as bad as it looks; I know it looks bad, and you might avoid walking on this end of the house (is that the master bedroom?) until we can replace the bricks with a temporary support column, but overall, it's not as bad as it looks, though it *does* look bad"—long after Dr. Linda had a couple of drinks, foregoing supper, and long after I had apologized *and* complimented her green-bean casserole, and long after she'd replied by saying, "I think it's best if you don't talk for awhile,"—long after all of this is when Buddy kicked my bed to say we were going to the Owen Motel, which had previously been owned by Buddy's Uncle Billy, who had killed himself the previous winter. Billy's children said he'd done it accidentally while cleaning his gun, but Buddy said they were just telling the story they needed to believe. Billy's children were trying to sell the motel, but there were no offers.

When our phone woke us at eight a.m., I figured it was Dr. Linda calling to continue the argument, but it was Clyde, calling to say an ATF officer was in the store, asking for the owner. My father looked awful that morning. When we left Dr. Linda's, he'd had an extra bottle tucked beneath his arm, and he'd finished it off while we lay in the motel bed. Now, he sat on the edge of the bed in his underwear. His long arms were stretched on either side of him for support, but he was swaying. He put on yesterday's clothes, then we drove to the store through the bright morning light without a word.

The ATF officer spread papers on a pinball machine. He said he'd sent an underage girl into the store the day before to buy beer, so he was now issuing a $1,000 fine and suspending Buddy's alcohol license for ninety days. Then he said, "Have a nice day," and left.

Buddy held himself up at the end of a pinball machine, arms stretched to either side. He dropped his head, making his shoulders stick up with a big gap between them.

I said, "Sorry about that."

He didn't say anything.

I told him again in case he hadn't heard.

He lifted his head. He said, "Let's get some breakfast."

Over breakfast at Aunt Sarah's pancake house, where Sarah himself delivered our food and made a joke about wanting to burn his bills, my father informed me that the rest of my summer would be devoted to working off the damage I'd caused.

"You will learn," he said, "accountability." These were his only words. From our seats, we looked out the window at the back of his store. Three tires leaned against the garage door, which Roger should have had opened by now.

After breakfast, while he went home to patch things with Dr. Linda, I cleaned bathrooms, swept and mopped the store, swept and hosed down the parking lot, filled fifty bags of ice and stacked them in the outside cooler, took out trash, removed merchandise from all the shelves, dusted the shelves *and* the merchandise, then arranged the merchandise back on the shelves more orderly, labels facing out.

My father stayed gone all day. Roger napped in the garage. Clyde kept going to the storeroom, closing the door behind him, and then coming back out. His eyes and nose grew redder as the day wore on. At three, he left without a word. When Garvey came in at 3:30 to start his 3-11 shift, I told him about crashing into Dr. Linda's house, but he wasn't impressed. He said there were more important problems in the world.

He said. "Her house was too fucking big anyway."

At 4:30, Buddy came in wearing the same clothes. He hadn't showered or shaved, and his eyes were red. He went straight for the trash can, but it was empty. He looked at Garvey.

"Not me," Garvey said. "First time I've noticed it."

Buddy said, "Son? You take out the trash?"

"You told me to," I said.

"Go climb into the dumpster and fish out a blue bag."

As soon as Buddy said dumpster, I remembered the truck that had backed up to it a few hours before, maneuvering the metal braces into the slots that lifted the dumpster and turned it upside down into the truck, dumping its contents. I'd watched the whole operation, thinking I might be doing something similar someday.

But I went to the dumpster anyway. I remembered watching Buddy put the money in the trash can the night before, but I hadn't remembered it when I dumped the trashcan into the dumpster. And I couldn't dare tell him that now, on top of the other damage I'd caused.

When I came back to say the dumpster was empty, my father didn't seem surprised.

He said, "Let's go."

At the landfill, he stopped to talk to the man in charge, the same man I'd seen in previous summers who wore the same eye patch and the same plaid pants streaked with dirt. When Buddy told him what happened, the man pointed to an area the size of a football field, layered with assorted trash dumped within the week. He told my father to make himself at home.

The odor was overpowering. I gagged and fought back vomit, pulled my shirt front over my nose. Seagulls swarmed above us, screeching like the world was ending. We waded through a sea of rotten food, baby diapers, animal feces, and what must have been a dead dog or two. We shuffled, side by side, through garbage that grew knee-deep. The seagulls followed us, swooping over our heads.

"Look for an umbrella," my father said.

We made laps of the area the one-eyed man had pointed to, taking small steps, kicking up the garbage on top to glimpse garbage underneath. Every few steps, my father stopped to scan the length of the landfill, searching for a spot of blue. He seemed too numb to be angry. It looked like he wasn't too surprised to end up here in the middle of a stinking landfill with his only son, looking for money he'd thought to hide in a trash can. His face looked like the same face he showed his poker partners when his final card wasn't the card he needed.

I said, "I think it'll take a fucking miracle to find that fucking bag."

He said, "Son, let me tell you something about miracles." He put his hand on my shoulder and squeezed it. He said, "The kind of man who begs for a miracle is the kind of man who will *always* be begging for miracles. We are not men who beg for miracles. You hear me? You understand?"

I sank into a pile of garbage and fell against my father, who pushed me straight. I said, "Is Dr. Linda pissed off?"

He looked toward the sun. "She was pissed off before this and she'll be pissed off about something else after this. When you get married the first time, you'll understand."

I looked into piles of trash to my left while my father looked into piles of trash to his right, stumbling along beneath the unforgiving sun. We looked for twenty minutes more, circling, retracing our steps, sweating, saying nothing. Then Buddy said, "Fuck it. Let's eat."

We sat in a booth at Aunt Sarah's Pancake House, the only customers. Sarah prepared our food because his cook hadn't shown up. From our booth, we looked at the back of Grand Central Station, where Roger had just then entered the empty garage and pulled a beer from his coveralls. When he finished it, he tossed it in the trash and grabbed a broom. When he finished sweeping, he hung up the broom, lit a cigarette and pulled the garage door down.

Later that summer, Sarah's Pancake House burned down, and Sarah disappeared. Garvey's son died, and Garvey disappeared. Clyde fell down his basement stairs and died a week later. Clyde's grandson, Bruce, went to prison for selling drugs. Lightfoot lost his other leg to diabetes. Roger inherited his dead father's auto repair shop, worked 80-hour weeks. Jocko died in Roger's shop, apparently from asphyxiation. Dr. Linda dated a millionaire. My father declared bankruptcy. My father inherited Clyde's GMC pickup, which he gave to me. I became the night manager of the Owen Motel, slept in room 101, and enrolled in the community college. My father went to work as a traveling salesman, selling tools and toolboxes to garages.

On Sunday nights, from my desk at the hotel, I called my mother. We each insisted we were happy. During my last call, I told her about my imaginary girlfriend.

"We go for drives on the Blue Ridge Parkway. And have picnics."

"Are you okay, Harold?" she said. "Don't lie to your mother."

"She's Catholic," I said. "Her name is Lisa."

"Before you do something silly and propose to her, I want you to bring her home for me to meet. Do you promise?"

I promised.

Once a week, my father called from a different motel room in a different city, trying hard not to sound defeated. In early September, shortly after midnight, he called from West Virginia. I sat behind the register, feet propped on the counter, staring through the open front door.

He said, "Are you studying?"

"I was just about to."

"Study," he said. "You need to be smarter than your old man. That shouldn't be too hard, should it?"

I heard him slurping from a drink. I said, "I'm sorry I fucked up everything."

"You're a home-wrecker, Harold." He laughed loudly at his own joke, then stopped. "No," he said. "You don't get to take credit for fucking up anything. I get all the credit for that."

In the pause that followed, I thought I heard my father weeping.

I said, "You okay, Dad?"

He said, "I've come up with a plan on how to live happily ever after. Are you ready?"

"I'm ready."

"I'm going to make your mother fall in love with me again. It might take awhile, but you have to have perseverance in this life, son. You need goals worth working toward, you need meaningful work, you need love, and you need courage. And money. You need money. Now, open those books and get to studying." And he hung up.

I didn't open my books. I walked out into the quiet and empty night, sat on the stoop outside the motel, and studied the sky, which looked, from where I sat, like a giant landfill littered with stars. I pictured my father in his motel room, and I pictured my mother in her bedroom, and I saw myself between them, imagining my own dim future, wondering how long I could make it before I begged for just one miracle.

Chapter 4
Harold

December 24, 1999; 10:45 p.m.

My father opened Libby's door. He bent and reached for her hand.

"What a pleasure," he said. "Allow me."

Libby stood, held Penelope high against her neck, yawned, then smiled.

Every time I saw my father after going awhile without seeing him, his height impressed me, and now, as Libby looked up at him, I knew it impressed her too. He stood in the dark like a gentle giant, smiling, stooping to take her free hand. I feared Libby's microscope would be unholstered from the beginning. She was ready to congratulate herself at the first sign of my father's neuroses, which would corroborate the bias she'd already formed of his being a bad role model for me. I knew she'd be eager to report her findings at the end of our visit so she could trace my shortcomings to his. While Buddy tried to impress her, she'd see his flaws and prescribe ways for me to shed his influence. I feared she'd find a single fatal flaw that she'd diagnose as hereditary and then decide she'd have to leave me so she could save herself. So I thought it best to limit her exposure to him.

"An absolute pleasure," he said. Still beside the car, one hand on her shoulder, he said, "Harold told me you were beautiful, and now I see how right he was." He lifted her free hand and kissed the back of it. Then he petted Penelope. He said, "What a pretty puppy. I'm happy to see my son has such excellent taste in women who have such excellent taste in puppy-dogs."

"Thank you," Libby said.

When he closed her door, he touched the window. He said, "Harold should get that fixed. Sometimes he's a little slow to get things fixed, isn't he? Where is he? Y'all should come over to my house for a glass of wine—I've heard so many good things. Come on over."

"I'm not sure," she said.

He'd heard nothing about her. When I moved in with Libby, I called to give him her phone number, but I provided no details. Buddy's response was a simple "Good luck," followed by a sigh. Since then, we'd talked a few times, but only long enough for each of us to assure the other that everyone was happy.

"Where *is* your future ex-husband?" Then he said, "That's a joke. You'll have to overlook my sense of humor. Most people do."

"Over there." She nodded toward me, still seated on the ground.

"What's wrong with you?" Buddy said. "You had to get out of the car and sit down?"

I stood and walked toward them. I tried to hug my father, but he grabbed my shoulders and pushed me backward.

He said, "What's wrong with your face?"

I'd grown a beard, or tried to, thinking it would make me look more professorial, but it was too thin and there were gaps on both cheeks.

"What are you trying to hide?" he said.

"What?"

"People with beards are trying to hide something. That's my theory. Wait until your mother and grandmother see it. Your grandfather will chase you with his scissors." He turned to Libby and said, "Don't worry. You'll love the family and they'll love you. Come to my house and have a glass of wine."

"No," I said. "We should get to bed. It was a long trip."

"I'd love some wine," Libby said.

"Son, go sit in the grass. Me and—" he paused.

"Libby," Libby said.

"Me and Libby will be in the condo sipping wine."

Her end-of-trip assessment might start with the fact that he didn't know her name. It would continue then, most likely, to catalogue the condo's condition. She would have to wonder about the psyche of someone who lived in such a place.

"Libby?" Buddy said. "I hope you're not too sensitive about slothfulness."

"Look who I live with," she said, and laughed.

"I like you already." He put his arm around her shoulder and guided her through the back yard, fifty feet to the tin-roof condo, which was once a dirt-floor shed.

I'd last talked to my father at Thanksgiving, when he called Libby's apartment to see if I could spare a hundred dollars. When the phone rang, Libby sighed, because she was listening (with closed eyes) to Tchaikovsky's violin concerto in D, Op. 35. I told him I could spare it. He apologized. He said, "My life hasn't turned out the way I planned." I thought he'd been crying, or was about to. He said, "It's the last resort of a desperate man to ask his son for money." He said he loved me and hung up. Which led to Libby's questions, a first impression of Buddy that involved suspicion, and finally a long argument over our own money and how we should and should not spend it.

A yellow light wrapped in spider webs lit the condo stoop, which was a square of 2x4's one cinder-block high, barely wide enough for a single body.

"Watch your step there," Buddy said. "There's a missing board. I keep nagging my landlady about it, but she's a bit negligent—something of a slumlord, really." He held Libby's hand while she stepped over the hole, then asked her to back up slightly so he could open the screen door, which he held tightly at the top because a hinge was missing. She walked beneath his arm and stepped inside, carrying Penelope, who pushed her nose toward something strange.

I stood in the yard, waiting for the stoop to clear, but Buddy waved me ahead and patted my back while I stepped over the hole, ducked beneath his arm, and crossed the threshold, bumping into Libby, who couldn't find an empty spot to move to. It smelled of leaking propane, insecticide, burnt coffee, mildew, and a sewage problem. The floor and the queen-sized bed were layered with clothes, newspapers, magazines, books, shoes, legal pads, envelopes, bowls of pens, jars of pennies. Libby scooted to her left and collided with several dress slacks pinned to a clothesline strung to the far corner, across the bed. The only chair—a plastic chair from Jude's deck—held more newspapers, library videos, an empty doughnut box, a calendar turned to June, assorted junk mail, a brown banana peel, a can of WD-40 and a can of Dust Remover.

Buddy stepped in beside me and tried to close the door.

"Tight squeeze," he said.

I moved to the kitchen, three feet away, where a pyramid of dirty plates and bowls teetered in the sink. Macaroni floated in brown water. On a back burner of the gas stove—behind empty coffee cans and a gallon jar of pickles, a boom box played classical music, something vaguely familiar. Next to the stove, on top of a giant microwave (circa 1978), sat a basketball-sized bowl, capped with a hand-crank, balanced on four legs.

I said, "What's this?"

"My washing machine. Found it in a dumpster. You wouldn't believe what people throw away."

I pictured my father standing neck-deep in a dumpster, whistling while he picked through trash, then I pictured Libby picturing this and felt a little sick. She stared at me with a smile verging on a grimace. To her credit, she did not, just then, look around.

She said, "Could Penelope and I use your bathroom?"

Buddy put his finger on his upper lip, lowered his chin and stared at her above his glasses. "On one condition," he said.

Libby cocked her head, waiting.

"If you promise not to make a mess."

She giggled politely.

I said, "Penelope will need a newspaper."

"That dog can read?" my father said. "Just so happens that today's newspaper is in there already. We'll step out to give you some privacy. The previous tenant—I won't mention any names here, Harold—but the previous tenant removed the door so he'd have more room, and my landlady has yet to replace it."

I opened the refrigerator and pulled out a beer to take with me. I said, "Why is there a flashlight on the top shelf of your refrigerator?"

"Makes the batteries last longer."

"Right," I said.

Libby said, "I'm sorry."

"Nonsense," Buddy said. "Harold should apologize. He's the one who removed the door."

"I'm sorry," I said. I looked at Libby. My apology was sincere. I was sorry she'd be using the smelly and doorless bathroom. I was sorry we weren't visiting her parents in their Manhattan co-op that overlooked Central Park. I was sorry for the interstate incident. I was sorry for whatever went wrong from here. But her eyes were not receiving. Her eyes were dark and tired and right now they said, very clearly, *leave us alone now.*

Buddy said, "I could stand to go myself."

We stepped outside, where Sister Agnes, the landfill mutt with the soulful eyes, sat on the stoop, missing her chair.

"That's my dog," Buddy said. "A gift from your mother. We go on walks together through the subdivision. Or used to."

We walked across the yard and faced the azaleas like two men stepping up to urinals. It was a pleasant night—a short-sleeve t-shirt night near Christmas on the land I'd known from my first memory. I looked through bare pecan limbs toward the stars and, for what seemed the first time in several months, inhaled deeply.

"Me and Agnes," Buddy said. "We went on a health kick for a couple days a couple months ago, but I think we're over it now. I fell in love with an amazing lady, and I started feeling good and I wanted to get healthy, then she dumped me, so now I'm back to my old self. Congratulations on your engagement, son. She seems pretty classy."

"I don't know," I said. "I'm all mixed up. Who was this woman you fell in love with?"

"Miss America, 1960-something. What do you mean you're all mixed up?"

"Miss America? Are you kidding?"

"I'll tell you about it sometime. Why are you feeling mixed up? Say more about that."

Say more about that was one of his favorite sayings. Another was—*I'll tell you about it sometime.* He'd picked up some rudimentary communication principles from self-help books, through a brief stint in marriage counseling (his fourth wife, Dr. Linda, had insisted upon), and from his fifth wife, a marriage counselor. He'd learned, through all of that, and through a career in sales, how to make people talk about themselves, something he often did with much success, unless he was talking to his first wife or to me, people whose stomachs grew unsettled when disclosing too much at once. Recently, however, with Libby's supervision, I'd been learning to share more freely. Sometimes, while I lay on the couch feeling guilty about watching muted baseball, Libby sat next to me and said: "Reveal a vulnerable feeling. I'll repeat what you said to convey understanding, then provide empathy, and we'll develop trust and create connection." So I tried. I ignored my stomachaches and proceeded. I closed my eyes and concentrated. When I used a thinking word instead of a feeling word, she said, "Start over." It was slippery business. Now, with my own father, I wanted to fall into the language of feelings.

I looked over at him while we shook ourselves and zipped. I said, "We had a bad fight on the way and it made me think I should be alone. I feel confused. Sometimes I'm sure and other times I'm not sure. When we're together I'm sure I should be alone, and when I'm alone, I'm sure we should be together. Is that normal? It makes me sad to feel so confused."

"What's her father do?"

I gulped my beer. "He's an executive for New York Life. But what's that—"

"Is he a major control freak?"

"I've never met him. He can't—"

"Does he have a ball-busting-control-freak-of-a wife?"

"She's also an executive for New York Life. They lost a—"

"Democrats?"

"I don't know. I'm beginning to think I shouldn't get married."

"I've thought that a few times."

"But then I think I'm getting old and—"

"How old are you?"

"Thirty-two."

"Thirty-two," he repeated, surprised at this. "Don't worry, it'll get worse."

Here was another of his famous phrases, a conversation-ending line he liked to toss out like a proverb. I gulped more beer and looked toward the river. I thought of running toward it and diving in.

He put an arm around me. He said, "Your mother made me promise I wouldn't give you any advice about love or money. Or anything else. For some reason she thinks I'm unqualified. But if you want to talk, I can listen with the best of them. And I mean that."

It would've been a good time to talk. It was quiet and peaceful, and the air felt good. I wanted to stay outside and talk to my father for awhile.

"I haven't been sleeping," I said. "I'm having trouble—"

"But right this second is probably not the best time. We shouldn't keep her waiting. Don't worry—I'm going to win her over by persuading her that you come from good people."

"No. You don't need to—please don't—"

"Relax. It'll be fine."

Buddy stepped to the porch and petted Agnes. I followed him over the missing board into the condo, was greeted again by strange smells and classical music. Libby stood outside the bathroom, Penelope in one hand, wadded newspaper in the other.

Buddy said, "Let me take that for you." He took it to the kitchen and placed it on top of the pile of trash that rose up the wall from the lidless can in the corner.

Libby said, "Are you fond of Brahms?"

"Is that a German wine?" Then he said, "Ah-ha-ha," and he flapped his hand toward her in an exaggerated motion so she'd know he was joking.

"We played this piece, his violin concerto in D, Opus 77, last Spring. This is the third and final movement here."

"Is that right?" he said. "What instrument do you play?"

She paused. She seemed a little stunned. She looked at me, and I looked away. She said, "I play the second chair violin in the Atlanta symphony."

"That's right," Buddy said. "Harold told me that, and I'd forgotten. I listen to this stuff because it's supposed to prevent Alzheimer's, but I see it's not working. Speaking of chairs, let me see can I find one."

He went to the plastic deck chair that faced his television, dumped its contents on the bed, then put the chair in the narrow space between the bed and the wall-unit propane heater, currently unlit. When he turned again, he struck his head against the wooden center beam, and said, "goddamnit" without inflection, as if he collided with the beam every night about this time. He held his head with both hands and pooched his lips into a pout.

Libby's face looked worse than his. She said, "Are you okay?"

"Can't feel a thing," he said.

Buddy pointed to the orange sock hanging from the beam. "This reminds me to duck." He sat in the deck chair that he normally kept outside for Agnes. Behind him, a little too close, I thought, was his giant TV, precariously balanced on an orange crate. The TV was cracked across the middle. On top of it, clung a VCR that held three wobbly stacks of movies on VHS.

"Son, you can sit on the bed."

"Where is it?"

"Very funny."

I sat on the corner of the bed, all of our knees pointed toward each other, nearly touching beneath the single overhead bulb.

"Now then. Libby, what's your pleasure—red, white, or beer?"

"White please."

"I was afraid you'd say that. How do you feel about red?"

"Red's okay."

"My doctor recommended a glass of red wine each day for my heart, but I got a second opinion and found a doctor who recommended two glasses. Then I found some bigger glasses." He opened his freezer, where he kept his silverware tray, and removed a corkscrew.

I felt comforted, briefly, thinking that I knew Libby well enough to know that she wouldn't be so forward as to ask him why he kept his silverware in the freezer.

She said, "Why do you keep your silverware in the freezer?"

"Keeps roaches from crawling on it. I think they come from my landlady's house."

Libby re-crossed her legs and searched the floor.

I put my empty beer on the counter and got another one, bumping Buddy's hip, then reclaimed my seat on the corner of the bed. Buddy handed her a splotched glass of wine. For every splotch I saw, I knew Libby would see two. Buddy poured himself a glass and raised it toward Libby. "Here's a toast to your future happiness. It is my great pleasure, my dear, to welcome you to our humble family."

She raised her glass to his. They turned to me, a cue to meet them in the middle.

"To enduring love and eternal happiness," he said, and we clinked.

Buddy sat, pulling his feet in and pressing his knees together to make more room. He said, "I love love. Even though I've never been very good at it for very long at once. I've loved and I've been loved, and I still admire the possibilities. And I admire—"

"Hear, hear," I said.

"I admire you both for having enough hope to nurture it as it needs to be nurtured."

"Thank you," Libby said.

I stood. I said, "Thanks, Dad. Goodnight."

"Sit," he said. "Why don't you relax a little bit."

I sat. I bounced my foot and scratched my ear. The overhead bulb burned too brightly, like an interrogation room. Penelope's recent bowel movement blended with pre-existing odors. For every odor I detected, Libby would detect two. The refrigerator clicked on and off, getting in the way of Brahms' violins, which were too manic now. I looked at Libby. Her eyes were closed.

I cleared my throat. I said, "Dad was just telling me that he had been dating Miss America."

"A *former* Miss America," he corrected.

"How interesting." Libby lifted her eyebrows, waiting for details.

I looked at the low ceiling and remembered the stomach-bubbling fears I entertained not so long ago in this very room when I'd struggled to quit my life as a bartender. I'd gotten lucky with the job I'd found. I looked at Libby now, grateful to have found a partner who loved me enough to sit in this room with me. Then I worried that my father woke every morning with the fear that he would live in this same room until he died and that nothing would change for him until that day.

"We went to the same high school forty years ago, and we met again last year at a high school reunion. I figured she wouldn't know me. She was very popular and I was this skinny little loser kid, then I dropped out in tenth grade, drove to Hollywood, lied about my age, then joined the Army and went to Germany."

"Germany," Libby said. "My favorite composers are from Germany."

"I wasn't listening to much music, I'm afraid. My job was to stand on the Berlin Wall and stare into the eyes of East German soldiers without wetting my pants. It was after Korea and before Vietnam, and—anyway, cut to this past summer. Somehow I got invited to my high school reunion. I didn't want to go, but I figured what the hell—maybe I'd sell some final expense insurance. Miss America was there and she introduced herself, which she didn't need to do, and she said she remembered *me*. How's your wine?"

"It's okay."

I looked around to see what Libby could learn of my father's life if she bothered to look beyond the clutter. The wall on the other side of his hanging clothes held a gold plaque for first place in the Soap Box Derby, 1950. Next to it, an equivalency certificate from the N.C. State Board of Education, 1974, next to Who's Who Among Students in Junior Colleges, 1975-76, next to Who's Who in Sales and Marketing, 1982.

"She remembered me from the radio. Before I dropped out, I was a rock and roll DJ at this little 500-watt station in Asheville. I was pretty well known for a brief period—at least my voice was. Honestly, I think I could've gone on to be a famous radio personality if I had stuck with it. Girls called up all the time to make requests, but I had to tell them I was busy working."

Libby's expression didn't change.

"Let me get you some more wine," Buddy said.

"Just a splash, thank you."

On his back wall, he'd hung a portrait Jude had painted of his mother. Jude complained that she hadn't gotten the hands and the eyes right, but I knew Buddy treasured it.

He reached to the counter behind him while remaining seated, grabbed the wine and refilled Libby's glass and his own, then placed the bottle beside his foot.

"Anyway—Miss America and I talked all night, danced, traded phone numbers and email addresses. Then every day for two straight months we talked or wrote, until finally, she invited me to visit her in Palm Beach, which I did—three different times."

A bookcase held badly stacked books, some horizontal, some upside down. A book called *How to Talk to Anyone* leaned against a book called *What Do I Say Next?*

"I really miss her." His eyes were wet, but he was smiling.

"Were you heartbroken?" Libby said.

"Devastated. It wasn't her beauty, either, you understand—I mean she has aged very well, but you'd never know just by looking at her that she was once Miss America—which is the way she likes it. We were in a restaurant once, and I asked a waitress if she had any idea who she was serving, and after the waitress left, she scolded me—told me never to do that again."

Viktor E. Frankl's *Man's Search for Meaning* leaned against *1,001 Humorous Quotations*. A picture-book history of the Ringling Bros. & Barnum and Bailey Circus leaned against *Despair and the Return of Hope*.

"She's very humble," Buddy said. "Classy, well-read, a pleasure to be around. She'd even talked about my moving to Palm Beach, where she had business contacts who could help get me involved in something. So yes, I was heartbroken. But if I'm lucky, maybe I'll be heartbroken again. I don't blame her. You have to respect the person you want to be with, right? I haven't made the kinds of choices that would allow that."

Beside the bookcase was a photo of Buddy standing behind a podium with Gerald Ford, which was next to a photo of Jimmy Carter gripping Buddy's hands, which was next to a photo of Ronald Reagan looking *up* at Buddy, laughing. Buddy had introduced all three Presidents on the campaign trail of 1976, when they each stopped at the community college he'd graduated from when he was thirty-four. When he graduated, the college president hired him as PR director. Gerald Ford wrote him a thank you letter, also framed and hanging. The letter said if Ford's stay in the White House should get extended and Buddy found himself in need of a job, Gerald would try to find him one.

"And that's not self-pity," Buddy said. "Miss America deserves someone more successful. Someone who's—I completely understand it. But there for a little while, I really thought we might—"

His phone rang, but he couldn't find it. He looked behind him on the crowded counter while he tried to finish his sentence. "I really thought we might—"

It rang again. He looked behind the television. He said, "I thought for a minute I might become Mr. America. Maybe this is her calling now."

It rang again, triggering his answering machine, where the message said, too loudly, "You've reached ol' Santy Clause. If you've been a good little girl, hang up now. If you've been a *bad* little girl, leave a number and an address, OH, ho-ho."

"Behind your foot," I said. "Beneath those legal pads."

He struggled to bend for the phone, but he finally reached it, picked it up and then sang into it: "Hello, Hello, Hello!"

Then he said, in a voice too deep, "Hello, darlin'."

Libby yawned. When she looked at me, I pointed my thumb at the door.

Buddy said, "That's awfully sweet of you, honey, but I've already eaten and my son is here visiting with his brand new fiancée—a very beautiful and talented young woman."

Buddy lowered the phone, covered the mouthpiece, said, "Y'all hungry?"

Libby shook her head. I was hungry, but I didn't want to prolong the evening.

"I'm sorry," Buddy said. "I hope you get some rest and I hope you have a good Christmas with your family. I'll drop in to see you in a couple days." He hung up. He said, "That was my current girlfriend, works at the Winn-Dixie deli."

"We should get some sleep," I said. I stood and set my empty beer on the counter.

Libby handed me her unfinished wine. I gulped the rest of it. She stood, tried to suppress a giant yawn, then gave into it and said, "Excuse *me*."

"You must be tired," Buddy said.

"It just overcame me suddenly."

"And I've been talking too much. Tomorrow, I want to hear your life story. I want to hear about wedding plans and life plans and your cello and—"

"Violin," I said.

"Violin," Buddy repeated.

"Okay," Libby said. "I'll tell you all about—"

The phone rang again.

"Damnit," Buddy said. "Excuse me." He answered it, singing, "Hello, hello, hello!"

Libby looked at me. I held my palm toward the door, but she didn't move.

"Hello darlin'. I'm sitting here with my only begotten son and his brand new beautiful fiancée." He winked at Libby.

On the floor inside the doorless closet were six columns of orange boxes stacked eight high, shipped from the Savannah VA clinic. Each box held syringes, three of which Buddy used each day to inject himself with insulin.

"Okay, sweetie. I'll call you back in just a little bit."

Libby looked at me. I winked at her. She rolled her eyes.

Buddy said, "That was my ex-nun girlfriend who lives in New Jersey. I met her online last month—an interesting woman. She's invited me to come visit her, and I'm thinking, first of the year, if I can raise the money, I'll ride up there and see if we can fall in love."

"New Jersey?" I said.

"We'll have to write up a contract first, of course, but she seems agreeable to that."

"A contract is a good idea," Libby said. "Harold signed a contract I wrote out."

"New Jersey?" I repeated.

"Have you had contracts in your previous relationships?" Libby said.

"All of them."

"I hope this one works," she said.

On the refrigerator was taped a piece of paper that held his handwriting. It said, IN THE EVENT OF MY DEATH, with arrows pointing to an envelope held with four magnets.

Outside, Buddy reminded Libby to watch her step. He followed her into the yard, looked into the sky and commented on the beautiful night. Sister Agnes propped herself on Buddy's leg, hungry for a touch, and Buddy bent to give her one. Then he took Libby's hand, kissed the back of it, and said, "May you sleep like the queen you seem to be. Harold's mother—my first and favorite ex-wife—she's going to love you. You know how I know? I know, because I love you. The whole family will love you—just wait until the big bash tomorrow, you'll see." He stooped then and kissed her cheek. He said, "Don't worry about a thing."

Libby said goodnight while I pulled her arm. I led her back across the dark yard. Behind us, Buddy yelled, "I love you!"

I led her up to Jude's unlit porch, through the unlocked door into the dark kitchen and through to the living room, lit by a small lamp. I pulled out the sofa-sleeper while Libby stood by, holding Penelope.

"What's this?" she said.

"My grandmother sleeps in my room. Didn't I tell you that?"

"No, you didn't."

"So she can sleep while my grandfather stays with a caretaker. Otherwise, he keeps her up all night, obsessing over silly questions."

"You didn't tell me that."

"I should have." I looked into her eyes, apologizing, but her eyes were not receiving.

"Bathroom?"

I pointed down the hall, told her the last door on the right. She went there, tiptoeing, carrying Penelope. When she returned, she placed Penelope on the bed, and got beneath the sheets, facing me. Penelope curled between us.

Libby said, "Do you think your father even knows when he's lying? Do you think you're already too much like him? Do you ever wonder how you can avoid ending up like him?"

Her eyes were closed, I noticed then, because mine sprung open. I took a moment to breathe, hoping to answer in a way that would prevent an argument and allow us sleep.

I said, "He's not so—"

"How can he live like that? I feel like I need a shower just from going in there. And his bathroom? I can't believe I used that bathroom." Her volume rose slightly, a sign that the argument train was leaving the station, announcing the moment I should ride or jump.

I moved to the floor.

"What are you doing?"

"I want to sleep here so my grandmother won't think we sleep together. My mother's fine with it, but my grandmother doesn't know we live together, and I'd rather not give her any cause to worry about my spiritual well-being."

"Great. Another lie. Do you think she *should* worry about your spiritual well-being?"

"Probably, but she already has too much to worry about."

"Great. I can't wait for the Christmas party. I wish I hadn't come."

I hoped I'd given her the last word, a parting shot that sank through my skin and into my blood which moved through my organs in super slow-motion while I lay silent on the floor with my eyes wide open, staring at the ceiling.

I scooted to the center of the room so my grandmother would see me clearly when she came down the hall at five o'clock in the morning carrying her rosary on her way home to cook breakfast for her husband before he woke and worried where she was. I wanted her to see me sleeping and to take comfort in the possibility that I might be happy. I knew my grandmother—blessed art thou among women—would add me to her morning prayers. I had little faith any more that such an act could work any magic (and Libby, with even less faith, would laugh at the idea). But I did have faith in my grandmother's faith, and it comforted me to know that her desire for our collective happiness was still very much alive, which meant that she would pray very hard for all of us to have a happy day and to have happy lives, which meant being able to give and receive kindnesses. And why—I wanted to ask Libby right this second—should such a seemingly simple thing be so difficult?

But she was already snoring. Why was it moments like this, when she was softly snoring, that I felt my greatest tenderness toward her? I made vows to the ceiling about being kind, and I expressed my gratitude to the great-giver-of-good-fortune (whatever form that took) that I would not have to endure this difficult life alone. I listened to Libby snore and promised myself I would express this gratitude to her first thing Christmas morning. It had been a long trip and she was tired and in strange territory, and I knew she'd need as much sleep as she could get to help her/us through the long and difficult day to come.

Chapter 5
Roberta

December 25, 1999, 4:45 a.m.

I touched my finger rosary and said my first Hail Mary while dressing in the dark, desperate to get home before my husband of sixty years woke and found me gone, which would mean he'd sing all day the same blues refrain: "Oh Roberta, where'd you sleep last night?" Even when I *am* there, he questions me about the affairs he is certain I'm having with the Winn Dixie bag boy, with Uncle Sludge, and with Father Cletus, simultaneously. Last week, when I complained of an earache, he said, "It's gonorrhea." Sometimes, it's not funny.

At the end of the hall, I squinted to see Harold, my youngest grandchild, sleeping on the floor with his mouth open, and I saw his fiancée on the foldout bed—some weird arrangement he must've designed to make me think he'd maintained his innocence. I started another Hail Mary. Harold was too young. No matter how old he got, he'd be too young to get married. But there's no keeping people from making their mistakes. Even if he stayed married as long as I'd stayed married, it would be a mistake. I married my father's favorite dairy hand, a man with a dangerous smile who went by "Sparky" because he'd always been full of fire and energy. He'd accepted dairy cows as his dowry, which meant he offered me a lifetime of waking up tired. Then three children in three years, three more life sentences, daughters who grew up trying to please their father and made too much noise instead, then moved into houses next to him and kept trying to please him by marrying men who favored him. My daughters kept me alive, but any mother kept alive by her children will tell you that you can only be as happy as the saddest of them, and the girls have had too much sadness—sometimes all at once, sometimes taking turns—mostly because of men. Because of men incapable of turning out differently than the man they'd grown up with, a man whose father died when he was six, whose mother made him a man too soon.

Harold's face looked dirty. Good God—was that a beard? Oh, Harold.

I prayed that he would make the most of all the sorrow to come. I prayed to St. Sophia, patron saint of wisdom, asking her to drop into his dreams. I held my breath while taking tiny steps through the kitchen, then slipped through the door, quiet as a ghost, but when I clicked it closed, I heard the little dog bark three times, which probably woke up everyone. Then I prayed them back to a deep and lasting sleep, the Holy Ghost's most precious gift.

I hurried myself through the dark and misty morning, kicked a clump of moss, then picked it up so Sparky wouldn't stoop for it later and break a hip, which would mean more suffering for me than him. I went to the mailbox and felt inside to see if the Jacksonville paper had come, but it was too early, so I dropped the moss at the foot of an oak and walked around the house to enter through the kitchen, where I started the coffee I'd prepared the night before.

I went to the couch and whispered loud enough to wake Janice, my favorite caretaker. I asked her, as I did every morning, if she'd like coffee and breakfast, but she declined, as she always did. On her way out, I handed her an extra twenty dollars. "Just between us," I said. It was guilt money. I wanted her to know I was sorry for what she had to put up with. She gave me a hug and thanked me, told *me* to stay strong.

Sparky was in the middle of a milking dream, wiggling his fingers around invisible teats. I grabbed his hand, then kissed him on the lips. I said, "Merry Christmas."

He said, "It is?"

I smoothed his hair and told him to get dressed and come to the table. Then I started his breakfast: slow-cooked grits, four strips of pan-fried bacon and three eggs fried in bacon grease which I flipped in the skillet so the spatula wouldn't bruise the yolks. I heated two left-over biscuits and buttered them. I warmed his plate in the oven. I poured a cup of coffee, placed it on a saucer and took it to the table so it would be there when he sat down. I poured a cup of juice and set it beside the coffee. I unfolded yesterday's Jacksonville newspaper and set it beside his juice. When he settled into his chair, I pulled his plate from the oven and loaded it, dropping a wedge of butter on the grits that melted slowly, added pepper. And just as I had for sixty years, I presented his plate to him and recited the blessing: "Bless us oh Lord for these thy gifts…"

When I finished, he stared at me.

"What's wrong?" I said.

He said, "Where's Roberta?"

The first time he asked this, a year ago, it took my breath. Now, matter-of-factly, I answered him. "I'm right here," I said. "Roberta, your wife, is standing right here beside you, just like she did yesterday."

"Where's Roberta?" he said.

"Right here," I said again. "Roberta's right here."

He didn't believe me. But he ate anyway. I sat across from him with a piece of toast and my book of morning prayers. When he finished eating, I refilled his coffee, cleared the dishes, washed and put them away while he flipped through yesterday's newspaper and read his Bible chapter. When I returned, drying my hands with a dishcloth, he looked at me with his mouth open, bits of egg on his right cheek.

"What's wrong?" I said.

"I know your tricks."

"Which tricks are those?" I said.

"You're trying to starve me."

"You've already eaten," I said.

"Don't lie to me."

I showed him the Polaroid picture I'd taken an hour before—a shot of him bringing a forkful of food to his mouth. Jude had given me the camera as a way to answer this daily accusation. At first, I dismissed the idea as cruel. But I grew tired and finally tried it. This morning, like other mornings, I put the picture where his plate had been.

I said, "This is you, one hour ago, eating breakfast."

He broke into a belly-shaking sob. He saw very clearly for one lucid moment that he was not himself. Which made me cry too. If he were himself, he would have said, "This looks just like yesterday." If he were himself, he would have said, "That's not me at all."

I wondered how he'd behave for Harold and his fiancée during our family get-together. At the end of summer, Harold got his first glimpse of his grandfather's slipping mind when he stopped to say goodbye until Christmas. He caught me trying to explain to Sparky where we lived. I kept saying it was in the same place where we were now, which was the same rock house he'd built sixty years ago, and I gave directions from town (north), from Florida (south), from Waycross (west), and from St. Simons Island (east), naming the main roads he'd taken when he drove the dairy truck, repeating *Highway 341* as the road for leaving and the road for getting home.

"No," Sparky kept saying. "I mean where is *home?*"

Then I started over.

And he looked at Harold then, standing by the door jingling his keys, and he said, "Harold, can you give me a ride home?"

I could tell this was a shock for poor Harold because he didn't know what to say, and suddenly he was in more of a hurry to get out of there, following the roads that took him away and brought him back. Poor Harold, who was still young enough to believe there might be some happy ending that did not deal with death. There are no happy endings. But that did not mean I ever once stopped praying for him, or us.

Chapter 6
Jude

By the end of December, in Harold's last year of college, I wanted to tell him this: learn to live with loneliness before you live with someone else. But I never told him. I was a bit distracted with learning it myself. Between April and December of that year, I divorced two men (*one of them, Buddy's brother*), and then I met the man I loved the most, Charlie Clarkson, whose proposals I refused.

I met Charlie in April, during my last dinner with J.D., who had insisted on taking me to the nicest restaurant in town for my birthday. On his way to the bathroom, J.D. collided with a table, made a bigger mess trying to clean up a stranger's spilled drink, then stumbled around the room on his way back, peeking into booths, apologizing, explaining he was trying to locate his wife, who seemed to have moved. By the time he fell into the chair across from me, he couldn't keep his head off the table, even after his prime rib arrived.

Charlie Clarkson came to our table wearing a white sports coat and silk tie, hands cupped behind his back. He said he'd be happy to pay for our dinner if we agreed to excuse ourselves and return another night. I walked out and waited for J.D., who got escorted outside so gently that he thanked Charlie for a wonderful meal, even if the portions had been small. He settled into the passenger seat and struggled with his seatbelt, which I had to fasten for him.

He said, "Just met the nicest man back there. Very nice man."

I drove in silence, drafting the farewell note I'd leave for him in the morning.

After a mile, he said, "Honey, I believe *you'd* better drive."

The note I left the next morning said, "Filing for divorce today. Do not be here when I get home. Do not call. Get some help."

At 10 a.m., Charlie called me. I didn't know how he learned my name or where I worked, but I soon discovered he had connections. For three years, I'd worked as Chief Deputy Clerk of Superior Court, having sat through one interview with Wayne Maddox, whose only question was whether I'd finished having babies. He touched my lower back every time he passed, made hourly references to his penis, which he'd named "Moby," yelled sexist jokes to lawyers, judges, and cops, who answered with their own sexist jokes from across the room.

When Charlie invited me to lunch, begging my pardon for being so forward, I thought I'd found the last gentleman on earth. On our first date, at his restaurant, he told me I was Grace Kelly's twin. I shrugged it off, enjoyed an excellent crab bisque.

He was a recovering alcoholic with two daughters in Toronto, where their mother had taken them when she left Charlie for being a lying drunk, which he admitted he was before A.A., the amends-making, the letting go and letting God and so forth. I told him my first husband often crawled from the bed to the toilet and my last husband greeted me every night with slurred speech, falling over kitchen chairs on his way to hug me.

He said, "Insanity is repeating the same behavior and expecting different results. *I* say the past is a toxic relic and the future is a fantasy. Here's to this moment." He lifted his water glass and bumped it against mine.

Then he said, "I'm dying."

I looked up to see him staring at me.

"Liver cancer. A local doctor said I had a year, so I flew to Rochester, Minnesota, for a second opinion and they gave me six months. I've decided not to have chemo."

I put down my spoon and wiped my mouth.

He said, "Go to Paris with me. Then to Venice, London, Hawaii, New York, Chicago."

I said, "I'm sorry."

His extended family lived in Chicago. He wanted to say goodbye to them.

"My mother," he said. "She was the greatest woman ever to walk this earth."

He started tearing-up. I refused to be talked into granting a dying man his final wish.

"My sister will love you," he said. "She owns a restaurant there."

"No. I'm sorry. It just wouldn't be—I can't do that."

"My two daughters will also love you. They'll be there."

"I'm sorry. No."

But I stopped by his restaurant every night on my way home. We ate together at a dimly-lit corner table—he always kissed my cheek, pulled out my chair, smiled, happier to see me than any man had ever been. He listened—he *concentrated* on listening—to me talk about my days, called the men I worked with bastards. He was kind to his employees, especially the women. He refused to be waited on—he went to the kitchen to get our meals and brought them back. He worried about his daughters and the kinds of men they'd marry, calling them daily, just to ask if they needed anything. Already, I wanted desperately for Harold to meet him so he could learn the finer points of being a gentleman.

*

Harold

The first thing I learned about being a gentleman was that you should stare into another man's eyes without blinking and smile while you try to break his hand in a firm shake. I had trouble maintaining eye contact with Charlie Clarkson; he was too intense. A day after I'd come home from my junior year of college, Charlie offered me a summer job as chief assistant to the head chef, "Big Mama," a 6'-5" four hundred pound African-American man who impersonated his favorite singers while cooking dishes like mussels milanese and pecan-encrusted red snapper topped with sautéed shrimp.

Charlie said, "Mama will take care of you. She'll teach you."

On my first night, while I diced onions to be sprinkled in hush puppy batter, Charlie approached me, sighed at my slowness, pulled the knife from my hand and looked me in the eye.

"This is a bread knife," he said. "See the serrated edges? You need a straight-edged knife. A man should learn his knives. I'll tell you something else: if you ever get into a knife fight, hold your knife like this." He pressed his thumb against the back of the blade and carved up the air in front of my nose. "This way, you can slice somebody's neck instead of trying to stab it."

Charlie pulled a new knife from a drawer, held my half-finished onion on the cutting board and demonstrated proper technique, keeping the knife's tip pressed on the board while he used a rapid rocking motion instead of the sawing motion I'd used.

Then he pressed the knife against my heart. He said, "Listen: I'm going to ask your mother to marry me."

I squinted toward him, closed one eye, then the other.

"She likes her house and where she lives, so I guess I'll be living there with you, but it won't change the relationship you and I enjoy. Do you have any questions?"

I wiped my eyes, then realized I shouldn't have.

"Don't wipe your eyes, son. Use your apron. If the onions get to you, go stand in the walk-in freezer. I'll give you one more piece of advice: never marry a psychologist. My second wife was a psychologist, and she spent seventeen years trying to convince me I was crazy. Tell you something else." Charlie pointed the knife at my neck. "You want a happy marriage, you need to make some money. What're you studying?"

I hadn't declared a major at that point, but I was leaning toward English.

"I'm leaning toward English," I said.

"Holy Christ. Why would you lean toward English? You want to work in a restaurant the rest of your life or do you want to *own* a restaurant? This is America, son. Get into real estate. Isn't your father a salesman? Christ, get *him* to teach you something. How tall are you?"

"Five-seven." This was a one-inch stretch.

Charlie handed me the knife, handle first, slapped my back and walked away. I went to the walk-in freezer and stood there awhile. Big Mama walked in and stood beside me.

Mama said, "Honey, this kitchen so hot, sweat be running down my crack and down my legs into my shoes making *puddles.*"

I agreed it was hot.

Big Mama said, "Harold? Let's go out back and tie a yellow ribbon 'round that old *oak* tree. You got a girlfriend?"

"No."

"Me neither." Big Mama laughed a loud and crazy laugh. "My old man died on me last year and left me brokenhearted. Anybody give you any shit around here, you let me know. Mama will kick they ass all over the kitchen for you, sweetie. I can tell you gone need looking after."

"I better get back to my onions."

"Yeah. You better get back to your onions."

*

Jude

I took off the first two weeks of June and flew to Paris with Charlie. We stayed in adjoining rooms on the top floor of a four-star hotel, balcony view of the Eiffel Tower. The next day, he paid for a boat to take us down the Seine, stopping at Notre Dame so I could climb to the bell while he waited in a pew. Everywhere we walked, couples kissed, held hands, cuddled on benches. Charlie said the tourism bureau paid some young natives to be romantic, but I thought all the couples looked sincere. Charlie put his arm around my waist and walked me across the Pont du Carrousel toward the Louvre, where we went straight to the Mona Lisa, then Venus de Milo, then he followed me for a couple of hours without a single complaint while I walked slowly by all the glorious portraits on the second floor.

Later, we took a cab to a restaurant Charlie knew, mirrored walls, frescos on the ceilings, 1930's light fixtures, a four course meal featuring boeuf bourguignon for me and coq au vin for Charlie, Grand Marnier soufflé for me, crème brulee for Charlie. The next morning, Charlie hired a car and driver to take us to Versailles. Inside the bright sun, while I stood on the steps of the Château de Versailles, with the Grand Palace behind me and the gardens in front of me, Charlie removed a large diamond from his pocket and proposed. I told him no.

*

Harold

Some Friday nights while I arranged shrimp cocktails or oysters on the halfshell, Mama would say, "Harold-honey. You know how I feel tonight?"

And I would say, "Lonely?"

Then Mama would impersonate an emcee introducing Roy Orbison, who was appearing on this special night only to perform just one song: "Only the Lonely." Then Mama would sing it slowly, stretching and enunciating the O's with bright clarity, supplying his own backup (dum, dum, dum, dum-be-do-wa), holding the high notes for a super-human duration toward the song's finish. Then Mama thanked his audience and gave way to the emcee who asked Roy very nicely if he could sing it one more time, so Mama did. It was beautiful, and I never tired of hearing it.

At the ends of these Friday nights, after I mopped and clocked out, Mama would say, "Harold? Do you know the heartache I've endured?"

And I would say, "Goodnight, Mama."

And Mama would say, "Do you know why I cry at night?"

And I would walk out the door and start across the parking lot.

And Mama would yell after me, saying, "I cry for you." Then he'd laugh a loud laugh that filled the night sky with heartache.

*

Jude

In the Grand Canal of Venice, while our gondolier sang an operatic tune and his companion played his guitar and we moved slowly toward the Bridge of Sighs at sunset, Charlie Clarkson reached for my hand and proposed again. Again, I told him no. Two days later, in London, inside the Poet's Corner of Westminster Abbey, he dropped to one knee and proposed again. Again, I told him no.

Over dinner in London, I explained what I assumed was obvious.

"Marriage should not be entered into under the assumption that it'll be a brief affair. And I will *not* be called a gold-digger. I wouldn't be able to stand that."

"You're supposed to grant a dying man his final wish."

"Oh, please," I said. "You keep that up and I'll have to kill you."

He said, "I love you."

I said, "Pass the pudding."

*

Harold

Before Big Mama impersonated Elvis, he impersonated the emcee introducing Elvis. He held a spatula to his mouth and said, "Ladies and gentlemans, now coming to the stage: the world-renowned singer, lover, movie star, and good Christian boy who loved his mama, the King: Elvis Presley." Then Mama sang "Heartbreak Hotel," slowly and powerfully, with enough feeling that I sometimes stopped what I was doing just to watch. When he finished, he thanked his audience. He thanked them very much, and he brought the emcee back to introduce Elvis for an encore.

On a Tuesday in late June, after I mopped and clocked out, Mama said, "Harold? Ain't you so lonely you could die? I know I'm so lonely *I* could die, but the saddest thing is I know I ain't the only one."

And I said, "Goodnight, Mama." I walked across the parking lot. I walked so quickly I was afraid I'd hurt Big Mama's feelings. When I got to my car, I popped the trunk and removed two beers from the cooler I stocked every afternoon on my way to work. I wanted to give Mama one and invite him to talk while we leaned against my trunk. But Mama walked too slowly with a head hung too low, a sight that scared me for the kind of heaviness I was then afraid to keep company with. So I took both beers to my driver's seat and drove home. Then I took my beer cooler to the porch and drank ten more, alone, staring toward the dark and silent river.

The next morning, I found a message Buddy had left from a motel room in York, South Carolina. He'd been drinking too, from the sound of it. He sang "Oh Sonny Boy," to the tune of "Oh Danny Boy." I stood beside the answering machine, surprised at his soft singing voice. Then he stopped singing and started talking. He said, "I met a woman in the hotel bar tonight from Slovakia, who said I reminded her of her third husband, who was from Russia. So I proposed and she accepted. Just thought I'd share the news. Tell your mother I said hello."

The next day, I bought a harmonica.

*

Jude

At the end of June, I cashed in a week's worth of sick days and agreed to fly with Charlie to Hawaii. We took a helicopter ride over waterfalls, canyons, rainforests and wild flowers on Kauai. And while Charlie sat beneath an umbrella, I went snorkeling in Oahu's Hanauma Bay, nose to nose with fish speckled in yellows, blues, and reds circling above the coral reef. We drove a rented car to the North Shore, saw cows standing in the ocean, took another helicopter to Maui, where we stayed a night, eating on a patio that faced the sunset-layered ocean.

I said, "Charlie? Maybe tonight you could get one room instead of two. Save money." So that night I slept with him, for the first time, and enjoyed it. He was a very attentive lover, more interested in my pleasure than his, but it was not because he wanted me to think of him as a great lover; it was because he was sincerely interested in me, a kind of attention

I hoped Harold would provide to the woman he hoped to make happy.

*

Harold

One night in late July, while I peeled more shrimp, Big Mama said "Harold-honey? You know what's wrong with these arms?"

I said, "They're lonely?"

Then he brought out his emcee, who introduced Otis Redding, who performed all night, "These Arms of Mine." Mama sang it beautifully, with a painful and deliberate slowness, closing his eyes sometimes to concentrate, giving a soft quiver in the perfect spot that made me wish someone would answer Mama's desperate yearning to be treated right. Later, after I mopped, Mama said, "Harold-honey? You want to come over and see my Otis Redding jumpsuit?"

I said, "No, I'd better get home."

"Yeah," Big Mama said. "You'd better get home."

I went home with my harmonica, sat on the porch beside my beer cooler, dogs all around, and played my harp along with Little Walter and Sonny Boy Williamson. I bent notes, flapped my left hand for vibrato, closed it for muting, lifted my chin to blow long single notes through the summer air and across the river, imagining a woman across the marsh who was just then looking up from the instrument she was playing on her own lonely porch. To this woman I had not met, I said, *I miss you.*

The next morning, I found a message Buddy had left from a motel room in Rome, Georgia. He sang, "Sonny-boy?" Then he said, "I decided not to get married. Tell your mother I'm still available. Tell her I said hello. Or in case she's listening, I'll tell her myself. *Hello?*"

*

Jude

I came home, worked two weeks without seeing Harold at all because I was asleep when he got home from work and he was asleep when I left for work. Then I flew with Charlie to New York City for a long weekend. We walked through Central Park, the Metropolitan Museum of Art, went to a Broadway show, ate in restaurants I felt guilty going to after stepping around so many beggars. Charlie pulled my hand, advised fast-walking, later ordered appetizers, soups, hundred-dollar entrees, desserts I took one

86

bite from. At the top of the Empire State Building, he proposed again. I kissed him on the lips. I told him no.

*

Harold

One night in early August, Big Mama broke into a duet of Nat King Cole and Natalie Cole, singing both parts, alternating smoothly. It was impressive.

Mama said, "Harold? What the hell I'm doing in this kitchen? I could be in—I could be in ... *Las Vegas!*" Then he laughed at himself and sprinkled chopped pecans over a trout. He said, "You know how come I ended up in this godforsaken hot-ass place?"

I said I didn't know and peeled another shrimp.

"I lived in Detroit till I was twenty-five. One day I said to my mama, I said, 'Mama? Ain't I got a sister?' She said, 'Yeah you got a sister. She live in south Georgia where it's hot as Hades.' So I got on the bus and came to meet my sister. That was fifteen years ago. I miss my mama though. I ain't seen her in five years." Big Mama paused. Then he dropped into the deep voice of an announcer and said, "Ladies and gentlemans. Please welcome to the stage Nat King Cole and his daughter Natalie, who will perform for you this evening." Mama broke into the soft and soothing voice of Nat King Cole, who gave way to Natalie, and they harmonized until closing.

In the parking lot that night, Mama said, "Harold? You want to come meet my sister? She'd be happy to meet you, I bet."

"I'd better get home."

"Yeah," Mama said. "You'd better get home."

I went home, played my harmonica and drank beer while staring through the hot summer night toward an imaginary woman a million miles away who was playing her violin while she stared out her window back toward me with a wish that we would meet one day. The next morning, I played a message Buddy left from a motel room in Athens, Georgia. He said, "Sonny-boy? Mother of sonny-boy? It's summertime and my goddamn flowers are dying."

*

I took a long weekend in the middle of July and flew with Charlie to Chicago. We took a walking tour of the city's architecture, sat in Grant Park, walked through the Art Institute, then took a cab to the Southside steakhouse Charlie co-owned with his sister, Candace, who hugged me as if *I* were dying.

Her husband, Bernie, said, "What a saint. Putting up with this stiff." Bernie hugged me too. "A pure saint," he said. "When he croaks, you come live with us."

"Maybe you won't have to wait too long," Charlie said.

"Mind your own business," Bernie said.

Candace said, "I want to show you something."

"Get ready," Bernie said.

We followed Candace through the dining room, which was busy with well-dressed servers putting out silverware, lighting candles, straightening chairs. At the rear of the room, we entered a narrow hallway, walked to the back of it and stood for a moment in a pitch-black room.

Candace said, "I just need to turn on this light."

The room exploded with fifty faces yelling *surprise!* while confetti flew toward bright balloons perched against the ceiling, strings hanging down between all the standing bodies, applause and laughter bouncing off the walls. All of Charlie's cousins, aunts, and uncles were there. His three other sisters and their families were there. Childhood friends and people from his home neighborhood were there. His two daughters—pretty women in their early twenties—approached with the first hugs and others soon formed a line.

Charlie, already tired, asked me to sit beside him while everyone approached, hugged, talked, cried, laughed, remembered this time or that. In a half-hour, Candace flicked the lights.

She said, "I want to thank everyone for showing up to honor this stiff here, my brother, a beautiful person. Without family, what do we got? Nothing, that's what. I love you all."

The rest of the night, his daughters, Anna and Karen, sat next to me, giving names to faces, listing peoples' ailments. I showed them a picture of Harold.

"Is he married?" Karen said.

I laughed. "He's not getting married until he's forty, I hope. Right now, he has too much in common with his father. A little immature in the ways of love, you know?"

In two hours, I looked at Charlie's slumping body. I said, "Let's get you to bed."

He circled the room, hugged and kissed all the men and women, touched the heads of kids, laughed at every stop. I watched the love he gave his family and the love they gave back, and it was this that made me fall in love with him.

*

Harold

My last night of work sparked a glimmer of the affection I'd craved all summer from three women servers I had not, until I said *goodbye*, had the nerve to speak to. They each hugged me and said, very seriously, "Good luck." They seemed to think I needed it. After I clocked out, I walked across the parking lot with Mama, feeling strangely confident, wanting suddenly to do something meaningful with my last night.

I said, "Big Mama, would you like me to come over and meet your sister?"

"No, honey. My sister been feeling sick lately. I better get home and see is she alright. You take care, now."

I watched Mama get into his car and drive away. I stood in the parking lot a moment, looking toward the ocean, listening to the empty sky.

I left home the next morning to start my last year of college. I left while Jude was at work, which is what she wanted, she said, so she wouldn't be alone in the house while I drove away. In my passenger seat, I placed seven harmonicas in seven keys. And I played them all the way to Asheville, sometimes driving with my thighs. I decided, somewhere around Denmark, South Carolina, that I would devote my life to mastering the instrument, both to keep me company when I was alone, and so I could speak, eventually, to the girl who would know the language of the notes.

*

Jude

In September, Charlie weakened. I helped him into the bath, scrubbed his peeling skin, put him to bed, fed him soup, gave him morphine pills

89

his doctor had prescribed, offered frequent updates to his daughters and to his sisters when they called. On September 15, he died at home, as he'd wished, with me lying next to him. I made the calls, arranged for cremation and a simple service. He'd wanted his ashes split among his daughters, his sisters, and me. His daughters and sisters flew in one day and out the next. They told me to stay in touch, to visit, to call anytime, but I already knew I'd never see them again.

After the service, about ten p.m., while I lay in bed, lights out and eyes open, I picked up the ringing phone and heard the voice of Buddy's brother, Uncle O, who was calling to offer his condolences, having heard from Buddy who had heard from Harold that I'd lost someone close to me. He could relate, he said, having lost his first wife to cancer some eighteen years ago, which was when he'd gotten a card from me, he said, offering condolences.

"The truth is," he said, "I've wanted to call you since you had the good sense to divorce my brother fifteen years ago."

"Twenty years," I said. "What took so long?"

Uncle O laughed. "My fourth wife just left me, my three children are gone, and I'm all alone in this big house thinking about mistakes I've made and how to make the most of the time I have left. I'm lonely."

"I have to go."

"You still have a sharp tongue. I've always loved that about you."

"I'm tired. Call me another time, a little earlier."

He called the next night, confessed to being excited all day about speaking to me again from the comfort of his kitchen chair while he sipped whiskey and tried to forget about his hard day at the funeral home.

"Have you ever wondered," he said, "how your life could've turned out differently if you had married me instead of Buddy?"

"No. Not once."

"Be honest."

"Okay, once. But not since Harold was born."

"Who?"

"Ha-ha."

The next night, he called to say he had started the seven-hour drive that morning for a surprise visit. "I thought my condition was gone, but it's not." He'd driven beyond the last stoplight of town without the slightest symptom, feeling confident he might continue, but as the small town shrank in his mirror and the long road loomed ahead, his fingertips had started tingling, his heart kicked, his stomach churned up bile. At the county line, sweat gushed from everywhere all at once, and he had to pull over and wait for a deep breath.

"Happens every time I try to leave the county," he said. "I don't know what to do."

"I guess I'll have to come there. For a weekend. Separate bedrooms."

Two weeks later, he sent a cemetery worker to meet me at the Greensboro airport. I spent a weekend at his farmhouse, nestled into a Blue Ridge mountain. This was the town I'd lived in when Harold was born, and everywhere I looked, I remembered happiness and sorrow. Buddy still lived there, but I said I'd rather not see him if we could help it, which would be easy, Uncle O said, since Buddy spent so much time traveling, living out of motel rooms.

We drove by the places I'd lived in before and after Harold was born. When Uncle O stopped for a prescription refill at the same drugstore I'd gone to twenty years before, the pharmacist said, "Where you been hiding, pretty lady?"

"Various basements and attics," I said.

He laughed like it was the funniest thing he'd ever heard, and it made me feel at home.

Sunday morning, the same cemetery worker drove me back to the airport. Uncle O called that night to make sure I'd made it safely, and he called at 7 p.m. every night after that. More than any man I'd known, he liked the telephone. And I liked his voice. He spoke with eloquence, enunciating crisply in a deep and rhythmic voice that made me think of the kinds of well-bred people who visited the art museums I'd seen with Charlie.

Over the next few weeks, I listened while he detailed the trouble he'd inherited from his father's funeral home, recounting showdowns with auditors. He cried softly while he talked of what his mother had meant to him. He talked of how he'd disciplined his children by using techniques he'd learned in the Marines, and cried again, softly, while confessing that he'd pushed them away by pushing too hard.

One night he said, "The leaves are turning. Do you remember the

October leaves?"

I said, "Are you proposing to me?"

He paused. He said, "Will you?"

And I thought, well, Harold would be in Asheville, just sixty miles away.

I dropped my resignation like a bomb on my boss's desk and walked away. Then I called Harold, singing with enthusiasm.

"I don't know," he said. "It seems a little—"

"Don't be a party-pooper, Harold. Can't you be happy for my new adventure?"

In the second week of October, Harold flew home to help me move. He backed a twenty-six foot U-Haul to the kitchen door and loaded my furniture, which Uncle O said we'd use so I'd feel at home. My two sisters spent all day helping me pack and load. Mom was there too, rosary in hand, helping. Dad boycotted the move and stayed away, even the next morning, when Mom and my sisters met me in the driveway for hugs and tears while Harold pulled the truck away. I followed in my car, Saint Jerome, my dachshund, riding shotgun.

Eight hours later, Harold drove the U-Haul up and around the tight corners of narrow mountain roads. The sun shone brightly on the orange, golden, and purple leaves, and I felt attuned to the first chills of autumn.

Uncle O stood on his front porch, arms crossed, dark glasses and heavy beard masking his expression. He hugged me, said, "Welcome home."

The next day, after Uncle O left for work, Harold and I unloaded my furniture. I was stupid with excitement. I said, "I can't wait to paint these dreary walls. God, they're dreary. Don't you find them dreary? Maybe peach or mauve or strawberry-red. Let's burn his couch."

"I'm afraid he'd shoot us."

"Oh, he's not that bad," I said. "You'll see."

A week later, on a Friday night, Harold returned to see me. I told O, in a strong voice that invited no response, that I was taking my son to dinner. While Harold drove us to town, I talked nonstop, like he was my long-lost and only best friend.

I said, "I think I made a terrible mistake. I'm stuck in that dark house all day and I'm finding out things I wish I'd known before. Did you know he left his mother in a rat-infested nursing home and he hasn't seen her in a year? That's unforgivable. Did you know that?"

"I knew she was in a home, but I didn't know he hadn't—"

"You know what else? Five months ago, he drove his youngest daughter to a sanitarium because she finally went off the deep end, and then he granted custody of her three children to her drug-addicted husband instead of taking them himself. Did you know that?"

"I'd heard something about—"

"And he has a widowed and unemployed sister who lives alone in the next county who needs all kind of help, but he can't get to her because if he crosses the county line he'll have a heart attack. You know what he does at night? He spends hours in his basement, dressed in his underwear and a cowboy hat, wearing a holster, facing a mirror and doing the quick-draw on himself, over and over, testing his speed. His basement is full of stacked cases of beans and forty pound bags of rice that he's storing for the coming apocalypse. Did you know the apocalypse was just around the corner?"

"He mentioned something about it."

"He's your father's brother, but he has a *file* on him. Letters, charts, pictures, clippings—pieces of evidence meant to *prove* your father is crazy. You believe that?"

"I believe that."

"You *do*? Guess what else? I'm not allowed to get mail delivered to the house. I have to use his P.O. box because he doesn't want his address known. Also—his funeral home's about to go bankrupt and there's a good chance he'll lose his house and land."

Harold pulled into the restaurant and turned off the car.

I said, "Am I the stupidest person in history or what?"

He said, "This place has good Brunswick stew."

"Not as good as your grandmother's, I bet."

"No. Not that good."

The day before Thanksgiving, I handed O a long grocery list for things we needed for the dinner I said I'd cook. I kissed him. When he left, I wrote this note: "I've run away. Do <u>not</u> call." I put Saint Jerome in the passenger seat and drove back home to my empty house.

∗

Harold

On my first day of Christmas break, I drove a U-Haul to Uncle O's house and backed it down the driveway. It was a cold and cloudy day and a heavy snow had fallen the week before. Uncle O stepped out wearing pajamas and dark glasses, carrying a camera. His thinning hair stood on end. He looked like he hadn't slept since my mother left him. He met me at the back of the truck.

He said, "If you love your mother, you'll get her some help."

I chuckled at the source for this advice. I sprang the lever back and raised the door as loudly as I could.

"I'm not going to get in your way," Uncle O said. "But I'm also not going to help you. I trust you understand how debilitating that would be."

I made countless trips through the garage and into the house, returning with clothes, lamps, unopened boxes, my mother's paintings. I dragged the couch and chairs through the house, stopped to rest every few feet, then dragged them again, pulling, then pushing, then pulling up the ramp into the truck while Uncle O sat in a lawn chair just inside the garage, taking pictures. He took a picture every time I loaded something.

In two hours, when I pulled the door down and locked it, Uncle O stood. He said, "You want a beer?" He meant, *don't leave.* I felt a little sorry for him then. It was easy to imagine how alone he'd feel once I drove away. But my mother was waiting for me, so I pulled the truck keys out. Uncle O took off his dark glasses and stared at me. His narrow eyes were wet and red.

He said, "Forget that thing I said earlier about your mother. I loved her before you were born and I still love her, even after this. It's painful. One day you might understand, but I hope you don't. I hope one day you will meet a woman who will not leave you while the world is ending. I wish that for you. But here's some free advice: don't marry a therapist. My second and fourth wives were therapists and they were crazy. I'm telling you this because I care about you. We're still family." He put his hand on my shoulder.

I said, "I have to go."

I looked back while I drove away and saw him taking my picture.

94

*

Jude

Between Thanksgiving and mid-December, I lived with my parents. Saint Jerome and I stayed in my childhood bedroom while we waited for Harold to come with my furniture. This also gave my recently-divorced niece time to return her belongings to the condo. I hated to kick her out of my house, which she'd been excited to move into. I told her the same thing I told my sisters and my parents. I said, "I'm pretending that I never left, and I'd appreciate it if you could play along by not asking any questions." No one ever did.

Three weeks later, Harold backed the U-Haul up to the door, just as he'd done three months ago. We moved all my furniture into the same places, put the pictures on the same spots on the same walls. My sisters, my nieces, and my mother helped, happy to have me back. They laughed and complained about being in each other's way and we talked a great deal about everything but my recent foolishness. Late that night, after Harold pulled down the door of the U-Haul, after we ate the chicken Mom brought over, after my sisters and nieces said *so long* and *welcome back*, I lay in my old bed, tucked beneath the covers in my old room, watching my old television. Harold came in to say goodnight and lay on the other side of the bed.

I said, "I guess I'm pretty stupid. How could you let me make such a huge mistake?"

"What?" he said. "I'm pretending it never happened."

"You should've stopped me. Next time, stop me. Did he say anything when you went there with the truck?"

"Who?" he said.

A couple minutes later, I said, "Have you ever felt like you were standing on a tiny little cliff where if the smallest little breeze came along it might push you right over the edge and you'd fall about a thousand feet? Have you ever felt like that?"

"I think so."

"One minute you're floating in the sun, and the next minute you're falling a thousand feet. But we survive and grow tougher for surviving. We survive because we have each other. Without each other, what do we have?"

"Nothing?"

"That's right."

I must've gone to sleep with Harold still in the bed. That's the last thing I remember. A couple of quick weeks later, he went back to college and left me more alone than I've ever been. It was the kind of deep aloneness I hoped he too would experience at some point. There's the kind of loneliness we can waste our short lives trying to escape and there's the kind of loneliness one should learn to live with before one lives with someone else.

Chapter 7
Jude

I hated to wake Harold so early on Christmas morning, but I needed his help. I was afraid I'd already woken him and Libby anyway because my phone had rung (only a sister dare call at such an hour), and I'd already clanked some cups and banged through the kitchen door a couple times, which made Libby's little dog yelp like a squeaky-toy. Still, I tiptoed into the living room and squatted beside him and shook his shoulder.

"Harold," I said. "Is that you?" I tried to whisper, but Libby sighed so loudly it seemed like a curse. "That beard looks awful, Harold. Just *awful*. And I can't find Saint Jerome. Come help me look. Coffee's on the counter."

"Merry Christmas," Libby said. She lifted her head off the pillow and squinted one eye toward me. I gave her credit for trying to be chipper so early, poor thing.

"Sorry to wake you. Try to sleep in—I need Harold to help me find Saint Jerome."

"Who's Saint Jerome?" she said.

"My oldest dachshund. He's missing."

"I'll help," she said.

It was good of her to offer. "No," I said. "Sleep in. Harold will help. Hurry up, Harold."

I went out and started looking down by the river. It was a bright and pleasant morning—already too warm. A family of buzzards circled me, but that wasn't unusual. When Harold came out, the other four dogs ran from me to him and back to me, wagging tails, frolicking in the early light while Harold walked toward me in a crooked line, carrying his coffee, hair sticking up. And I thought, for just one moment, that he was still a little boy. But when he got close and we hugged, I thought he'd aged forty years in five seconds. I grabbed his shoulders and pushed him backward.

"Will you shave that silly beard before your grandfather sees it? Your hair's too long too. And you could stand to lose about twenty pounds. How do *I* look?"

"Fine," he said, of course, but I knew better. I was aging rapidly, too. I'd noticed a new neck wrinkle just this morning and brown spots were crawling over my hands.

I said, "Do you think Libby likes me yet? Did I make a good first impression? Do you think she'll like it here?"

He batted away a bug, sipped his coffee, looked at the river. "Sure," he said.

He didn't sound convincing. I wanted her to like me and this place well enough to move here so Harold (and my grandchildren) would be close. Harold could get a job at the community college and she could start a private practice on St. Simons that specialized in rich people's problems. Two homes were for sale in the subdivision behind us—houses I'd already mentioned in emails to Harold, adding links, without any pressure—just innocent information. Why wouldn't she like it? Hadn't she grown up in crowded New York City surrounded by concrete and buildings and homeless people and dangers everywhere? And didn't she live now in Atlanta, which is *almost* a suburb of New York? What I planned, secretly, was an after-lunch walk around the subdivision so she could see how nice it was. The For Sale signs would speak for themselves. I would hold my tongue and apply no pressure.

Why wouldn't she like the view of this river, even now, when the tide was going out and the low water revealed the fiddler crabs on the opposite bank, lined up like spectators filling bleachers? And above them, the marsh grass sprouting like hair at the top of a forehead, then spreading like a shiny flattop for a half mile in three directions, a little pinch of salt in the air that offered the constant hint of the natural and wild earth we would soon return to.

Harold looked over the marsh while he sipped his coffee, considering similar things, I imagined. I said, "Harold, don't get fat like your father. He's let himself go. You should prepare yourself."

"He seemed okay last night."

"You saw him last night? Did Libby see him too? She didn't see the condo did she?"

"She saw it."

"Oh God."

Father Cletus was rolling on a dead carcass, probably a squirrel, though it was hard to tell. There was no stopping him, so I got a stick and lifted the carcass and tossed it in the river.

"Poor ol' Saint Jerome," I said. "I rescued him right after you left home the first time, when you left me alone with J.D. the drunkard. Then Jerome went with me to North Carolina when I married your Uncle O, that fool. We've been through a lot, Jerome and I."

Harold took his coffee and walked down the path the dogs had made into the marsh, wide from the knees down where they had carved an opening. About twenty yards later he stopped, marsh grass up to his armpits. He sipped his coffee and surveyed his surroundings.

I said, "I don't think he'd go in *there* to die, Harold."

When he came back down the path and stood beside me, he stank of mud and something rotten. "Libby will love you now," I said.

I looked to my left, through the low-lying oak limbs, and in a gap between dangling moss, I saw my father slow-stepping across his yard toward his chair at the river. He wore a coat and a winter hat, though he needed neither, and he carried a long cane pole, using it like a walking stick. He plowed ahead, slow and steady, like he was on a boat being rocked by waves.

"There goes your grandfather," I said.

When he got to his chair, he fell into it. He laid his cane pole horizontally across the arms of the chair, put his own arms over it, and stared toward the river.

"He sits like that for hours," I said.

"He's waiting for the tide to come in," Harold said, eager to defend him.

"He has no bait. He sits there all day, just like that, while your grandmother watches from the window, afraid he's going to fall in."

"He's meditating."

"He thinks your grandmother is sleeping with the ninety-year-old bag boy at Winn Dixie. He also thinks—when she finds time to get away from the bag boy—that she's having sex with your Uncle Sludge. Can you imagine? Like Uncle Sludge would even take out his tobacco for sex? He's also suspicious of Father Cletus, which I sort of understand. If you ever act like that to your wife, I'll come back from the grave and rip off your testicles."

"I would never do that."

"Men do that. They go crazy over their penises, especially when they can't get it up anymore. It's a big payoff for your grandmother to put up with his shit all these years and be rewarded like this in the end. She told me last week that she almost left him fifty years ago, and she wished she had. She said she had me and your two aunts loaded in the car with our bags packed, but she had no money and got scared and all she could do was sit in the car and cry, then go back inside. I don't remember it."

Harold stared at his grandfather—the only man who had been a constant presence in his life. I wondered whether I should be revealing such things. It was strange how I could go months without sharing much by phone, but the second Harold came home, I had to tell him everything, all at once. He sipped his coffee and stared at his grandfather. Then he abruptly turned away, toward the marsh, and called for Jerome, who did not answer.

I wondered whether Harold had some romantic idea that staying married for sixty years was heroic. Sometimes it could be, I guess, but the fine line between martyrdom and heroism got harder for me to see the longer I watched my mother.

Harold sipped his coffee and stared at his grandfather, who was staring at the river. He said, "Maybe he just wants an excuse to leave the house for awhile and do some thinking."

"Some thinking," I said, and laughed. "One morning a few weeks ago, Mom woke up at 4:30, like always, and went home to wake him, but she couldn't find him. She looked all over the house, then went to the garage and saw his truck was gone, so she came and knocked on my window, hysterical and sobbing. I called 911 to report him missing, and the dispatcher said, 'Does he drive a red Chevy S-10?' She told me where he was, so I called Sister for us to go get him, and when we got there—he'd pulled into a church parking lot—he was sitting on his tailgate wearing his boxer shorts and his t-shirt, no shoes, no teeth, no glasses, looking like a scared little boy, six cops standing around him. Someone had seen him driving down the wrong side of the road with no lights on. One cop gave me his license, said I should lie and tell him that the sheriff insisted on keeping it, so he'd be mad at them instead of us. But it's our fault anyway. He said the reason he had to leave home at four in the morning was because his wife and daughters and grandchildren and great-grandchildren were all running through the house making too much noise. I hope he'll be nice to Libby."

Harold turned away and walked in the opposite direction, toward Mary's house, calling for Jerome, who did not answer. The other dogs ran ahead with wagging tails. I was telling him too much too fast, but I couldn't stop. We walked between the marsh and the old dirt road, just barely detectable now. I wondered then whether Libby had ever seen a dirt road, outside of movies. Maybe Harold would paint her a picture: stand in the center of it and tell her how it had started at the highway and went straight for one mile, thick woods on one side, the river on the other, passing Mom and Dad's house, then mine (once owned by a dairy hand, then remodeled), then past his Aunt Carol's house before dead-ending at his Aunt Mary's house. Wouldn't Libby like marrying into a family all aligned on a single road? It was a different picture now, of course, winding through the paved road of Riverside Drive, (without once seeing the river), past all the brick houses and brick mailboxes and quarter-acre lots before slowing to the narrow gap between two old oaks (always missed by pizza delivery-drivers) that opened up to the gravel road that went behind our houses, hugging the chain link fence that enclosed the twelve acres Sparky kept, thinking it was enough to buffer us. I've often wondered whether his dementia began during those months that he sat outside and listened to the constant cacophony of bulldozers, saws, and hammers, and watched new houses spring up like popcorn, confused at the two-lane traffic racing in and out of the new subdivision, kids in new cars boom-booming their stereos, oblivious to history.

Harold walked toward Mary's, calling for Jerome.

"Harold? I'm not going to give you any marital advice at all, even though I do have a little experience along the lines of making a mistake or two."

"Okay," he said, then pointed at an egret who was standing in the shallow water, repeatedly plucking up something and dropping it. He said, "That egret is trying to eat a frog."

So it was. The frog's legs were flapping while the egret held it. Then he spat him out and plucked him up again and spat him out again, all while standing on one leg.

"Except to say," I said, "that you should be absolutely certain that you're madly in love with Libby. Because if you're not madly in love with Libby, it's going to be hard to get through all those times when it's a pain in the ass to live with someone and you want desperately to leave. But if you're madly in love, you'll only want to leave for a little while instead of forever. Are you? Madly in love with Libby?"

He called again for Saint Jerome. He said, "I guess so."

"You guess so. I have one more final piece of advice."

The egret dropped the frog and shook its head, as if the frog had shat into its mouth.

"My only other advice is that you should not take any advice from your father. He means well, but I'm afraid he just really doesn't know jack-shit about much of anything. It's kind of sad. He had such potential. You know what I think I loved about him most? I saw how much he loved his mother, and I loved that. You can't be all bad if you love your mother very much now can you?"

Harold pointed to two turkey vultures standing on my sister Carol's roof, close enough to surprise me with their size. They were busy grooming each other, beaks buried into one another's shoulders, which was something I'd never seen. In the air above them, other vultures circled. Carol's house was dark, run down, in need of great repair. There were holes in the laundry room floor where raccoons came and went as they pleased, and probably large colonies of rodents breeding in every corner, attracting snakes.

I said, "Did I tell you that your cousin Sarah and her two kids moved back home and are living here with Carol?"

"No."

"Sarah's husband announced one day that he was starting a new family with his high school sweetheart in California, and off he went. He said he hated being a father to the kids Sarah had already spoiled, and he called her all sorts of bad things and took off, and she lost her house and moved in with her mother."

Harold called again for Saint Jerome. I had a feeling he didn't want to hear anymore, but I couldn't stop.

"Her own father left in about the same way when she was ten, shortly after her sister drowned in the river, which is something no one ever talks about, as you know. But now her father's back and trying to make an effort to be involved. He sings in church, apparently."

Harold called for Jerome.

"Sarah's daughter, Catie? She's funny. I had a few wild cats around here before the dogs killed them all, and a few weeks ago, Catie found one that had been decapitated, so she walked over while I was watering my flowers, and she said, 'Aunt Jude? I found a cat whose head fell off.' So I told her yes, sometimes their heads fall off, and she was satisfied by that. But oh Lordy, we've got some sad stories around here, Harold. People must think I'm one of them. No one gets through this life unscathed. There's sorrow and hardship and we make the best of it and then we die. The trick is to find someone who can help you carry your cross while you help carry theirs. Do you and Libby help carry each other's crosses?"

"I guess so."

"You guess so." He didn't have a lot to say about Libby, I noticed. Maybe it was too early, or maybe he was hiding things. He called again for Saint Jerome.

We walked to Mary's house, and then behind it, where her back yard met the marsh, and where, at the highest of new-moon tides, the water came to her back door, sometimes stranding snakes. Harold squatted to look beneath a pile of tin stacked on cinderblocks.

"I don't think he'd go under there to die, Harold."

At the far end of the yard, next to her horse stable, Mary yelled at us. She said, "What are y'all *doing*?"

Her quarter horse, Lady, was saddled and ready for riding. Mary led her across the yard, singing Harold's name with some excitement. She'd always been a sort of second mother to him, watching from one side while he grew up, patching wounds, driving him places, scolding him when she spied him coming home too late from God knows where, slipping him some occasional spending money. She'd been a constant source of support all of our lives, even as she lived through her own trouble—she'd hurt her back forty years ago lifting crates of glasses at a diner where she worked each day's breakfast and lunch shifts before walking to the hotel next door to work each day's 3-11 shift, finding time, somehow, to raise two daughters and to fall in and out of love with four husbands who came and went and took something of her with them, though one of them died slowly after falling out of a tree he was trimming with his chainsaw. Her first, Uncle Sludge, earned his nickname from the plug of tobacco he kept in his cheek, even inside, where he gossiped circles around the women without ever spitting. I don't know why Mary asked him to leave, but I admired her courage at the time—she was the first of Roberta's daughters who put into action a plan for a different kind of life than the type Roberta could only imagine. She was tough, my sister, and if ever we needed a fierce fighter to stand beside us, or in front of us, we could do no better.

She led Lady across the yard now, let go of her reins and reached out to hug Harold. Then she backed up, still holding to his shoulders, and made an exaggerated ugly face. She said, "Harold-honey, you need to lose the beard." Then she hugged him and frowned. "And you could use a shower. You been in the marsh?"

"We're looking for Saint Jerome," I said.

"Oh hell. I just saw him yesterday, seems like, running around and playing."

Just then, from my house, came a scream that Mary would later describe as "loud enough to wake every dead soul between here and New Orleans."

Mary was the first to move. She stepped into the stirrup and swung her leg over the saddle in one motion, and I stepped quickly into the same stirrup, threw my leg over Lady's rump and said, *go*. We raced away, four dogs following, our hair bouncing, Harold following on foot. When we got closer, I saw Libby standing beside Harold's car, still in her pajamas, both hands covering her mouth, staring toward the pampas grass in the flowerbed. She kept staring even as Lady came up and stopped. I got down and went to her. She pointed.

"Damn," I said. "We should have looked closer to home."

Saint Jerome's hair was matted and soaked, and part of his intestines had seeped through his stomach and were lying in front of him like tangled worms. Ants walked across his head and body. A dark pool of blood had gathered on the ground beneath his nose.

Harold came running up behind us, wheezing. He grabbed Libby's shoulders, trying to lead her back inside, but she jerked away.

"Is he dead?" she asked.

"Looks that way," I said. I was still bent over him, examining his body.

"How long has he been lying there like that do you think?" Libby said.

"Hard to say," Harold said. "Let's go inside."

"Poor Jerome," I said. I dropped to one knee for a closer look. Harold stepped behind me and put his hands on my shoulders.

Carol came jogging across the yard from her house. Mary, intercepting her, said, "We just found Saint Jerome, who is not in the best shape, and we just got a little excited is all."

It was just like Mary to help Libby, the stranger, seem less strange.

Carol said, "But I just saw him yesterday. I'm pretty sure it was yesterday. He was running and playing." She smiled at Libby. She said, "I'm Harold's Aunt Carol."

Libby hugged her. She said, "Merry Christmas."

"Yes," Carol said. "Merry Christmas."

Mary stepped beside me to look at Saint Jerome. She said, "Looks like he might've tangled with a coon."

Libby put a hand over one eye. Her other eye was teary.

Mary said, "I'm Harold's Aunt Mary."

Libby hugged Mary. She said, "Merry Christmas."

"Yes," Mary said. "Merry Christmas."

Libby said, "Don't raccoons carry rabies?"

"Very few of them," Harold said. "A very small minority, really."

Carol said, "I swear—I just saw him running and playing yesterday. Or the day before."

Libby said, "Is that Jerome who smells like that?"

"Poor baby," Mary said. "He was a good dog."

"That's me," Harold said. "I went into the marsh looking for him."

I said, "Harold, get the shovel."

"I'll get a garbage bag," Mary said.

Libby's hand went over her nose.

Harold said, "Mom? Did you meet Libby?"

I looked at Libby. I said, "I'm sorry you had to be the one to find him. It's not a pretty sight, is it?"

Libby hugged me. She squeezed for a long time. I wasn't sure she would let go. She said, "I'm so sorry for your loss."

I felt it best not to touch her after I'd touched Jerome, so I just stood there and let her squeeze, stretching my eyes toward Harold as if to ask how long the hug might last. She finally released me, stepped back, wiped her eyes.

I said, "Did you find some breakfast?"

"I'm okay," she said. "I don't have much of an appetite."

Mary said, "Hell, it's only seven o'clock. Maybe the day won't get any worse."

Shuffling around the house just then, rushing to the rescue of the screamer, came Sparky, using his cane pole as a walking stick. He lifted his head every couple of steps to confirm his coordinates, stopping completely once to make an angled turn. He stepped widely around Lady's backside, then slapped her flank. His face was drenched in sweat, eyes wide with worry.

Carol said, "Morning, Daddy. You going fishing?"

He looked at Mary, then at me, then at Carol, then at Harold, then at Libby, then back at Harold. His mouth stretched to a wide smile he tried to close but couldn't.

"Well, well," he said. "There's the old maid of the family. With some kind of shit all over his face. Was that *you* screaming?"

"No. It was—"

"Everything's fine, Daddy," I said.

"Sounded like a damn steer getting his nuts chopped off," he said.

"No, Daddy," I said. "It must've come from back there somewhere." I pointed toward a house on the other side of the chain link fence, where three children played loudly every summer afternoon in their in-ground pool.

I pulled Mary to my side to block the pampas grass. It was best to spare Sparky (and consequently, Roberta), an image of death that he'd spend all day obsessing over. And Jerome's death *would* disturb him. The dog had been a fixture in his life for thirteen years, climbing on his picnic table to lick his face, curling in his lap when he sat in his swing, staring through the glass door of the side porch until Sparky relented and let him in, then they'd both sleep in his recliner. Despite his troubles, Sparky had yet to forget a name, and Jerome was the name he called most frequently. So it was best to keep Jerome's death a secret.

"Sounded like a damn sow getting her throat slit," he said.

Carol said, "Daddy, this is Libby, Harold's girlfriend he brought home from Atlanta."

"Fiancée," I corrected.

Carol put her hand on Libby's shoulder. Libby hugged her again.

Mary said, "Congratulations."

"His what?" Sparky said.

"Fiancée," Mary shouted. "The woman he's going to marry."

"Who's getting married?" he said.

"Harold's getting married," I said.

"*I'm* getting married," Harold said. "To Libby here. She's from Atlanta."

"New York, actually." She gave Sparky a big smile. She had good teeth; I'll say that for her—early orthodontia, no doubt, heavy maintenance.

"*Harold's* getting married?" Sparky said.

"Yes," I said. "To Libby."

Libby laughed a nervous laugh. She said, "I'm very pleased to be part of the family."

Sparky looked at her, then at Harold. He said, "They ain't no future in that, Harold. After that comes babies, and after babies, it's all downhill, boy."

Libby gave a little giggle and lowered her head.

"Look coming here," Sparky said. "We got some real help on the way now."

Around the near side of the house came Buddy, barefooted, thick hair standing up, his belly button exposed between his t-shirt and purple sweat pants.

Buddy said, "Everybody okay out here?"

"Just fine," I said. "Thanks for rushing out."

Buddy said hello to his ex-sister in-laws. They had never acted like it was strange that he should end up living behind me, nearly thirty years after we'd divorced. Even Sparky, who hadn't liked Buddy thirty years ago, had recently warmed up to him.

Buddy positioned himself next to Harold, ready for a whisper of the truth. When Sparky looked up to check the sky, I heard Harold give Buddy the scoop.

"Ah hell," Buddy said. "Jerome died? I just saw him yesterday, playing and running around."

Sparky said "*Who* died?"

"This old friend of ours," I said.

Buddy caught up with my cue. "This ol' boy we used to know from a long way back."

Sparky said, "The Lord taketh and then He taketh again. That's how that song goes."

Lady decided just at that moment to release her bowels. The excrement came as if poured from a bucket and smacked the ground and then kept coming while everyone remained silent. Libby's eyes got a little wider and her mouth scrunched into a frown.

Sparky said, "Looks a little wormy."

Mary said, "She's on some antibiotics, but she's getting better."

I said, "Harold, get the shovel."

Carol guessed she'd go back home now, but not before giving Libby a little shoulder pat and a sympathetic look that clearly said *good luck with the rest of your Christmas Day.*

Buddy said, "I'm going back to bed. Call me if you need me." And he walked away.

Sparky said, "Harold, throw that shit beneath that peach tree yonder."

Libby said, "I think I'd like to take a shower and change clothes if that's all right."

"Harold?" I said. "Did you warn Libby about the sulfur water?"

"It's nothing," he said. "I can't even smell it. Some people say it has a strong odor if you're not used to it, but you might not even notice."

Mary said, "It just takes getting used to—it won't hurt you."

"It won't hurt you," Harold repeated.

"I'm sure it'll be fine," Libby said.

"It's good for you," Sparky said. "Puts hair on your chest."

"Okay, Daddy," Mary said. "I think I hear the fish calling."

"I do too," he said. He tipped his hat, said *good day*, then turned to begin his journey back, looking down, then up, stamping his cane pole next to his right foot.

Mary mounted Lady and moved her forward. "Sorry about the mess," she said. "But that reminds me. I'm bringing barbecued baked beans, so bring something else." She clucked her tongue twice and gingerly walked

Lady back home.

I said, "Libby, help yourself to whatever rags and towels and soaps and shampoos you can find."

"Thank you." She put her hand on my arm. She said, "If you'd like some help processing this painful experience, please let me know. I specialize in grief management, so I'll be happy to speak with you. Free of charge, of course." She cocked her head to the side and lifted her eyebrows.

"Thank you," I said. "I'll keep that in mind."

Libby smiled and went inside, and Harold came back with the shovel. He scooped what he could of Lady's pile and carried it to the peach tree.

I carried the bag that held Jerome, and we walked to our pet cemetery on the far side of the old road near the marsh, in a big square patch of soft dirt where I once kept a garden. None of the other graves had been marked because I didn't want to be reminded constantly of each dog's death (and life). I didn't want anything reminding me to be sad for what I'd lost.

While Harold dug the hole, I fetched a cinder block. I set it on its end, sat on it, and lit a cigarette. The other dogs had come to investigate what we were doing. They each came up to the bag and sniffed Jerome, then backed up slowly.

"Deeper," I said.

Harold kept digging. I looked behind us at the house. From inside one of the living room windows, Libby watched us. She held Penelope in one hand and her cell phone in the other. She was talking to her mother most likely, detailing the dramatic play-by-play of all the ugliness she'd seen so far as a foreigner inside this village with strange customs.

"Deeper," I told Harold.

Harold dug deeper and stopped. I lowered the bag. Sister Agnes stuck her nose into the hole, then turned her head sideways—first one way, then the other. Then she bounced back, wagged her tail and barked, as if asking Jerome to wake up and play.

I set the cinderblock on top of Jerome so he wouldn't wash up. Then I sat back on the ground, stared into the hole, sighed. I grabbed a handful of dirt and tossed it in.

"My baby," I said. "Sweet Saint Jerome. I got him right after you left for college."

"I know." Harold scooped the dirt and dropped it in.

Libby watched from the window, talking into her phone.

"Harold?" I said. "Do you think the day will get any worse?"

"We've got a long way to go," he said.

"Do you ever pray?"

"No," he said. "Not much."

"Might be a good time to start."

While Harold spread the last of the dirt, I looked to the window again and saw Libby still staring at us, Penelope in her arms. She was no longer on the phone. Then she disappeared back into the house.

"Maybe the day won't get any worse," I said.

Harold stepped on the dirt and stood back and we both stared at the covered grave.

"Maybe not," he said.

December 25, 8:35 a.m.

After Libby found Saint Jerome, she locked herself in the bathroom with Penelope, and I sat on the couch, listening to Mom call members of the St. Sebastian Bereavement Committee, begging each lady to donate a dish to the Griffin family, whose father had died in the night. I imagined Libby sitting on the closed toilet lid, explaining to Penelope that they would soon be home in their own safe place that they'd never have to leave again, not for any man. I wanted to knock on the door and ask her nicely to come out so we could start having a merry Christmas, but I was afraid she'd say *go away*, which I didn't want my mother to have to hear.

Libby had decided that I should shower first so I'd be out of her way, so I did, hoping she and Mom would spend that time becoming friends, but as soon as I'd stepped into the hall, Libby (and Penelope) brushed by me quickly and silently, trailing a gust of irritation. When I entered the living room, Mom was on the phone, saying, "Tiny, if you could open a can of green beans, you'd be a life-saver." She laughed at herself, briefly, then pulled a new cigarette from her pack and lit it. This was likely the kind of thing Libby had been listening to, while inhaling cigarette smoke, for the fifteen minutes I'd been gone.

Now, it was an hour later. I wanted to knock on the bathroom door and say *I love you*, but I was afraid she'd say go away.

I looked at the ceiling and spotted the hole I'd made with a three iron twenty years ago. The ceiling had been repainted, but Mom had given strict instructions (I wasn't sure why) to leave the hole intact. I wanted to point to the hole as a place where Libby might have a laugh, but I feared she'd unholster her microscope instead, jerk her knee, and conjure some insta-theory on how the hole proved that my mother continued to arrest my development and keep me infantilized. At which point I would push my fingers into my ears and sing la-la-la, hoping she might laugh, though it wasn't likely. Which made me wonder, again, why I planned to marry her.

Because I needed her to give me lectures on my arrested development? Because she helped me see myself more clearly, which I admitted (only to myself) was something I needed to do more often? I trusted her when she said the thing she cared most about was helping me. Still, I was too scared to expose the hole in the ceiling, so I lowered my eyes to the carpet beside my shoe and saw a quarter-sized patch of burnt carpet caused by a dropped cigarette. I covered it with my foot. I worried, already, that Libby would express some fear about us all burning to death this very evening while Mom smoked in bed.

Mom said, "Oh, for God's sake, Jo Ann." And blew smoke across the room. "Don't feel guilty. Grandchildren *should* be a priority. You would hope so, anyway."

I rose from the couch and went down the hall. I put my ear against the bathroom door, but heard nothing. I gently knocked. I said, "Y'all okay in there?"

"No," Libby said. "*Y'all* okay out there?"

"I love you," I whispered.

"What?"

"Are you coming out?"

"Go away," she said.

I returned to the couch and sat with my hands in my lap, knees touching. Mom blew smoke across the room. She said, "How old were you when you had *your* first grandchild?"

I imagined a movie-scene starring my alter-ego, a lonely Neanderthal dragging an axe to the bathroom door to swing away like Jack Nicholson's character in *The Shining*, a guy who was asking only for a chat. Then I blinked away the image and hated myself for picturing it, insisting I could never come close to doing such a thing. I looked out the window toward the peaceful marsh and inhaled deeply.

Mom said, "Please, Jo Ann. This is not the time of year to feel guilty."

I knew it was difficult for Libby. She'd never been away from her own family at Christmas, a fact she liked to repeat. I wanted to look into her eyes, hold her hand, and thank her for being *here*. I would concede that conditions weren't perfect and I would promise that next Christmas we would go to New York, or anywhere, or nowhere. I wasn't sure I could manage without her, and I planned to tell her so.

I knew Libby was nervous about making a good impression, that she was taking extra time now to prepare herself, applying makeup, which she normally didn't use and—so far as I could tell—did not need. I knew she would look pretty and that my mother and my entire family would be impressed with her and be proud of me for having "won," finally, a smart and pretty bride-to-be. Oddly, I felt a surge of hope for our future then, a feeling I planned to disclose to Libby as soon as she sat beside me.

Just now, after she'd showered and dressed (in a red turtleneck sweater bought special for this day), she was probably leaning toward the bathroom mirror, looking very closely in the bathroom's bad light to see how my family would see her. I would compliment her as soon as she walked down the hall and entered the living room, a moment that would serve as her official debut to Jude, who would offer her approval and we would all begin again, more properly, to get acquainted, and the mood would shift toward the festive, even if there was no tree. Or decorations. Or presents. Or music. Or snow. Or sleep. What we *did* have was a dead dog and phone calls repeating news of death. I turned on the television, searching for a parade.

The bathroom door clicked open. A male television-authority said the looming fiscal crisis would create global chaos unlike anything the world had ever known.

Mom said, "Death never knocks at a convenient time."

Libby walked down the hall, carrying Penelope. And yes, she did look pretty, but I wanted Mom to say it first. She held her phone, blew a line of smoke toward Libby, and said, "I'll call you next time, probably tomorrow, the way people are dying around here."

Libby walked to the couch and sat beside me. On television, the male authority said the National Guard had been dispatched to twenty cities across the country, including Jacksonville and Atlanta, in order to discourage looting. Libby stared at the television, eyes glossing.

I put my hand on her thigh. I said, "Merry Christmas."

Mom said, "I can't wait to play with *my* grandchildren."

I watched Libby watch my mother mash out her cigarette. I knew Libby feared second hand smoke as a fatal toxin. She said, whispering, "You didn't mention that your mother smoked. I noticed it immediately last night as soon we stepped into the house, which made it hard to sleep, but I didn't say anything."

"I thought I mentioned it." I knew she worried that the smell would stick to her clothes, her hair, her skin, Penelope's coat. I wasn't crazy about it either—it made me remember my bartending days and how it felt every night like I was standing neck-deep in a lake of smoke I knew would drown me slowly, which is maybe something I should've shared with Libby as a point of empathy. Why, instead, did I feel like defending my mother's smoking?

Libby said, "That sulfur water was gross."

Something in her tone made me hear this as a personal insult. The water I'd known my entire life—the water that had done a decent enough job keeping me clean *and* hydrated—had been accused of nastiness, and it struck a nerve I couldn't name.

A newsman reported that levels of fear—in some cases, *outright panic*—had seized the holiday spirit in parts of Kansas. Then a commercial said there was no better time to buy a car.

Mom said, "It's not like the family is going to have much of an appetite, right?"

"I'm sorry," I said. "About the water." I tried to think of ways to make it better. I imagined heating gallons of spring water on the stove and pouring her a bath, adding bubbles, handing her a glass of wine.

"Where's the tree?" Libby said.

Mom said, "Listen, Jo Ann. If you don't go right this second and start playing with your grandchildren, I'm going to reach through the phone and strangle you."

"We've never been big on trees," I said. "Too much trouble, really."

"Merry Christmas to you too," Mom said. She hung up, and said, "That woman. She makes me have to smoke. Libby, was your shower okay—find everything you need and so forth?"

"Yes, thank you. Merry Christmas. We brought presents. Harold, go get the presents."

I pulled in my feet, prepared to get the presents.

"No," Jude said. "Let's do that later. I have to organize this dead-dinner."

I watched Libby squint at Jude, who was pulling out a new cigarette. I said, "Mom is chair of the church bereavement committee. She asks people if they'll take food to a family's house when someone dies."

"They're starting to get to me." She lit her cigarette and stared toward the dark end of the hall, where she must have imagined all the sad-faced family members from all the dead-dinners she'd organized, staring back at her.

"Who died?" Libby said.

"This guy named Peanut Griffin. Died last night of bladder cancer. A real pisser."

Libby's head moved backwards as if she'd been poked. She rubbed Penelope's head.

CNN reported record levels of sales from a gunshop in southern Illinois.

"I need to make a couple more calls, then take a shower, then it looks like *I'll* be taking food to the Griffins. Y'all may as well go on over, see if you can help your grandmother entertain your grandfather." She blew smoke, then crossed her eyes and pushed her tongue out of the corner of her mouth, a funny crazy-person face she held for a second before dropping it.

CNN showed the same looped footage of an Iowa family stocking their backyard bomb shelter with beans, Bibles, and board games. Libby stroked the top of Penelope's head.

What I planned—as soon as we stepped outside—was to initiate a complaint about the smoke so we would have a complaint in common, which would make Libby feel more at home. I planned to take her on a leisurely stroll to the river and point to the tree my cousins and I once jumped from. While she absorbed some natural beauty, I planned to thank her for being with me. I'd pick a spot to hold her hand, and I'd pick a spot to kiss her, and we'd feel the air around us begin to sparkle with the festive feeling of Christmas.

Mom said, "Libby, do you see that hole?" She blew more smoke while holding her phone and pointed her cigarette to the ceiling. "That's where Harold swung a golf club twenty years ago after I told him not to swing golf clubs in the house. It's my—Hello, Sara? Peanut Griffin died, and I need beans."

Libby squinted toward the hole.

"Let's go," I said.

115

She looked from the hole to Jude, then to the hole again. I stood and walked to the door, and Libby followed, clutching Penelope.

Jude said, "I know it's Christmas, Sara. Don't start feeling guilty on me."

Libby pointed discreetly to a spot beside her shoe, having found the burned carpet spot, and lifted her eyebrows toward me. I waved her toward the door. She rose slowly with Penelope and stepped my way. Mom said, "Sara, when did you have *your* first grandchild?"

We walked out into the warm air, already seventy degrees according to the rust-tinged thermometer with Buddy Owen's red-lettered name at the top. At the bottom it said: "Final Expense Insurance. I'll Get You Covered."

I looked over the bright and green back yard, imagining the path we'd take to meander beneath the old oaks between us and the river. I reached for her hand. But four thigh-high dogs rushed us from around the corner of the house, their wild whipping tails like wet ropes because they'd just returned from a river swim, open mouths and snouts jousting for position, first toward my crotch, then toward Libby's arms, raising up on their hind legs for a better view of the potential playmate she tried to shield from them. The dogs persisted, figuring this was the start of play, circling her while she turned on tiptoes and shouted for them to get away.

She said, "Do something, asshole."

She'd muffled the first two words of her sentence, so I thought "asshole" had been intended for a dog. But I caught on and issued a command as authoritative as I could muster, and the dogs settled down.

"God," she said. "Thanks for the help." She lifted Penelope to her face and whispered that everything was fine. "Does this pack of wild dogs just run free all the time? Until they die, and then you wait a few days to find them? Then you stuff them in a garbage bag, toss them in a hole and drop a brick on them? Is that what happens?"

I looked toward Saint Jerome's fresh grave. "It's so they won't wash up if we get a lot of flooding." I didn't tell her about the times that dogs had brought bones to the house that could have been the bones of buried dogs, hence the need for bags and blocks.

"God," Libby said. "It's all so cold. Not even a tombstone or a marker."

"We know where they are."

"*They?* How many are out there?"

"Just two or three." Probably twelve, maybe fifteen.

"God."

I wanted to tell Libby that my mother preferred not to be reminded, every time she passed a window, that the dogs she'd loved were dead, but I feared this would invite another round of disagreement on the subject of grief management, which might also deepen Libby's position as an outsider and further the illusion that I was betraying her to side with my mother in some kind of competition that would have Libby outnumbered, which was not at all what I intended. Was it? I wanted to suggest that not everyone would need to construct an elaborate shrine and pay for a proper burial in a high-dollar pet cemetery, as Libby would when Penelope died, but I knew better than to compare Penelope's pedigree with my mother's mutts. The thing that frequently moved us toward personal grief, Libby often helped me see, was our constant need for comparisons. No need to go in that direction, especially on Christmas morning, when so much of the day still lay ahead. I reached for her free hand and squeezed it.

She said, "Are these dirty animals going to follow us?"

"It's just next door. Let's walk to the river, first. I'll show you—"

She pulled her hand away to tug at her sweater. "God, it's hot. I shouldn't have worn this sweater."

"Would you like to change?"

"You don't like it?"

"You just said it was too hot."

"I know," she said. "I'm sorry. I feel strange. I've never been away from my family at Christmas. I'm feeling very—"

"I know," I said. I put my hand on her shoulder and looked toward the river.

"I didn't sleep at all," she said. "And then I found Jerome, and—"

"I know. That was—"

"And your mother absolutely hates me. It's obvious."

"That's crazy. She doesn't—"

"You're calling *me* crazy? From what I've seen so far, I think you've got some case studies in crazy. While you were in the shower—before she started making calls? She asked me how much I weighed. Can you believe that? She asked me what I *weighed*."

"Well, you're very thin. She probably—"

"It was her first question, and it's inappropriate. Then she asked me—"

I pointed toward the river, and we started walking. The four dogs ran ahead.

"Then she asked how many children I wanted to have, and how soon I thought I'd be having them, which is also inappropriate. It's—"

"It's a normal—"

"It's inappropriate. Then she asked what I did for a living. She has no idea what I do."

The dogs were happy, running fast and free, frolicking in open spaces.

"No idea at all," Libby said. "I get the feeling you've never even mentioned my career or my music to your parents. I'm wondering why that is."

I wondered. Hadn't I mentioned her career and her music? I looked over my shoulder, back toward the house and saw Jude framed by her living room window, looking out at us, phone to her ear. She waved.

"She probably just forgot. She gets very busy and—"

"When I told her what I did, she asked why I wouldn't want to have my own private practice rather than working with an HMO, like I have a choice right now."

A hundred yards away in the low water of the creek bed, stood what I thought was the same white egret who had earlier been trying to eat a frog. I knew, as we kept walking, the egret would rise and fly across the marsh in an awe-inspiring moment of natural beauty we could share.

"Well," I said. "She's just, you know, she's just—"

"I have to tell you," she said. "Even if I wanted children, I'm not sure I could bring them here. I'd have to hear way too much advice on how to raise them properly."

"Well, that's—I mean, she'd probably want to help, but—"

"You know what else? I would not at all be surprised if she was hoping that I'd be the one to find Jerome."

I laughed out loud at this. I said, "That *is* crazy."

"I see," she said, "where this is going."

The dogs ran to the bank and the egret lifted its body out of the water and swooped across the marsh. Libby looked at the ground, focusing on the space where each foot would fall.

"Where this is going," she continued, "is that you will always defend your mother and you will always believe that something is wrong with me instead of her because you aren't capable of seeing what I see."

The egret disappeared across the marsh. I saw that Libby's face, still pointed toward her feet, would soon collide with a clump of moss hanging from a low oak limb. I pointed at the moss, but she didn't see, so when she ran face-first into it, her entire body bounced back and she released a loud gasp, wiped her face with her free hand, and tried, without success, to spit.

"Careful," I said.

"Asshole. You knew I was about to run into that."

"No, I—"

"Are there bugs in that stuff?"

I tore the moss from its limb and carried it to the burn pile, stacked with old limbs and palm branches, drying.

"You'd have to roll in it for awhile to get many redbugs, as we call them, or chiggers as others call them." I did not say that they were microscopic mites in the flea family whose dangers were more mythical than real, though excessive contact could, I knew from experience, induce chronic itching.

She said, "I wish I could look forward to a shower."

The dogs patrolled the river bank, running up and down with wild tails wagging.

I said, "See that tree leaning over the river?" It was held by a cable hooked to two trees behind it. Jude's fourth husband, J.D., had wanted to save the tree, but the two trees holding it up were now being choked to death by the cable, which meant all three trees would soon be lost.

"My cousins and I climbed and dove from that tree when we were kids. You can still see the little steps we nailed into the trunk."

"You went *swimming* out there?"

Libby's parents used the indoor pool in their high-rise midtown apartment building, a pool with chemically treated water, heated, vigorously attended by hourly workers new to the United States.

"Yes," I said. "We went swimming there. It's low tide now, and you can't tell, but—"

"Aren't there alligators and snakes?"

"I swam with a knife in my mouth, like Tarzan." I laughed at myself and leaned toward her for a kiss.

"Tarzan, who was raised by apes? That makes sense."

I pocketed my hands and walked closer to the river. I said, "Remember me telling you about my five-year-old cousin who drowned? She drowned right out here. My aunt Carol's youngest child."

"Yes, that's—"

"No one's talked about it much at all that I remember, so it's best not to bring it up. Yesterday was her birthday, come to think of it. It was a big deal—for five years, anyway."

"Is that mud you just walked across? And what are those things?"

Between us now on a rectangular mudflat, currently dry, were a family of fiddler crabs—miniature crabs as long as a thumb—pincers raised like swords while they skated sideways.

"It's dry and solid right now." I stepped into the middle of it to show her.

"I'm not walking through that. Let's just go to your grandmother's house so your grandfather can give us some more marital guidance."

I went to her. I grabbed her free hand again. I said, "I love you. I'm happy you're here with me, and I'm happy to be introducing you to my family. If I love you, they'll love you."

She looked away, toward the low-tide river. She said, "I didn't sleep, and I'm hot and grumpy. Let's start over." She kissed me. She said, "To grandmother's house we go. Just don't leave me alone with anyone."

"I won't leave you alone with anyone."

When we stepped through the door, we both grimaced from the blast of heat that greeted us. There was the extra heat that old people need, tightly sealed, there was heat coming from the kitchen, and there was the heat that trailed us.

Sparky was asleep in his recliner, head hanging to one side, mouth cracked, loud television tuned to CNN, where another Y2K computer-crisis expert was predicting bankruptcy for all businesses who had not completed their compliancy checks. In the room's corner, a skinny tree was lit and decorated, presents scattered beneath it. Food aromas came from the kitchen and hit my stomach. I walked that way and Libby followed, carrying Penelope.

Red-faced Roberta lifted her arms and laughed like an old friend. She hugged me tightly, and touched my face. She said, "Oh, Harold. You have to shave that silly beard." Then she said, "Hello, Libby. And puppy." She tried to hug Libby, but Penelope was between them, so she held both of Libby's shoulders and gave her a smile. She said, "That's a pretty sweater."

"Thank you," Libby said.

"I know it's hot as the devil in here. It puts the devil to sleep is one reason." She jerked her head toward the living room and laughed. "Tea or lemonade?"

"I've not had lemonade in years," Libby said.

"Harold, fix Libby some lemonade."

Libby shook her head at me, uninterested in lemonade.

Roberta cracked the oven for a peek, releasing heat, closed it again, wiped her hands on her apron, adjusted the heat on all four burners, and said, "Libby, I was happy to hear that you're a psychiatrist. I think I'll need one before this day is over."

"I'm not actually, well—I guess I am sort of one, yes."

"Sparky's about to kill me. Sometimes he makes sense, but it's in the middle of when he doesn't make sense, but sometimes his nonsense is an improvement, like when he gets sweet, and I have to laugh because I know it's not the real him, you know, like the other day he called me 'sugarplum,' which he hasn't called me since our second date, sixty years ago." She laughed and turned to the counter, where she used the open end of a can to cut biscuits from a sheet of flour she'd flattened.

"But sometimes it's not funny," she said. "He thinks I'm sleeping with every man in town, including Uncle Sludge, who's coming today, so it'll be fun to see how they get along. Last week he cleaned his guns while he watched his soap operas, but I hid his bullets, so I don't think we'll get shot—not today, at least. This is the happily ever after part of marriage I've been waiting for all these years through sickness and health and right this second, to be honest with you, I'm not sure I'd recommend it. Harold, where's Libby's lemonade?"

"I don't care for any," Libby said. "I try not to consume too much refined sugar."

"People should take a good long look at each other before they get married," Roberta said. "A good long look into each other's eyeballs." She pointed a finger at my eyes, then moved it to Libby's eyes then wagged it between our eyes, then turned back to her biscuits. She said, "At least Sparky is healthy from the neck down. I just hope *I* stay healthy long enough to take care of him so the children won't have that burden. Would y'all go check on him for me? Sometimes when he wakes up and no one's in the room, he gets scared. We'll have twenty-three people in the house today and that'll make him nervous, but at least we'll have a psychiatrist on hand." Roberta lifted her can toward Libby and laughed a loud laugh that I knew I would miss one day.

I kissed my grandmother's red cheek and led Libby back to the living room.

Sparky was still asleep, despite the histrionics of a CNN reporter who was broadcasting live from a busy intersection in Atlanta where she claimed traffic lights could cease to function at the turn of the new year, potentially creating headaches, injuries, and deaths. I stole the remote from the recliner's armrest and lowered the volume. When I returned the remote, Sparky's eyes popped open, wide and scared, as if he thought a burglar had just stepped in to murder him.

But he said, "Hello, Harold," just as softly as if he'd come from a pleasant dream. "When did you get home?"

"Last night," I said. Then I introduced Libby, again, as the woman I intended to marry, the woman I brought home so she could meet the family and the family could meet her.

Libby smiled and petted Penelope.

Sparky made an effort to rise. He shifted his weight, gripped the armrest, leaned forward, but Libby said, too loudly, "Don't get up." She stepped toward him, shifted Penelope to her left arm, and stuck out her right hand.

"Merry Christmas," she said.

"How do you do?" He offered his famous smile that surprised people because it sprang so wide so quickly and instantly cooled the tension he initiated to begin with. He shifted in his seat and motioned to the two seats adjacent, quite concerned with being a proper host. We sat and faced him, and Libby kept her smile.

He said, "I'm pleased to make your acquaintance. I'm happy some-one's finally come along to marry the old maid of the family. We've been worried about him for some time, but I see now we don't have to worry any more." He smiled again and Libby loosened her grip on Penelope and relaxed her whole body.

"Thank you," she shouted.

"He's not deaf," I whispered.

"I'm not deaf," he said. "Harold, that beard makes you look like a unsavory character."

"I like his beard," Libby said, laughing.

"You would." He turned his head above the television, to his cuckoo clock, which just then ejected the male bird to count the hour before retreating rapidly, door slamming behind him as his partner sprang out to offer her solo, then retreated, door slamming behind her. Then the wooden pendulum resumed its loud tick tock.

Sparky said, "We have a clock just like that at home."

Libby tightened her grip on Penelope.

"Harold?" he said. "You know anybody at the sheriff's office? Those bastards took my license." His eyes narrowed with the urgency of a child who was a few seconds away from a sobbing fit.

"No sir. You need to go somewhere?"

"Need to get home for Christmas."

"You want me to take you?"

"We could go together."

"I'll get the truck." I rushed to the door, looked back at Libby to give her my best reassuring expression. Her eyes said: *do not leave me.* I winked to let her know that she'd be fine, that it was all an act designed to pacify him, and I even imagined her being impressed that I had jumped so quickly to take this action, though her eyes did not, just then, seem to communicate this idea.

I went out and jogged to my grandparent's tin-roof shed that held Roberta's Cadillac, Sparky's old fishing boat, his Chevy S-10, and his John Deere tractor. I opened the toolbox bolted to the tractor and fished out his truck key, which I knew was Jude's hiding place. Another story she told me while we looked for Jerome was how, three months ago, after Sparky spent a full day nagging Roberta over his desperate need to get home, Jude came up with the idea to drive him away and bring him back. And since then, every couple of weeks, when he started in on needing to get home, Roberta called Jude, Mary, or Carol and said, "I'm sorry, but your father needs to go home," and one of them would pull up to the door in his truck and drive him around the new subdivision before returning him, fully satisfied, to his recliner.

By the time I got his truck out and pulled up to the house, he was waiting in the yard. I parked and ran around to help him manage the door, but he'd already opened it and fallen into the seat and reached for his seat belt, though I had to stretch it over his stomach for him and snap it into place.

I drove down the dirt road until I struck pavement, turned right, and proceeded slowly through the subdivision that wound through the 488 acres Sparky sold too cheaply twenty years ago to break even on debt. I followed the meandering loop the developers had designed as a way to avoid cul-de-sacs, creating tight curves that slowed traffic, splitting the road in some places around massive oaks, adding stop signs at three-way intersections that needed none. Many of the homes were new, or either I didn't remember them. A-frames were tucked into the corners of wooded lots next to Victorian-style homes next to elevated ranch homes, second-story porches with adjacent staircases. The bermuda grass Sparky's cows once grazed upon had been replaced in every yard with shiny squares of turf.

He said, "This here's the rich side of town, Harold."

I tried to remember where Sandra Delgado's house had been, but I was having trouble.

Driveways overflowed with Lexus minivans, BMW's, Escalades, Hummers, and deep-sea fishing boats equipped with three V8 motors. I saw Maine, Minnesota, and Quebec license plates. People in khaki shorts and boat-shoes carried presents toward porches filled with smiling people ready to receive them. Children chased dogs and dogs chased balls. In one yard, a group of people dressed in white shorts and white shirts played croquet.

Sparky said, "Roberta will be happy to see me and I'll be happy to see her."

I drove around the backside of the subdivision, where houses faced the widest point of Turtle River, long walkways stretching over the marsh that lead to docks where boats and jet skis were tied. Here, on the west side of the subdivision, the sun set across the water and landed on half-million dollar homes. Sparky had built his house on the opposite side, facing east, because Roberta preferred sunrise over sunset.

I was pretty sure that Sandra's house had not been on the water, but now I wondered whether it was true.

Sparky said, "I know you know the way, don't you, Harold?"

I told him I did. I drove past a house with pink stucco, a lawn being watered by an in-ground sprinkler system, then a three-story brick home with columns connected to a three-car brick garage. Maybe that was Sandra's house. The house looked older than most, but I didn't remember it. I coasted down the back stretch beneath leaning oaks, passed a small yard packed with plastic flamingos. Sparky stared out of his window, and I began to understand how the land he'd spent sixty-plus years watching could vanish right out from under him.

He said, "I'll be happy to see Roberta and she'll be happy to see me."

I'd be happy to see Libby too, I realized, and I planned to tell her so as soon as we walked in. I would smile and say *I missed you.* I'd kiss her as if I'd been away for a week. I'd say *I'm sorry I left you alone.* I'd grab her by the shoulders and look into her eyes and say *I will never leave you and you will never leave me.*

"I bet she's making biscuits," Sparky said. "Her biscuits will cure what ails you every *single* time."

I turned from the pavement between two live oaks and followed the dirt road toward the river, coasting. Sparky had trusted me to know the way, a silly thing that made me want to cry, as if he'd made some speech saying we are of the same special place, me and you, this place we're coming back to now, which you'll never be able to leave, even when you've moved away, the place you can't move deep enough inside of, even when you *are* inside and blind from the fear that it has disappeared.

I cut across the yard so I could let Sparky out at the door.

"Watch for pecans, Harold," he said. "We can't afford to lose too many."

"Okay." But I heard them popping beneath the tires.

And in a moment of sharp clarity, he said, "There goes your inheritance."

I stopped at the side door, unfastened Sparky's seatbelt and went around to help him out.

"Home sweet home," he said. "Roberta will be happy to see us. You smell those biscuits?"

"Yes," I said. Because I did.

When we entered, Libby shot me an angry look: the wrinkled brow, raised eyebrow, the cold-eyed stare that demanded an apology for leaving her alone with the large man who sat now beside her who was dressed in khakis, red tennis shoes, and red blazer, left cheek swollen with tobacco.

"Hey here," Uncle Sludge said. He made no effort to get up, but I knew he was hobbled from two bad knees and a bad back, so I went to him and shook his hand.

He said, "I reckon y'all been running the roads. I was about to take off with this pretty lady here, but y'all got back too soon." Then he giggled, which fattened his cheek and made visible a portion of the tobacco inside of it.

Sparky hung up his coat and hat. He said, "He'll do it too, Harold. That son of a bitch right there will steal your woman right out from under you. Where's Roberta?"

Uncle Sludge laughed. He said, "That'd be about the onliest way I could get a woman would be to steal her." He giggled again, but Libby didn't laugh and neither did Sparky.

I put my hand on Sparky's shoulder and said, "Roberta's in the kitchen." Which made him happy enough to move to his recliner.

I sat beside Libby and leaned toward her ear and whispered this: "I missed you." She stiffened her back and gave me a version of the same look she'd offered when I walked in.

Sparky said, "Is Roberta in the kitchen?"

"Yes," I told him.

Uncle Sludge said, "You catching any fish, Sparky?"

"No."

"Me neither. Damn river's so low, the catfish are covered with ticks."

I looked at Libby. I said, "Uncle Sludge is a county commissioner."

"He was just telling me all about that," she said.

"I've got her educated on all the local politics," he said. "We've been talking about the ten commandments in the schools and the new prison some idiots want to build on the waterfront and I've generally just been running off at the mouth like I do when I get around pretty women."

"I'm telling you, Harold," Sparky said. "First, he'll steal your daughter, then he'll steal your wife. Might take your money too."

Uncle Sludge laughed, but Sparky didn't. The clock on the mantle ticked in a higher octave than the cuckoo clock while the grandfather clock ticked in baritone in time to Penelope's panting. I flapped my t-shirt to generate a breeze.

The door flew open and four kids stormed in, three girls and a boy, each carrying an electronic game they held in front of their eyes like a map. They walked between us without a word, shorts and socks nearly touching at the knees, t-shirts too large for their skinny frames, glasses sliding down their noses. They marched in a straight line to the far end of the living room and plopped on the couch, working their thumbs, staring at their games.

Uncle Sludge said, "Hey-here, kids." None of them answered. To Libby, he said, "Those are my grandbabies. I come here to spend Christmas with them. They seem to like it."

"They look like nice children," Libby said.

"Shit," Sparky said. "It's fixing to get louder than hell in here."

From the kitchen came Mary and Carol's voices, each exclaiming over the weather, then sighing over the inside heat, followed by Mary's twin daughters Lois and Linda, repeating weather-related news, then Sarah, Carol's oldest daughter came in, followed by her sister, Sue, who was clearly carrying an infant because all the women went wild with cooing. The loudest and wildest cooing came from Jude, who entered last.

The side door popped open, and in stepped Uncle Hammer, Aunt Carol's first husband, father of her two daughters. He wore jeans and steel-toed boots and a dirty white t-shirt that showed off his muscular arms and chest. He was unshaven and seemed exhausted.

"Hey-here, Hammer," Sludge said.

"Here comes another one," Sparky said.

Uncle Hammer removed his hat, revealing a bald head, hung his hat behind the door, sighed loudly, then turned, all smiles and bloodshot eyes. He stopped at Sparky's chair, bent and gave a hug, which I was happy Libby saw since I knew she'd be watching the way the men in my family expressed emotion. When I introduced Uncle Hammer to Libby, he kissed her cheek and said, quite softly, "I hope you'll pardon my odor." He moved to me, gave me a hug, and said, "I hope you too will pardon my stench." He smelled of sweat, mulch, and some chemical that resembled flatulence. I made a note to myself that I should act more like Uncle Hammer so people might use the word *gentle* when they talked of the kind of man I was.

Hammer bent to hug Sludge, who said, "Brother Hammer? Smells like you've come fresh from the grave." Hammer confirmed that he had. He sighed and sat in the corner chair between Libby and Sludge, then got up and moved to the other side of Sludge, saying he'd prefer to offend Sludge with his odor rather than Libby and her lovely dog. He lowered his red eyes and confessed to not sleeping for three days, then giggled. He looked across the room at the four children on the couch and said, "Hello children," but they didn't answer.

To Libby, I said, "*The grave* is an abbreviated slang term that refers to the graveyard shift, also known as *third shift*, which typically begins at 11 p.m. and ends at 7 a.m. Uncle Hammer works at the papermill."

"Right," Libby said. "I—"

"He's also the best singer this side of Nashville," Sludge said. "He makes me blubber every time I hear him. I mean, every *single* time."

"That's because you only hear me at funerals. If you'd come to church more regular, you wouldn't cry so much."

Sparky said, "*Who* had a funeral?"

Uncle Hammer said, "Libby, what's your denomination?"

Sparky said, "Harold, is Roberta in the kitchen?"

I said she was. I looked at Uncle Hammer, wishing he hadn't asked Libby, who was devoutly agnostic, this personal question. She hated to discuss religion, even as a philosophical subject. Uncle Sludge looked at her now, along with Uncle Hammer, both waiting for an answer.

"Well," she said. "To be honest, church is something I don't get into. Ha, I made a pun. I don't get into church. Ha-ha. Anyway." Libby cleared her throat and looked at the carpet, where her joke had landed.

My father burst through the door then, offering a loud "Ho-Ho-Ho!" which trailed into a long "O," inspired by the room's heat.

"Hey-here, Buddy," said Uncle Sludge.

"Here comes another one," Sparky said.

Buddy sat beside me, slapped my thigh, looked at Libby, and said, "Hello darlin'."

"You sounded just *like* Conway," Uncle Sludge said.

"Who's Conway?" Libby said.

Sparky said, "Harold? Is Roberta in the kitchen?"

"Yes," I said. To Libby, I said, "Conway Twitty. Country music star who had several big hits, mostly through the 1970's, including *Hello Darlin'.*" I heard my voice take on a condescending tone I didn't intend and I immediately regretted it.

"I'm sorry," Libby said. "I'm very ignorant about country music."

"His real name was Harold Lloyd Jenkins," Uncle Sludge said.

"Born in Friars Point, Mississippi," Uncle Hammer added.

"Married three times," Buddy said. "Four children."

"Drafted by the Philadelphia Phillies to play professional baseball," said Uncle Hammer, "but he turned them down to make music. I've always admired that."

"Who had a funeral?" Sparky said.

"His first hit," Uncle Sludge said, "was *It's Only Make Believe.*"

"Released in 1958," Buddy said.

"That's right," Hammer said. "1958."

The men honored Conway with a moment of silence. I turned to Libby. I wanted to take her outside so we could get out of the hot room, have a moment alone, and then reenter by way of the kitchen so we could reverse our positions in the heavily segregated (men=living room; women=kitchen) historical order of things.

Sparky said, "Buddy, you still selling cars?"

"I hadn't sold a car in thirty years, Sparky. You need one?"

"Damn sheriff stole my license. Sludge said he'd talk to him, but I think he's in on it. I think they're *asshole* buddies is what I think. I didn't vote for neither one of them."

"I'll talk to him," Uncle Sludge said, and giggled.

Once I got Libby outside, I'd assure her that I was happy she'd come and empathize with the awkwardness she felt as a first-time visitor. I'd tell her again that she looked very nice, and I'd say she shouldn't worry about remembering names just now, or who had been married to whom (or for how long) because I could clarify on the way back to Atlanta, which I'd remind her is where we'd be returning very soon, maybe earlier than we'd planned even, if that would make her happier. But I didn't know how to excuse ourselves gracefully from the living room, so I did nothing, which Libby would say was all-too-typical.

The door popped open again, and in walked Josh (recently divorced from my cousin, Sue), dressed in shiny new overalls. He was a weatherman at a Jacksonville TV station, and was therefore a celebrity, which Libby would never guess, I knew, so strongly did she cling to her first impressions, arrived at here, no doubt, from her assumption that overall-wearing Southerners descended from Jed Clampett of *Beverly Hillbillies* fame.

"Hey-here," said Uncle Sludge. "How 'bout this heat?"

"I expect this warming pattern to remain consistent for several days," Josh said.

Jude's boyfriend, Bruce, came in behind Josh, sighing at the heat. Five years ago he'd installed central air and heat, at cost, which meant, finally, that Roberta could close the windows, turn off the fans, remove the propane heaters and start arguing over thermostat settings while Sparky complained about the electric bill. Bruce's oval glasses and grey sideburns gave him a scholarly look, which I was glad to see so Libby's first impression would be a good one.

"Hey-here, Uncle Bruce," said Uncle Sludge.

"Is the air working?" Bruce said.

Four new children, chest-high and lower, sprang through the door and ran to the far end of the living room where they stood over the four children seated on the couch, asking what they got for Christmas, but the seated kids, glued to their games, did not reply.

Uncle Hammer said, "Hello children," but they didn't answer. "Those are my grandchildren," he told Libby. "They're a bit bashful."

She smiled and petted Penelope, whose panting seemed worse. I wanted to tell Libby who the children belonged to—two from Sarah, whose husband moved to California to be with his high school girlfriend—and two from Sue, whose ex-husband, Josh, walked past me and Libby without saying anything and sat on the floor next to his children, who did not speak to him after he said *hey*. The other four belonged to my twin cousins Lois and Linda (two each), who were still in the kitchen. When I lifted my finger to point to Josh, the door popped open and in walked Moose and Fuzzy, (ex-husbands to Lois and Linda, ex-sons-in-laws to Uncle Sludge). They each wore camouflaged hunting pants and boots, camouflaged t-shirts and camouflaged caps. They moved past Buddy to the far side of Hammer, patted Sparky on his shoulder as they passed, then sat on the kid-size blue and yellow plastic chairs brought in from the garage. They removed their camouflage caps and placed them over their camouflage knees. Fuzzy turned to Josh, said, "It's hot."

Josh said, "I expect this warming pattern to remain consistent for several days."

I lifted my finger toward Josh to make introductions, but Uncle Sludge spoke before I could. He said, "Y'all kill anything?"

Moose said, "I killed a buck with a clean shot to the neck and Fuzzy gut-shot one. We had to run him down and hit him over the head ten times with a lead pipe before he'd die. Look here, Sparky." Moose extended his left leg and pointed to his blood-smeared calf.

"You shoot yourself?" Sparky said.

The men laughed. Libby didn't. A strict vegetarian and annual PETA donor, she opposed animal-killing of any kind. I wasn't fond of animal-killing myself, but I'd never say so to someone who was, which Libby would say was all-too-typical of too many people in the world who were afraid to make a stand, a sentiment I'd agree with, but not as loudly. I knew Moose and Fuzzy well enough to know that they were ethical sportsmen who followed rules designed to manage deer populations and that they always ate what they killed and often donated venison to friends and family, all of which I intended to explain to Libby at the first opportunity.

Just now, I wanted to tell her that Moose was a high school principal, and Fuzzy was a math teacher at Moose's school, that they'd been best friends since middle school, which is when they'd first met Lois and Linda, though neither couple had an interest in dating until Linda started teaching science and Lois became a librarian. Each couple got married on the same day in June, went on the same honeymoon cruise, then divorced on the same weekend in June seven years later. Their divorces didn't discourage the men from dropping in at their ex-wives' grandmother's house. In fact, Roberta had ordered Moose and Fuzzy—just as she had ordered Sludge, Hammer, Buddy, and Josh—to remain part of the family, instructing them to show up for holiday occasions without calling ahead. I was about to tell her this, but Lois said something from the kitchen that made the women laugh. Roberta's laugh rose above the other laughter, and it cheered me to hear it. If I had taken Libby outside and reentered by the kitchen, Libby would now be laughing too, and we would have missed all the unpleasantness to come, but again, I did nothing.

Sparky said, "Harold—are you staying with me tonight, or is Jerome coming?"

Everyone looked at me, just as confused as I was.

Janice, Sparky's caretaker, was the only name Sparky had trouble remembering, but the family was relieved, so far, that he hadn't called her anything worse. His ideas about race (unlike Roberta's) had evolved only slightly since 1908, when he was born into the Jim Crow south, so Roberta and each of her three daughters had individually taken Janice aside—to the living room couch or to the porch, where they sipped tea and ate cake while warning her that offensive language might fly from Sparky's mouth without warning, and they offered to give her a raise if she would stay. She said she'd take the raise, plus a little more, and everyone laughed and agreed to whatever terms she asked for. But Sparky surprised everyone with his good behavior. Sometimes he answered Janice with *yes ma'am* and *no ma'am*. So the worst Sparky could do, apparently, was to confuse her name with the name of Jude's dachshund, which had been his beloved companion, after all.

"You mean Janice?" I said.

"What did I say?"

"You said Jerome."

Uncle Sludge said, "It sounds like you mixed up your dog and your nigger, Sparky," then giggled too loudly at himself.

Libby's head rocked back like she'd been shot.

I opened my mouth, then closed it. I knew Sludge, and I knew that prolonging the issue would lead to worse jokes, so I figured it was best to let the moment pass, which I knew Libby would say was precisely the problem with too many people in this part of the country for too long. She looked at me now, waiting for me to make a stand and tell my uncle that the n-word was unacceptable. I looked toward the kitchen and back to Sludge. I cleared my throat.

"Harold?" Sparky said. "Where *is* Jerome?" He looked at the glass door. "He usually sits right there on the porch and looks in at me, but I haven't seen him all morning."

"He must be sleeping," I said.

Libby, confused, cocked her head sideways at me.

"Is Roberta in the kitchen?"

"Yes."

"Sometimes she disappears on me," Sparky said. "Sometimes around dusk, that man right there will circle the house on his mare and wait for her to step out and ride off with him."

The other men looked at the floor. The kids on the couch looked over the shoulders of the kids on the floor, who had stolen their games. From the floor, sad-looking Josh watched CNN, which had no sound.

"Is she in the kitchen now?" Sparky said.

I should have said, *let me check* so I could take Libby along to help me look, then leave her with the friendlier women while I came back to report that yes, Roberta was still in the kitchen after sixty years.

Jude danced into the living room carrying the one-year-old that belonged to Sue and Josh. She said, "Look—it's *a baby*," stretching each syllable so it sounded like the product of a magic trick, voice full of wonder.

Softly, I said, "Please don't." I implored her with my eyes, which she looked into blindly. She danced the baby forward, saying goochy-goochy, making a fat pucker, rubbing a finger on the baby's belly. She stopped in front of Libby and started moving the baby slowly toward her lap, giving Libby time to dump the dog.

Libby said, "Oh no—no thank you, no, really."

"Harold," Jude said. "Take the dog."

The baby kept coming, so I pulled Penelope off Libby's lap and Jude placed the baby into Libby's arms, then walked away. Libby leaned forward, held the baby out from her body, overly cautious not to cause an injury. I gripped Penelope, who barked like a machine gun and tried to lunge for the baby. Everyone looked at Libby, which I knew made her uncomfortable, just as it would make *me* uncomfortable.

Penelope's barking grew more manic. The baby started to cry.

"Okay," Libby said. "You can have it back now." She blushed bright red.

Jude had walked to the far end of the room to inspect the behavior of the eight children stacked in two rows. She was asking them questions, getting no response, asking them again, more loudly, choosing this moment for a lesson in manners.

"Okay," Libby said again. "She wants you back now."

But Jude was busy. Libby looked from the crying baby to her barking dog and said, "It's okay, honey. Mama still loves you." But it didn't help. Penelope barked and the baby cried.

Sparky said, "I can't even hear myself think."

When I tightened my grip around Penelope's chest, Penelope bit the backside of my left hand, so I dropped her instantly and held my hand, which was bleeding, I noticed, then Penelope jumped up and bit the baby's leg, triggering a scream so loud that even the children on the far side of the room looked up from their games and stared with their mouths hung open.

Libby stood and lifted the screaming baby away from the jumping dog and shouted at me: "Hold the dog, dummy!"

I said, "Mom! Come take the baby."

But Jude, even over the noise, was scolding a child about the rudeness of not speaking when being spoken to, and she would not, just now, tolerate the rudeness of being interrupted. I looked at Josh, the father, who threw up his hands and laughed, meaning it was none of his business because he had done nothing to cause the chaos in the first place, and he seemed relaxed enough to know that the baby's mother, his ex-wife, Sue, would soon be on the way.

Uncle Hammer, the baby's grandfather, said, "I don't miss these times."

A second later, Sue came rushing from the kitchen, saying, "Hey! What did you do to my baby?" in a tone I clearly understood as joking, knowing Sue well enough to know that she didn't take much of anything *too* seriously, though I knew Libby well enough to know that she would hear the tone as an accusation. Sue plucked the baby from Libby's arms and held her, swinging gently from side to side, patting her back, whispering that everything was okay, but the screaming baby didn't believe it. Libby sat. Penelope jumped into her lap.

Libby pointed to the fatty tissue of the baby's thigh, where a small amount of blood was pooling up. She said, "Oh my God! I'm so sorry."

Sue dabbed the injured thigh. There was enough blood to cover two fingertips. She said, "Oh, I've seen worse."

Libby said, "Should we take her to the emergency room?"

Sue laughed. She insisted her screaming baby would be okay.

Then Josh got involved. He said, "Has that little dog had her shots?"

"Of course," Libby said, insulted.

Sue said, "We'll just go have a little hydrogen peroxide bath. She carried her crying baby to the bathroom. Josh stared at Libby, looking like he wouldn't mind shooting her dog for her. I held my bleeding hand, hiding it, so no one would get excited.

Uncle Sludge delivered commentary as if Libby couldn't hear. He said, "She didn't want no part of that baby, did she?" The other men agreed and laughed.

Uncle Hammer said, "They just take a little getting used to."

Libby tried to be a good sport. She said, "I think I've got all I can handle right here," and looked at Penelope.

Linda came from the kitchen then. She said, "Is a baby getting abused?"

Fuzzy, Linda's ex-husband, said, "That little bitch just bit a chunk out of the baby's leg."

Jude came back across the room and smiled at Libby. She said, "Really, Libby—if you can't control that dog of yours, how do you ever expect to control a baby?"

Libby's eyes got big. She said, "It was—"

"I'm *kidding*," Jude said. "Wasn't that the prettiest baby you've ever seen?"

Libby smiled unconvincingly, petted Penelope, and looked at the carpet.

I flapped my T-shirt to generate a breeze.

Lois came from the kitchen then, went straight toward Libby, and introduced herself as my favorite cousin. She said, "Congratulations on the engagement. Marriage can be a wonderful thing if you find the right person. Maybe one day I will."

"I wish you'd hurry," Moose said. He laughed and the men laughed with him.

Uncle Sludge said, "Lois, are the lights still on at the library?"

"You cut our budget one more time and they won't be."

"I was the only one voted *not* to cut y'all's budget."

"Likely story," Sparky said.

"You need to keep it open for the children," Lois said. "The children need it most. Like the other day, I got the funniest question from this little girl, must've been ten years old. She came up to the reference desk and said, 'Excuse me, but could you tell me how I could find out for sure when someone is in love with me?'"

"Ha." Uncle Sludge laughed for a second, then got serious. "What you tell her?"

"I told her, I said, 'Honey—you need to go read every book in here and then come back in ten years and tell *me* the answer.'" Lois laughed and Jude laughed with her.

"I don't know about that," Uncle Sludge said. "I don't think that's the kind of thing you can learn from books. That's the kind of thing you learn in the streets."

"Maybe *you* learned it in the streets," Buddy said. "But that's the kind of thing you can't ever know for sure. On its best day, love is a fragile and fleeting fragrance." He looked at Jude, who was looking at Libby.

"And some days it's like a fart," Bruce said.

"Harold?" Sparky said. "Where's Roberta?"

"In the kitchen," I said.

"It *is* an interesting question though," Libby said. "It's a question worth—"

"*I* know," Jude said. She lifted her arm like a schoolgirl. "I know when someone's in love with *me*."

I looked at Buddy, who was squinting, as if preparing his denial. Then I looked at Bruce, who was squinting at Buddy. Everyone else looked at Jude, waiting.

"But I'd rather hear what Harold thinks," Jude said. "Harold, how can you tell for sure when someone is truly in love with you?"

Everyone looked at me.

"Yes, Harold," Libby said. "How can you tell for sure when someone is in love with you?" She laughed a little giggle, having fun, feeling safe, no doubt, with the answer to come.

I thought: shouldn't a speech be stored on the tongue's tip for a time like this? *My* tongue, quite suddenly, was a board. I wanted to avert the issue altogether by offering something witty, then someone else would offer a better follow-up joke and I could fade from focus. But Libby would see a witticism for the cop-out it was. I wanted to say something honest I would direct at Libby to prove I could easily answer this. I searched my brain's left hemisphere, where reason lived, to locate the correlation between love and evidence for love. The living room clocks ticked like gameshow clocks. I leaned forward, put my forearms on my thighs, right hand covering my bleeding left. My tongue was a brick. I thought: an honest answer to such a question should have come by now, when the one answering was engaged to the one listening to his left. And on Christmas morning of all days, when true sentiment could be wrapped more easily in the sentimental, which could be taken more easily for the truth. I asked myself how I knew for sure that I was in love with Libby. I looked at Sparky, whose pale blue eyes stared back as if to say he couldn't help. I giggled, a pause-producing sound meant to soften tension. Libby, at first amused, grew tense, I could tell by the vibe I felt, being a self-proclaimed expert feeler of vibes, more of a curse than a gift, certainly, because most of the vibes I felt were decidedly unpleasant, though I wondered now how often I felt bad vibes beyond Libby's company, another sign—if one were needed—that I was sufficiently stumped just now to explain my love for her or her love for me. This was the same question (dressed as an elephant in an evening gown) that she brought into the room of our second date. The same elephant who slept between us and led us into every room, who packed himself into my car and grew fatter after what would forever be referred to as the interstate incident. The elephant was here now, in my grandmother's living room, telling me I was proceeding toward mistakes I would devote years to explaining to myself, building rationales as long as novels. I thought of all this in a matter of a few seconds that stretched into the kind of life-defining silence I wanted, right that second, to liberate myself from. I squeezed my bleeding hand. I licked my lips. I shifted slightly toward Libby. I opened my mouth.

"Oh for God's sake, Harold," Jude said. "Isn't it something you just *know*?"

"Well, yes," I said. "If you wouldn't interrupt, that's what I was about to say—it's something you—*I* ... just *know*." I felt a sweat ball pop through my left armpit and begin sliding down my side. I looked at Libby and smiled.

Libby hugged Penelope, who was trembling. "I agree," she said, though very softly. "It's something you just know."

Sparky said, "Harold? If you're sweating now, just think about the sweating you've got ahead of you. That's all I'm going to say."

"And the sweating never stops," Uncle Sludge said, then giggled. "The longer you stay married, the more you sweat and the more you sweat the stronger your wife's nose gets, which makes you sweat even more every time she smells something."

"*Or*," Lois said, "The longer you stay married, the smellier your spouse gets, and you have to decide whether you want to chop off your nose or stay married."

"That's right," Moose said. "Till one day you walk outside and fall face first into some fresh flowers, but then you realize you can't smell them because you're missing your nose."

"Do you fall because you're drunk?" Lois said.

"Maybe. But you're drunk because you don't have a nose."

"That doesn't make sense," Lois said.

Moose said, "Harold? Does that make sense?"

Everyone looked at me.

"Yeah, Harold," Libby said. "Does that make sense?"

A sweat-ball popped through my right armpit and slid down my side. I wanted to find the ten-year-old child who had asked the original love-question and throw a book at her. I looked across the room at a child on the end of the couch who was dropping a booger into the hair of the kid in front of him.

"It's all downhill," Sparky said. "Soon as the kids start coming, the bills pile up and first thing you know, a damned county commissioner comes along and steals your wife."

"Don't be a grouch, Sparky," Lois said. "Libby will think we're strange."

"Who?"

"Libby. Harold's fiancée who's sitting right here."

Sparky looked at Libby. He said, "It's all downhill." His tone suggested he meant *uphill*, where a steep climb required extra exertion that could lead to exhaustion, though he might've meant downhill, as in a landscape that lent itself to heavy objects that gathered speed and raced recklessly away, never to be reclaimed.

"Well," Libby said. "Every marriage takes work, doesn't it?"

"Every one of mine did," Buddy said.

Jude said, "Libby, when's your birthday?"

"No," I said. "Please."

"March 4th," Libby said. "I share a birthday with Antonio Vivaldi."

"The race car driver?" Buddy said.

"In case we don't we see you then, we should sing you our family's special version of the birthday song," Jude said.

"No we shouldn't," I said.

Linda warmed up, saying, "Me-me-me-me." Then Jude kicked it off, and people followed, sort of, each person proceeding at a different tempo with wild variations in pitch meant to be disturbing—voices cracking and quivering, a cacophonous collection like drunkards trying their best to sound their worst, a frightening experience for a newcomer who wasn't warned about it, though no one, if asked, would be able to explain how or when the strange custom started. This particular version got so good at sounding bad that Penelope started barking, which made the singers proud. I tried to sing nicely and softly, being closest to Libby's ear, but it was lost on her, overwhelmed as she was with the loud ugliness of it all. When I looked at her, I saw she was staring at Aunt Carol, who was standing at the edge of the dining room, mouth closed, eyes locked on the carpet, possibly thinking of her dead daughter's birthday. When the song wound down and people came to their individual ends (Jude taking the longest), Fuzzy belched, which meant it was over. Penelope stopped barking and started shaking, her eyes rattling in their sockets.

Sparky said, "Harold, can you give me a ride home?"

All the singers laughed and looked at Libby, waiting for some reaction.

She said, "Wow. Thank you. That was a very—quite a unique rendition I'll remember that for a long time. Also, could I just say? I hope this is not out of place, but I just learned a moment ago that yesterday was the birthday of Carol's child who drowned, and I wanted to say how sorry I am that you all had to endure such a difficult trauma. My brother—"

"We don't talk about that," Roberta said. She gave Libby a long stare to make sure she understood. It was a stare that contained some heat, and even I was surprised by it.

"Let's open presents," Jude said. "Harold, you play Santa."

I looked at Libby, whose eyes had gone to the carpet again. I rose from my chair without a word and went to the tree, took presents to people, tossing what I could, stepping gingerly between feet and legs and boxes. I took presents to Sparky and Roberta and to their three children, and to the grandchildren, and the great-grandchildren, and to the ex-in-laws, and people kept opening presents and yelling thank yous across the room and holding up shirts and sweaters and pocket-knives while Libby sat empty-handed, except for Penelope.

Roberta had simply forgotten, which seemed perfectly understandable, because she did her Christmas shopping in July to avoid the crowds, and since then, she'd had too much to worry about. I knew Roberta would be embarrassed if she was made aware of the oversight, and I did not want, under any circumstances for her to feel bad—a woman who had suffered so long for others. My grandmother, the most unselfish soul I'd ever known, could be forgiven such a silly thing, and if Libby couldn't understand that, I had my answer by negation—she was not someone I could love. Plus, Jude had told me that she and Mary and Carol would take a private moment later to give Libby an envelope containing a small amount of cash she could apply toward wedding expenses, but I hadn't mentioned this because I'd wanted it to be a surprise.

Once I passed out all the presents and saw that Libby still had none, I showed her three presents addressed to me and said, "These are for us."

"They have *your* name on them," she said.

"Right, but they're still for us. Open this one."

"*You* open it."

Moose opened a long box, pulled out a rifle and placed the rifle over his knees, barrel pointed toward Penelope. Fuzzy reached over to pet the stock. Moose's chin quivered for a second while he fought back tears. He said, "Thanks, Sludge."

"Every principal ought to have one," said Uncle Sludge. "We should make the *teachers* carry them too."

"I'm keeping this one at the house," Moose said. "Shoring up my home security in case things get crazy with all this Y2K business."

Libby put her nose against Penelope's skull.

I whispered, "Why'd you bring up my dead cousin? I told you no one talks about her."

"Thanks for standing up for me," she whispered back. "You're a different person around these people. It's like some kind of gang. It's disturbing. God, I wish I hadn't come. Although I did just remember that we still have presents in the trunk."

I said, "I'll get them."

"No," she said. "Stay and open your presents. Really. I would love to step outside for a minute." Then she rose and slipped out the side door carrying Penelope. No one looked up.

Five minutes passed. People crumpled paper and laughed and yelled thank yous across the room. Sparky made slow progress with his pocket knife, gently running the blade between the paper and a piece of tape, rotating the package slowly to locate every piece of tape, then he pulled the paper off as if it were a shell, folded it neatly, and put it aside so it wouldn't be wasted. Then he looked at the picture on the box, a rubber band-powered pecan cracker, without changing expressions and set the box aside.

Buddy unfolded a pair of socks and leaned to my ear. He said, "Go check on her."

Yes, I thought, I'll take action and go check on her.

Five more minutes passed.

Sparky went to his next present. Jude sat across the room against the couch, playing with one of the children's electronic games. Fuzzy opened a pack of shotgun shells and Sludge opened a case of chewing tobacco. Buddy opened a used paperback by Lewis Grizzard called *They Tore Out My Heart and Stomped that Sucker Flat*, and Roberta held up a dress that made everyone gasp. She stood and held the dress over her, cocked her head to the side like a teenager going to a dance while Mary snapped her picture.

Sparky said, "Did Sludge give you that?"

Buddy leaned toward me again, said, "Go check on her."

So I got up and walked out. I figured she was allowing herself a moment to regroup before she rejoined the mob. I stopped and stared at the incoming tide and knew that in just a few hours, Libby would be treated to a beautiful view. I wanted to borrow Sparky's boat and take her out on a slow ride through the winding bends of tidal creeks that wound toward the wide expanse of Turtle River. She might decline at first, but I'd show her the life vests we could wear, and I'd say Penelope could go too, and if I timed it right, we could turn around as the sun sank and ride back home inside the soft orange and yellow light that would blanket the river. There would be enough salt water in the air to give the sinuses a splash of something wild, and our senses would remain dilated through the night. Sometimes it took a small moment like that to excite her for a long time, which is something I loved about her, I realized then.

When I resumed my walk, I saw a deer lying on the tailgate of Moose's truck, stomach slit, guts removed. It took a moment to realize there were *two* deer lying together. The closest deer was beheaded, and the head of the deer behind him looked like it belonged to the first buck's body. It wasn't until I noticed the buck's head sitting in the back of the truck that I understood there were two carcasses, spooning. My stomach gurgled, once when I looked into the deers' eyes, big as brown moons, and once for imagining Libby's eyes when *she* looked into them.

When I got to Jude's porch, the big dogs were waiting for me. This meant they'd escorted Libby and Penelope back to the house, which would have further frazzled Libby's nerves. I walked into the living room, then into the kitchen. Presents were stacked on the kitchen table. I called her full name: "Elizabeth?" And got no answer. The back bedroom was empty. The other rooms were empty too. I went outside and slowly circled the house.

"Libby?" I called. And got no answer.

I didn't know where else to look, so I stepped into Buddy's condo, thinking, foolishly, she might like a secret peek at the environment that revealed his personality. She wasn't there. I walked back toward Jude's house, stopped in the driveway, and looked in every direction. Something felt strange. At first, it was an emptiness I attributed to her absence. Then I noticed my car was gone.

Libby, who hated to drive, who didn't even have a driver's license, who feared all roads and all cars, had stolen my car. And taken it—home? Surely not. It was three hundred miles to Atlanta, and once to Atlanta, she'd have eight lanes of craziness to navigate while trying to find the right exits that led to the right streets that led to our apartment, a difficult task even for me.

I went back into the kitchen. On the table, beside the stack of presents, I found her engagement ring placed on top of a note: "We've gone home. <u>Don't call</u>. I need to keep both hands on the wheel. Also, I plan never to speak to you again. I'm glad this nightmare is finally over—it would only get worse."

I pocketed the ring and the note and went to my old bedroom that my grandmother now used and lay on top of the sheets in the silent house. I closed my eyes and felt my body grow too heavy to move. Then my eyes sprang open. Yes, the nightmare was over. Her reaction to my family proved that she was not someone I could love. The farther she drove away (even in my car), the happier I would be. I had no fear of getting back to Atlanta—I knew I could count on my father to get me there, or at least to a bus station. But then I saw the interstate Libby was now driving down and imagined her intense terror. I pictured a slow-motion scene of Libby dying from a head on collision with a tractor-trailer or a tree, her body mangled amidst crushed metal, eyes pointed at a hand reaching for her phone, intending to call … me?

I pulled out my phone. But I did not call. I said a little prayer that she would get home safely.

I got to my feet and moved down the hall and outside and back over to my grandparents' house, happy to join my family for Christmas dinner.

When they asked me where Libby was, I told them the truth: "She is gone for good. Pass the biscuits, please."

But five hours later, tormented with waiting, and needing to know that she had gotten home safely, I stood alone by the river in front of Mom's house and called her.

She answered on the second ring. Her tone that suggested she had no idea who might be calling. I said *hello*. And paused. She paused too.

She said, "Traffic isn't too bad on Christmas Day."

"Are you home? Did you make it okay?"

"I like to drive. It gave me time to think. Would you like to hear what I've decided?"

"Of course."

"If you still want to marry me, I have two conditions."

I paused again. I said, "Okay."

"Immediately after getting married, we have to get pregnant. Or try to. Also, very soon after our first child is born, we have to have a second child, so the first will have a playmate of about the same age and avoid being an only child who grows up lonely. Also, we will never take the children to visit your family, although your parents will be allowed to visit *us*, so long as they do so separately, no more than twice a year, and only if they stay in a hotel."

I waited to see if there was more.

"Hello?" she said.

"That sounds like more than two conditions."

"Those are the terms. You can think about it between now and the time you get home."

"Fine," I said. "I'll have to think about it."

"Fine," she said. "Think about it." Then she hung up.

Chapter 9
Jude

Buddy entered my kitchen without knocking, carrying his first cup of coffee and the classifieds, sighing like a schoolboy as he stomped across my kitchen in his size sixteens, headed toward my recliner while I balanced the books for Bruce, who hadn't spoken to me since April, when I broke off our seven-year engagement so I could marry Phil, a seventy-five-year-old retired Navy officer from Minnesota I met in church. Buddy fell into the chair and whipped out the footrest. Then he moaned from the effort, louder than usual.

He said, "I've been thinking we should ride to the wedding together. Save gas."

I stapled a receipt to an invoice and moved the invoice from right to left.

"Oh," I said, "but doesn't that sound like fun?"

"Unless your new husband's going. I'd hate to be a third wheel."

"He's not going."

"Unless you're riding with Mary or Carol or someone else."

"No. Linda is taking them and Lois and Sarah and Sue in her big SUV. I need to get there earlier to see if I can help Libby and her mother feel less anxious about the rehearsal dinner and any number of other things."

"In that case," he said. "I'll let you drive. I know my driving used to make you nervous."

"You're too generous."

"And I'd insist on separate rooms."

"Do you have money for your own room?" I asked.

"I'd also need to borrow money for a room."

"Right," I said. "Of course."

"Where *is* your latest husband?" he said.

The only time Buddy came over was when Phil's Buick was gone. Phil was slow to understand Buddy's presence in my back yard and he had, more than once, expressed some strong curiosities that sounded like jealousy, an issue I had not anticipated and was sad to hear.

"He took his oxygen tank to get calibrated," I said. Phil wore a portable tank on his belt, which he removed at home in favor of using the larger tank in our bedroom that spat out an occasional hiss followed by a gush of air that made me imagine I was sleeping with Darth Vader. The tank was combustible, which meant I had to be careful where I lit my cigarettes. I don't know what I'd been thinking.

June 16; 7:45 a.m.

I sat in my car and honked until Buddy stumbled out of the condo and across the yard. It was surely the earliest he'd been awake in years. His shirt was untucked in the front, barely tucked in the back, his jeans were wrinkled and dirty, and his hair was standing on the crown of his head. Phil stood outside my car door, prepared to see us off. Ten years retired from forty years as a Navy recruiter, he still looked ready for sailing. He wore his white bucket hat, a white polo shirt (tucked tightly), white boatshoes, white socks to mid-shin level, and white shorts, ironed. His oxygen tank was strapped to his belt like a canteen.

Buddy saluted Phil, then fell into my passenger seat. He said, "I'm ready."

"Do you have a bag?"

"I'll be right back."

Phil laughed loudly while he stood at ease, hands cupped in front of his crotch.

Everything I thought I'd liked about Phil were things I learned I was wrong about. I thought he must have accumulated some wisdom and understanding toward women because he raised five daughters after his first wife died—the oldest daughter had been ten. But it was his daughters who had taken care of *him*. They took care of his house too, "ran a tight ship," as it were, living for his approval, staying scared for the moment anything went awry, teaching themselves how to handle bras, menstruation, boys, sex. And the Minnesota accent that once seemed interesting, with its long O's and nasal U's, had recently begun to irritate me. What I'd first admired as his calm stoicism now resembled a cold soul crouched in a gloomy corner, a face that changed expressions as often as a tombstone. And the confidence I thought I'd seen in a man I thought was too secure for petty hang-ups had vanished at the first hint of jealousy over Buddy, an immature act I wouldn't be able to live with for long.

"Behave yourself," he said now, too seriously. He looked toward the condo and back to me, lifting his eyebrows.

"Give me a break," I said. Then I lit a cigarette so he'd step away.

Buddy came out carrying a red plastic duffel bag by a single strap. The back of his shirt was now untucked to match the front. He fell into my seat again. He said, "I'm ready."

"Do you have your insulin?"

"I'll be right back."

Phil said, "Is it too much for me to ask that you behave yourself?"

"Don't be childish. Do you have your list?"

He pulled a piece of paper from his shorts and reviewed his instructions on dog-feeding, plant-watering, and parent-watching. Roberta didn't feel up to making the trip—she'd called Harold to apologize, but he said he'd felt relieved that she wouldn't have to endure the stress and fatigue of travel for a simple wedding ceremony. I asked Phil to check on her and Sparky while we were gone, and he said he would.

Buddy came back with a handful of orange-capped needles sticking out of his front shirt pocket. He saluted Phil again, then fell into the passenger seat. He said, "I'm waiting on *you*."

Phil touched my shoulder, stared into my eyes for several seconds, then said, "Goodbye, love." I pulled away, watching him in the rearview as he stood with his hands cupped over his crotch, head turning to follow my car.

"I've done it again," I said. "I just amaze myself."

Buddy sat up and looked to see if I'd run over something.

"I've picked another winner."

"Captain Phil? He seems like a good guy. A little uptight maybe, but what do I know? I was the first winner you picked."

"Not quite the first. Fasten your seatbelt."

"I can't."

I stared at him.

"Doctor's orders. Since my heart surgery a few years ago—if I get a sudden jolt to the sternum, it could kill me."

I stopped the car, springing him forward so quickly he had to throw a palm against the dash. I said, "It would be better for me, and my car, if you died from the seatbelt rather than the windshield."

He fastened his seatbelt.

I put out my cigarette and moved from the dirt road to the paved road of Riverside Drive toward the highway.

Buddy said, "I've already flown through one windshield in my life and I was pronounced dead on the scene. I was racing my ambulance against another ambulance down the mountain from Asheville, missed a curve and went through a brick building. I remember floating in the air awhile, looking down at my body."

I accelerated down highway 341 toward I-95. "You've told me that before. Your mother told me first, actually, before I met you. She said you were lucky to be alive, though what she meant was that I was lucky to be able to meet you. Then she warned me about your driving. Then you told me about it yourself, more than once. You said God must've kept you alive for some good reason, and you were determined to make the most of your life."

"I said that?"

"More than once."

Buddy looked out his window. "Just think if I would've died. We never would've met, and our lives would've been all the poorer for it. Well—I'm not sure I'd be poorer, but you know what I mean."

I imagined, very briefly, a life without Harold, my anchor through waves of unsteady men. My only begotten, whom I loved more than any of my husbands or lovers, which the Bible says is wrong. Poor Harold, who was now determined to make his own mistake, though I was determined to say nothing and show that I trusted his judgment. It was difficult. As soon as I imagined his unhappy future, a sharp pain squeezed some organ I couldn't name. But maybe he would make it work. He was smarter than his parents. Wasn't he? Hadn't he paid attention to the mistakes we'd made? I thought about these things while I watched the road and veered into a meditative mood having to do with the slippery business of love and loss, sorrow and joy, youth and death, death and sex, slow time, fast time, lost time, shrinking time, Time. I said a little prayer for Harold's happiness.

"I'm talking about Harold," Buddy said, looking at me. "We'd be poorer without Harold."

I accelerated down the ramp to I-95 and merged with traffic. The headlights on southbound cars were on. In the distance, the grey sky grew darker.

"Thank you for driving," he said, sounding so sincere I had to look at him to remind myself who was sitting in the passenger seat.

"No big deal," I said.

"My truck would've blown up by now and I would've missed the wedding, then people would've missed the father of the groom speech I'm going to give tonight and the best man toast I'll give after the wedding. I was up all night working on them. Can I try out my father of the groom speech on you?"

"Maybe later."

"It starts off with a tribute to—what's her name?"

"Libby."

"Then it moves to a brief tribute to her parents, then I'm going to say something about lasting love and true happiness."

"You are?"

"Then I'm going to talk about being proud of Harold and quote some poetry they'll both like. Then for the big finish—I'm going to give a very moving and honest tribute to Harold's mother, the person who single-handedly turned him into the gentlemen he is now."

"No. You shouldn't—"

"Just wait until you hear it before you start criticizing."

"You shouldn't talk about me. If you insist on talking at all, you should stick to Harold and what's her name."

"Lily."

"Libby."

"It's going to create the perfect mood for their marriage. I want everything to go perfectly for him, and I figure this toast is about the only contribution I'll be able to make."

I said nothing. I hoped his speech went as well as he wanted to, and I hoped Libby would like it too. She had planned, with a lot of her mother's help, a seemingly simple wedding at a banquet room of an Atlanta hotel, partly because she was agnostic and didn't want a church wedding and partly because it would reduce complications and anxiety for the wedding party, who could stay in the same hotel. Libby's parents, afraid of flying, took a train from New York. I decided I would try hard to like them. My contribution was to pay for the rehearsal dinner, which I had the good grace not to mention to Buddy, who might feel like making a speech about guilt and good intentions. I suppressed a sigh, anticipating the coming events, then said a little prayer for everyone (especially Buddy) to have a good time during the dinner and before and after the wedding—all for Libby, who would remember her wedding day in great detail and hold it forever against her marriage should something go wrong.

The sky darkened as quickly as if a curtain had been pulled, and a few raindrops hit the windshield. I turned on my lights, set the wipers on low. A second later, the sky broke open and the rain fell in heavy sheets, pounding the glass so hard I wondered if it was hailing. I turned the wipers to high, slowed to forty, and moved my chin to the wheel to see better.

"I have to pee," Buddy said.

"Ha-ha."

"Seriously."

"We've gone three miles and you have to pee?"

"It's my kidney medication and a little prostate trouble if you must know."

"And you have to pee right now?"

"No, I can wait until the next exit."

I slowed to thirty-five.

He pressed his knees together and cupped his crotch. He said, "I hope it rains tomorrow. It's actually good luck if it rains on your wedding day— especially if you're a farmer."

"It rained on *our* wedding day."

"Did it?"

I didn't remember the weather for any of my other weddings. All but the first took place in a courthouse, and the weather had been forgettable.

"You probably don't remember it too well," I said. "You were still drunk from the night before, then you got drunk again that night with your best man, Uncle O."

"Is that right? Why in the world did you ever marry *him*?"

A tractor-trailer passed on the left, blanketing the windshield. I slowed to thirty. Buddy squeezed his crotch and inflated his cheeks.

"I don't know. He sort of reminded me of you."

"Were you kind of fantasizing that it *was* me?"

"No. I was just nostalgic for that time and place, when I was pregnant and you were off driving a truck. It was mostly a happy time, but I was stupid to think I could go back to it."

"If I had it to do all over again," he said, "I'd do the opposite of what my father and grandfather and all my uncles did, which was what I thought a man was supposed to do, you know, be a drunk carouser who didn't want to go home and listen to his wife complain about all sorts of things. I would do the opposite now. I'd go home and listen."

A motorcyclist had stopped beneath an overpass. He was sitting at the top of the embankment, smoking. I wished, for one moment, that I could join him. I slowed to twenty-five.

Buddy bounced the back of his head on the headrest, cheeks still inflated.

I had to shout over the rain. "I'm glad Harold's not like that. He's not is he?"

"Harold's not like that. He's already gone through his—"

"Wild phase?"

"When he tended bar, I think he—"

"Sowed his wild oats?"

"He's more mature than I was at his age," Buddy said. "I think he learned—"

"That sex doesn't cure loneliness?"

"Well," he said. "There are treatments and there are cures. I guess it depends on—"

"Maybe he's more mature than you were at his age."

"Maybe so," he said. "I hope so."

Buddy rocked and held his knees together, cheeks still inflated, hands in his crotch.

I got behind one tractor-trailer while another passed me on the left, covering my windshield with another wave. I took the next exit, stopped at a gas station in Darien, pulled to the far side of the parking lot behind an RV.

Buddy said, "You need anything?"

"A twelve-ounce Dr. Pepper in the can, please."

"I'll get it." He raised his hand to emphasize the grand gesture of buying me a drink.

I watched him walk through the rain, ducking, stepping through the center of two large puddles. A man who stepped out of the store and held the door open for Buddy looked a lot like my fourth husband, J.D., who had returned to live in his Altamaha River houseboat when our two-year marriage ended, though I'm not sure where he went a year after that, when the state required all houseboats be removed. The rain obscured my vision, and this man seemed older than J.D. ought to be. But he walked with the same ginger gait and short strides J.D. used because of a bad back—head down, no swing to his arms, elbows pointed toward the sky. And I could see, even through the rain that pelted him, the jaw-clench that tightened with each step. And when he climbed into what looked like his old truck, his mouth fell open into a grimace, and he closed the door. A dog waited for him in the passenger seat. J.D. (or the man who looked like him) spoke to the dog and drove off. I nearly started crying. He was old and feeble and lonely-looking. I wondered whether I'd pushed him closer to the grave when I'd kicked him out nine years ago. I wondered how much longer he'd live. I said a little prayer for forgiveness and a prayer that he'd find some happiness before he died.

The rain stopped just as quickly as it had started, and the sun came out so suddenly that waves of steam rose from the asphalt. When Buddy stepped into the parking lot, hands full with coffee, a honey bun, and my drink, his glasses fogged over while he walked through the rising steam, and he had to tilt his head to find my car.

"Goddamn," he said. "I couldn't see a thing out there."

"You couldn't see a twelve-ounce Dr. Pepper in the can? This is a sixteen-ounce Mountain Dew in a bottle. And it looks like you made some smart choices for a diabetic with a bladder problem."

"No one's ever accused me of making smart choices."

I pulled out of the parking lot, accelerated down the ramp to the interstate and merged with traffic.

"You're a good driver," Buddy said. "You've always been a good driver. I remember—"

"Seatbelt."

He fastened his seatbelt. "I remember your driving was one of the many things that first attracted me to you. You remember—"

"Oh no."

"What is it?" He looked behind him.

"Are we headed down memory lane? I don't think we should."

"Right after we got married, you drove me all over Asheville while I was selling door-to-door vacuum cleaners. You remember that?"

"Because you'd gotten your license suspended for the second time, asshole. And after I worked all day doing the books in that miserable welding supply office, I came straight home to drive you around all night, sometimes in the ice and snow, and if you ever got in for a demo, I sat in the cold car, writing letters home, asking my very poor mother if she could spare a few dollars to help us pay our bills because you pissed away whatever little money we had at the bars, which I didn't mention to her, of course, though I did ask her sometimes, I'd say, 'Mom, just how in the hell do you manage to stay married to one man longer than a month without going completely batshit?' "

"So you do remember that?"

"I remember."

"What did your mother tell you?"

"Nothing useful."

"Don't you *and* your mother still have those vacuums?"

"They're good vacuums."

"Okay then." He said this as if Mom and me had come out ahead in the deal. He set his coffee in the middle cup holder, unwrapped his honey bun and held it toward my chin to offer me a bite, which I declined.

The license plate of a passing truck said *Jeff Davis* at the bottom (representing the truck-owner's home county), which made me think of my third husband, Lewis Foster, and the farm he'd moved back to when we divorced—the farm where he'd taken Harold some weekends. It was hard to believe seven years had passed since Lewis Foster died. He died of a heart attack in the same fields where his father died, in the same August heat, at the same age. Harold cried over the telephone when I called him in North Carolina to tell him this, which made me cry too. He felt guilty for not going to the funeral, but he also felt like a hypocrite for letting so much time pass without speaking to Lewis. Then he felt even worse when the obituary listed him as a surviving son. I said a Hail Mary now, for more forgiveness, then I said another one for Lewis' widow, a woman I'd never met, whose sorrow I imagined so well that I started crying again.

Buddy chewed his honey bun, looked out his window into the woods. He said, "I have to tell you something."

"You have to?"

"It would make me feel better if I did."

"Okay then."

"When we were married, while you were pregnant—"

"No thanks," I said. "I don't care to hear any more, thank you. We're exiting memory lane now."

"In that case, I have to tell you something else."

"Don't get that on my seat, please."

"Is it okay if I tell you something else?"

"There are napkins in the glove box."

He opened the glove box and found my handgun. He said, "Hell-fire. What's that?"

"A golf club," I said.

He removed a napkin next to the gun and closed the glove box.

"That's something else that attracted me to you a long time ago—you knew how to use a gun, and weren't afraid to if you thought you needed to protect yourself from some asshole."

"Some asshole man, most likely, who might think he could force himself on me."

"Yes," he said. "I know the type."

Sparky had given me a gun before I left home the first time, bound for Asheville to live with a boarding school friend who lived next door to Buddy, whom I hadn't yet met. He gave me the gun after I'd packed my car, told me then that most men had only one thing on their minds. I played dumb. When I asked him what one thing that was, exactly, he told me to shoot the penis off of any man who couldn't take no for an answer. Then we walked to the river. He showed me the safety. He showed me how to load and unload, how to grip with both hands, how to raise the gun and extend the arms, how to train one eye down the sight toward the target's center, how to breathe, firing at the end of an exhale when the chest isn't rising or falling, how to squeeze (not jerk or pull) the trigger, how to hold steady for follow-through after recoil, then repeat a shot for as many shots as it took to stop a man. It was low tide, so fiddler crabs had danced across the opposite bank. Sparky hit one and I hit four. Back at my car, I put the gun in my glove box, and when I hugged him, he started crying. I told him not to worry. He kept crying. I drove away.

Now, I checked my speedometer, then looked at Buddy, waiting for him to remember his train of thought.

"What?" he said.

"You had to tell me something?"

"Right. I'm thinking about moving to New Jersey to live with an ex-nun I met online."

"New Jersey?"

He licked a finger. "She's an interesting and classy lady. She thinks I'd be a good father-figure to her sixteen-year-old son, who's a little retarded."

"Developmentally-challenged, please."

"She wants me to teach him how to drive. You think I could live happily ever after in New Jersey with an ex-nun who has a developmentally challenged sixteen-year-old?"

"I have my doubts."

"She does too. We're going to write up a contract as soon as I get there and determine what we need and expect from each other, which means any time we get into a disagreement, we'll simply point to the contract and it will serve as the official last word."

We were silent for a half mile. I passed a woman in a truck who was yelling into a cell phone. She raised her other hand off the wheel and lifted it to the heavens while she yelled.

"If it doesn't work, can I rent out the condo again?"

I laughed, but my lips were closed. "No. Phil may need a place to live pretty soon."

"Are things not going well?"

"That's none of your business."

"Okay." He balled up his honey bun wrapper and tossed it between his feet.

"I don't know why I keep making the same mistakes."

"You want me to tell you what I think?"

"No."

"I think you see too much of the best in people and it blinds you to the worst in people, which you only see after they've moved in and you have to share a bathroom."

"That's not true." I wondered if it was true.

"Or you feel sorry for people and try to save them."

"People like you?" I said this too quickly and regretted it.

"Yes," he said. "People like me."

I wondered. My second husband, Johnny Tate, hadn't needed saving, and I'd never noticed the worst in him. Johnny was the kindest man I'd ever known, who needed nothing, who loved Harold, who was talented in the ways of building and repairing anything and did so without being prompted and who cooked for me, who wanted so badly to make me happy, who built frames for my paintings and hung them everywhere around his hardware store, who touched me every day with some endearment, who took me dancing and danced quite well, who took his time making love while looking in my eyes. Who could trust love like that to last? I'd asked him to leave one summer while Harold visited Buddy, then he disappeared. He sold his hardware store and vanished. I said a prayer for him now that he'd forgiven me and gone on to find happiness. I prayed that Harold hadn't been hurt too badly by Johnny's disappearance. It's weird that neither of us ever mentioned him again. As far as we knew, Johnny Tate was dead.

"I don't know," I said. "I just wanted to have one more small little bit of romance before I died. That's all I wanted."

"Maybe you still can."

"Then this old guy with tubes in his nose comes along and seduces me in church. He said 'Peace be with you, beautiful,' and I fell for it like a stupid schoolgirl."

"We're not too old," Buddy said.

"Right there in front of God and my mother too, I fell for that shit."

"It's not too late," Buddy said.

"He and Sparky have the same birthday, which I suppose what's-her-name would have a field day explaining with her deep-fried Freudisms."

"Our hearts are young," Buddy said.

"I just wanted that romantic feeling one more time is all. You know that feeling? Is that so crazy?"

"Maybe you and I should become lifetime partners without getting married."

"God, I'm stupid. Don't you think Harold's a lot smarter than we are? He's more—"

"I could cancel my New Jersey trip and stay in the condo and we could be partners without living together, which I think would improve our chances of making it last."

"He's more realistic or something, I think. It's *her* I worry about."

"We'd have to make a contract, of course. The official last word on everything."

"Of course Harold knows her better than I do, so I have to trust that he's smart enough to make the right decision. I can't bear to think about it too much."

"Just think about it," he said.

"Do you have to pee again?"

"I can't help it."

I stopped in Pooler, a small town near Savannah, where Harold once scalded his face after removing the radiator cap from the overheating car he was driving back to college. After the EMTs took him to St. Joseph's Hospital, a nun tried to call me to say he'd be fine (after some blistering and peeling), but I wasn't home, so they called Roberta, and the nun, Sister Alice Sullivan, got excited because she'd known Roberta very well from the years she'd spent at the St. Sebastian Convent, where she had lived when Sparky dropped us off every morning with milk to take into the convent, which is where we stayed until school started. And while Harold's face was burning, Sister Alice and Mom laughed about old times, and Alice declared that Harold's guardian angel had been inside the hot water that scalded him.

Buddy got back in the car and handed me a Diet Dr. Pepper in the can. "Almost," I said. "Do you remember that time Harold scalded his face from opening his radiator cap?"

"No. Did it turn out okay?"

I looked at him.

"Was that a stupid question?"

"He's alive isn't he? He wasn't blinded or disfigured was he?"

"I did the same thing when I was a kid. Hurt like hell, but I got over it."

I accelerated toward the interstate and Buddy fastened his seatbelt without being told.

I said, "After the wedding tomorrow, I was thinking—"

"Where are they going on their honeymoon?"

"You just interrupted me."

"Sorry."

"I was thinking we might drive to Asheville to your mother's old house so we can see the place where you fell in love with me. Maybe put up a plaque or something."

"It's not there anymore. They tore the whole block down and put up a strip mall."

I slapped the steering wheel. "You never told me that."

"About fifteen years ago."

"You never told me. You should have told me."

"I guess I should have."

Buddy fell silent for awhile, looked out his window toward the woods. He was probably thinking about his mother, dead now twenty years. They'd been very close—almost as close as Harold and me. And he was likely thinking about those first days of his first real love, so full of laughter and ignorance. I wanted to ask what he was thinking about, but that seemed like a question for married people.

I said, "They're postponing their honeymoon—trying to save up for a trip to Paris next summer, apparently. Libby's anxious to return to work so her clients won't kill themselves."

We sat in silence for awhile. Somewhere close to Macon he said, "You think I should go to New Jersey?"

"How should I know? I have enough trouble managing my own life."

"Yes you do."

I gave him a look he didn't see because his eyes were pointed toward the woods.

"But I do too. That's why I didn't give Harold any advice last night when he called."

"Harold called *you* last night?"

"I told him I was the last person he ought to be asking advice from, but—"

"Why are you just now telling me this?"

"He wanted to know how he could tell for sure whether he should get married."

"And he called *you?*"

"I think he'd been drinking a little. He sounded pretty scared and—"

"What wisdom did you offer?"

"He talked for a long time, and sometimes he didn't make a whole lot of sense, so I just tried to listen. He wants very badly to do the right thing, you know, and he has this silly idea that he's inherited some kind of bad luck, but I told him he was thinking too much. I told him to relax. If it didn't work, he could get divorced, and he'd survive. I told him it was probably a good thing that he was scared."

"You told him that?"

"I never felt scared before any of my marriages and look how long they lasted. Were you scared before any of your marriages?"

"Just the first one." It was true. I was scared because I was deeply in love and he was reckless. After that, all the men I'd known loved me more than I loved them and I never felt afraid again, which has its advantages, but they didn't turn out so well either.

"If you're not scared," Buddy said, "you might be too cocky or already numb, like you have nothing to lose. Like me going to New Jersey. It doesn't scare me at all, which means I probably shouldn't go."

"Are you going?"

"Probably."

I checked my speedometer. A billboard for a radio station said, "Bulldog Country."

"Unless," he said, "you're too scared to tell me I shouldn't go."

"The person I'm most scared for is the ex-nun."

"Make jokes. Go ahead. That means you're scared."

"Tell her I'll be praying for her."

"What you're most scared about is the same thing I'm scared about—dying alone. Neither of us wants to die alone."

"I just hope it happens quickly. I'd rather not shrink away in a smelly nursing home."

"Maybe we could be roommates."

"Oh, wouldn't that be romantic?"

Buddy looked out his window. I checked my speedometer, figured the math for miles remaining to Atlanta, sighed.

He said, "Would you like to hear my father of the groom speech now?"

"Maybe later."

He pressed his knees together and held his crotch.

"Again?" I said.

"Yes, please."

"We're making great time. Might be there by midnight."

"Do you need anything?"

I pointed to my Diet Dr. Pepper and my Mountain Dew.

"Right. That should last you awhile."

Chapter 10
Jude

All through the wedding rehearsal, the dinner, and through the hours leading up to the wedding, Libby's father, Lou, enjoyed my little jokes ("Couldn't you spring for a quartet instead of a trio"), but Libby's mother, Lorraine, stayed too tense for a single smile, though Buddy's jokes certainly didn't help ("Let's all get naked so we'll *know* who the best man is," etc.).

I also joked with Pastor Chuck—a client of Libby's going on five years who had agreed to perform the ceremony (his first), in exchange for a month's worth of free over-the-phone therapy. His real name was Theodore, but he reminded me of Charlie Brown, so I called him Chuck. He was a short pudgy man in his forties with three sprigs of curly hair and basset-hound eyes, recently ordained online, anxious that he would never find a congregation or a wife. After he led everyone through the rehearsal without a glitch, I kissed his chubby cheek and said, "Will you do *my* next wedding?" He said he'd be honored.

Our circular table was occupied by Lou, Lorraine, Buddy, me, Harold, Libby, Mercedes (the lone bridesmaid), and Chuck. At an adjacent table sat Mary, Carol, Sarah, Sue, Lois, and Linda, all of whom were busy with their own party, laughing, eating off each other's plates. They looked happy and I was glad they'd come for Harold. The other table in the room was occupied by some of Libby's clients, none of whom appeared to know each other. Every time I looked in their direction, they were staring into their plates with their heads down, silent and serious.

I forgot to request vegetarian meals (even though I'd stuck a post-it reminder to my desk) for Libby, each of her parents, and for Mercedes. I apologized like hell, offered Lou a bite of my chicken breast. He laughed; Lorraine did not. Mercedes (another of Libby's clients), forty and never married, pouted like a little girl. I ordered four new vegetarian dishes, and they arrived just in time for desserts. To her credit, Libby laughed it off. She said if the meal was the only thing that went wrong, she'd be a happy bride.

Pastor Chuck said, "You can count on one thing going wrong at every wedding."

"I'll drink to that," Buddy said.

I dipped my chicken breast into Buddy's steak sauce and studied Lorraine's posture—her spine and long neck resembled a post, especially when she lifted her napkin, *after every bite*, to dab each corner of her mouth. I had wanted to like her, but I was finding it a challenge. Maybe she was just tired, the poor woman. She'd had a long train ride, and she was clearly nervous about something else going wrong, beyond the fact that her rich daughter was marrying the likes of poor Harold. Once, when I looked up at Lorraine, I was startled to see her staring at me.

She offered a phony smile. "I hope you'll pardon me," she said, "if this is too personal. But I was curious to know how long you and Mr. Owen have been divorced. You seem such good friends." And she dabbed her mouth again.

I said, "Beats the hell out of me. That was five husbands ago." And I winked at Lou, who laughed and tried not to.

"Thirty-one years ago this December," Buddy said. He lifted his whiskey glass, bumped it against my tea. "I hope Harold and Libby stay married for as long as we've been divorced." Lorraine and Mercedes squinted at him. He said, "And with that—"

"Oh goody," I said. "Just make it brief, please."

He tapped his fork against his glass. He pushed his seat back, stood, and continued tapping, much longer than he needed to. The people at the other tables turned to see him better. He cleared his throat. He said, "Ladies and Gentleman." He put his glass down and reached inside the pocket of his slightly wrinkled sportscoat, and he pulled out an empty hand. He fished inside his pants pockets, first the front, then the back two. Lorraine rolled her eyes. Libby giggled.

He cleared his throat again. He said, again, "Ladies and gentleman." He folded his hands across his crotch, looked down at his empty plate as if his words were there, to Harold, to me, across the faces at the other tables, then toward the back of the room at no one. He used his lower lip to push out his upper lip. He looked at the back wall while the silent room waited. He licked his lips and frowned again. I shot a glance at Mary, who was smiling in Buddy's direction, clearly encouraging him that the crowd was friendly and that it was safe for him to get on with it. He must have seen her, because he forced a smile, but the smile collapsed. It was a tortured smile, his mouth-muscles contorting into a shape his eyes rebelled against. He lifted his left arm and pointed at Harold. He opened his mouth and closed it. He held his arm out, still as a statue. Libby raised her eyebrows, head cocked to the side. Harold looked at his father with the same forced-smile Buddy had used a moment ago, an agonizing moment, really, the tortured son trying to relax the flailing father. Buddy was frozen, arm stretched toward Harold and Libby, his lips pushing against each other now. Was he crying?

I clapped. I clapped three times before another clap came from across the room, and other claps followed. Even Harold joined in. The applause awakened him. He lifted his heels. He said, "Ladies and gentleman."

He said, "When I was a child, I dreamed that I would grow up to be the ringmaster for the Ringling Brothers and Barnum & Bailey circus. Maybe there's still time. I'll tell you a secret. I'm a high school dropout. I got my GED when I was in my thirties, and then I went to community college and learned too late the value of an education. I started Toastmaster's clubs, I won public-speaking awards—I've shared a stage with three U.S. presidents. Once upon a time forty years ago I thought I might be the kind of man who could stand before big crowds and make great speeches. None of that has prepared me for this moment, when I stand before my smart son and his smart bride, embarrassed that I can't remember the important things I wrote down so I'd be sure I wouldn't forget to say them on this important occasion."

Lorraine dabbed the corners of her mouth and dropped her napkin in her plate. Libby put her elbows on the table and folded her hands across her mouth. Harold slouched and drank from a beer that was already empty.

Buddy said, "In the speech I left at home, I had written some well-chosen and specific words—a list of sincere things that paid tribute to Libby's parents for raising a beautiful and intelligent woman that I'm very proud to have as a daughter-in-law, a woman whose heart is big enough to tolerate her well-meaning but absent-minded father-in-law, though I do hope, Libby, that you will take some comfort in the knowledge that in a few years I'll be dead and won't have a chance to influence your children. To Lorraine, Lou, and Libby, I lift my glass."

163

Buddy raised his whiskey glass, and everyone raised their glasses too.

"The next part of the beautiful speech I left at home was devoted to Harold's mother, Jude, for—"

He stopped cold here and swallowed, apparently choking up—apparently very close to blubbering.

"For raising Harold so well." He lifted his glass and paused, and others lifted their glasses with him, and the moment was all the more touching for what he did not say.

"And finally, to Harold." Here, he gave the first genuine smile I'd seen, the easy smile of the entire face relaxing. "Harold, in the speech I left at home, I had written some honest things that I had hoped would make up, in some small ways, for all the times in my life when I have failed to say the right things—or all the times—many more of these, of course, where I failed to say anything at all. I had quotes from a poem you would have liked—a poem that spoke about the love I've always felt for you and the sorrow I've felt for lost love, bad choices, and last chances. I don't remember any of that poem or even what it was called. All I can say now is that I salute you for becoming the man you've become without my help. Or despite my help. I applaud your choice in wives, and I wish—"

He stopped again, choking up again, it seemed. He raised up on his tiptoes and lifted his glass. "I wish you and Libby a lifetime of great health, happiness, tolerance, and forgiveness."

He raised his glass and everyone else raised theirs.

"In the speech I didn't bring I made notes of other things I wanted to say, but I'll end your suffering and stop here. I would like you both to know, however, that if there's ever the slightest little thing that either of you should ever need—no matter how small or how big—whether it includes walking the dog or babysitting—"

I looked at Libby and saw her lift her eyebrows at Harold.

"I'm here to tell you," he said, "that you should call Jude or Lorraine or Lou."

He lifted his glass a final time and others lifted theirs with him. Applause came from the far side of the room and spread. Libby kissed Harold, with feeling. Lorraine seemed to take her first deep breath in several hours.

Buddy sat beside me and drained the rest of his whiskey.

"Not bad," I said. "Not very brief, but not bad."

Buddy shook his head. "There was a lot more I wanted to say—it's all in the speech I left at home."

"You can mail it to them."

He shook his head and frowned. "We'll just cut our losses and move on. Tomorrow will be a better day. Tomorrow, I'll do better."

"Just be briefer," I said.

Libby touched her wine glass against Harold's beer bottle. She put her arm around his shoulder and kissed him. She whispered something in his ear that made him lower his eyes and nod. She smiled at whatever he had agreed to and looked happy. And I thought, why not? Why couldn't he— why couldn't we all—live happily ever after? What on this Earth could prevent such a seemingly simple thing from happening?

At the wedding, I stood outside the banquet room and listened for my 11 a.m. piano cue, a Bach piece I thought too common (though I refrained from saying so), then I walked into the small, low-ceilinged room lit too brightly with fluorescent bulbs, and proceeded slowly down an aisle (without an usher), that was too short of a walk and assumed my (aluminum) seat in the front row of the right side. In the second row just behind me sat Mary, Carol, Sue, Sarah, Lois and Linda. Sue, the biggest softie, held a Kleenex. The only other person on Harold's side was a man named Richard Jenkins, Harold's boss, who had been nice enough, a half-hour prior to the wedding, to engage me in conversation at the hotel bar, where I'd gone for a glass of orange juice to wash down the Valium I'd gotten from Mercedes, who had gotten two from Lorraine, who had gotten three from Libby. Richard Jenkins badly needed a haircut, a beard-trimming, and possibly a shower. He insisted on buying my orange juice, guessing correctly that I was the mother of the groom, then he proceeded to tell me, while emptying his whiskey glass, that Harold would one day make a fine teacher if he only stuck with it long enough. He also told me that Libby would be good for Harold. "Most men," he said, "need women who will teach them how to be more like women." Then he confessed to having been married five times, though he was currently in a good relationship with a former student who was teaching him how to be a Buddhist, and did I have dinner plans? I gave him a shocked look. "Five times!" I said. "Wow. You must get a lot of crap for that." Then I looked at my watch, told him we'd better find our spots.

Lorraine sat across from me on the front row, stiffly facing the front, tired eyes locked on the carpet where a lonely thought was planted. All the seats behind her were occupied by Libby's clients, many of whom had been at the rehearsal dinner. Mercedes had introduced me to some of them while we stood in the hall. Each of them shook my hand and smiled as joyously as if they'd just returned from being baptized in the nearest river. One woman, so thin I wanted to call an ambulance, said, "Libby saved my life. I think she'll be perfect for Harold."

A console piano had been set up in the right corner of the room. The pianist, another of Libby's clients, was a twelve-year-old named Ally who wanted one day to perform professionally, maybe with symphonies, though she suffered extreme stage fright, even at small recitals, and sometimes anxiety attacks overwhelmed her without warning and she'd run from rooms. After the rehearsal, she told me, "One time in third grade? During a recital? I wet my pants." I hugged her. I told her she played beautifully. I pointed across the room to Harold. I said, "See that guy? The groom? One time in a school play, he wet his pants right on stage. *Now*, he's a teacher." She liked this.

Now, Ally pushed her glasses up, turned a sheet of music over and started playing a new piece, which was the cue for Mercedes, Pastor Chuck, Buddy and Harold to enter through a door in the back of the room—a white door that blended so well with the white walls that I hadn't even noticed it. Harold walked to his spot, faced the seats, and squinted toward the back of the room, rocking on his heels, looking unbalanced. He'd nicked his chin while shaving. He removed his handkerchief and wiped his forehead. He licked his lips. I wanted him to look at me so I could smile and send him a peaceful message.

I didn't cry until I saw Harold standing beside his father and noticed the terrible resemblance. Harold suddenly looked old and lost. I cried for the long-gone happiest day of my life, when he'd come screaming into a hospital room, and I cried for his lost childhood, which vanished like a city sliding backwards from an airplane window. I cried for the time that was left of our lives, and I cried for any unhappy day he had ahead of him. I cried because we were aging too rapidly, which meant, I realized now, that

Harold was dying.

Buddy yawned. Then moaned. From the looks of him, he'd stayed up too late drinking in the hotel lounge, insisting that Harold (from the looks of him) tag along. After the moan that followed his yawn, I looked at Lorraine, whose eyes went wide with horror, apparently from Buddy's noises *and* from the couple of plunked notes Ally had missed. Ally stuck out her tongue and lowered her head and kept playing, and I was proud of her.

Finally, Harold looked at me. He wiped his forehead with his handkerchief again and smiled, reassuring *me*, that everything was fine. I wiped my eyes and smiled back, winked, took a painful breath and tried to think of something funny. I looked at Pastor Chuck. His big grin. I imagined him wearing Charlie Brown's striped shirt, then I gave Harold my own big grin.

Ally stopped playing. Pastor Chuck nodded at her. She turned over a new piece of music and started the wedding march, fat chords played with more power than seemed possible from twelve-year old hands. When everyone stood and turned toward the front, I saw Buddy pat his pockets. I knew the horrified look on his face, the open mouth, the frightened eyes, the same expression he got when he searched his mind for misplaced wallets, lost cars, lost nights. I heard his whispered confession as he bent toward Harold's ear, and I heard Harold say, "Very funny." It was the oldest joke in the history of weddings, after all, and Buddy had already given one variation during last night's rehearsal, happy to have gotten ha-ha's from everyone.

All other heads were turned to Libby, who was coming now in slow-motion down the aisle on Lou's arm, smiling big toward Harold, taking her time because this was her moment, of course, and she was luxuriating in every second of it.

I heard Buddy say, "They're in the bathroom."

Harold's mouth dropped open and his eyes went blank, which meant, tragically, that he looked just like his father. He wiped his cheeks. He wiped his forehead.

Pastor Chuck whispered *don't worry* and smiled toward Libby, who had no idea what she was walking toward.

I wanted to rush down the narrow aisle past Libby and Lou, (*pardon me, please, I'll be right back—it's nothing, really*), then sprint down the hall, past the lobby and into the men's bathroom, pluck the rings from the counter and race back, whisking past Libby and Lou again (*pardon please*), then sneak the rings into Buddy's hands and return to my seat before Libby and Lou hit their marks. But there wasn't time and my rapid movements would cause more chaos than calm. I hoped Pastor Chuck might summon some miracle to salvage the moment with grace, but it was *his* first wedding too, so I had little faith.

Libby looked beautiful, which I was sad to see, because I knew her radiance would vanish when the pomp of her day collapsed like a circus tent, branding memories more forcefully than any photograph to come. She smiled all the way down the aisle and Ally played beautifully. Then Lou unwrapped his arm from hers, methodically, and kissed her. He dabbed his eye, then turned and stepped toward Lorraine on the front row. She dabbed her eye too—the saddest woman I think I've ever seen, and reached out to Lou, as if to share in the grief that their daughter was now officially lost to Harold.

Libby's eyes were beautiful and serene, composed and confident. Harold's eyes spun with fear. It was touching then to see Libby give him a gentle smile, as if to say she loved him for seeming so vulnerable—as if to say, *do not worry yourself over any little thing my darling.*

Buddy's adam's apple bounced like a cork. He looked at me—the gaze of the newly convicted searching the courtroom for a friend. I shrugged and lifted my eyebrows as if to say *hey, this might get interesting.* He put a finger inside his stiff collar and jerked his head to the side. He licked his lips. A line of sweat bubbled on his forehead. Harold, meanwhile, quite oddly, stared at the ceiling. A line of sweat bubbled on his forehead. He licked his lips.

Pastor Chuck invited people to sit. He smiled. Paused. Looked over the guests. Libby remained beautiful. I looked at the photographer (another of Libby's clients whose experience thus far had been limited to birds and babies), who was squatting against the wall, adjusting his camera settings. I sent him a telepathic message: *Take her picture NOW, asshole.*

Pastor Chuck cleared his throat. He said the standard things, read the standard vows (love is patient through sickness unto death etc.), then he paused and lifted his chin. He said, "Ladies and Gentleman. I planned, as this portion of the program, a time for the bride and groom to stare into one another's eyes while I remove myself momentarily from the altar.

Symbolically, this moment represents an opportunity for them to stare into one another's soul and find there the assurance that each is committed to the other as they embark upon this lifelong journey." He smiled first at Libby, then at Harold, whispered that he'd be right back, then walked down the aisle and out of the room.

They had practiced this eye-staring ritual the previous night, while giggling, though Pastor Chuck had remained in front of them, watching them watch each other. Now, while he was gone, they stared at each other silently, holding hands. It was a long time to stare at someone. I couldn't remember ever staring for half as long into the eyes of any of my husbands. Harold's forehead shined with sweat. Buddy cleared his throat. Harold rocked on his heels, stared into Libby's eyes, held her hands. Mercedes squinted down the aisle, a crease between her eyes. Buddy cleared his throat again. The room was silent too long. Harold pulled a hand away, wiped his forehead, wiped his hand on his pants, then reached for Libby's hands again. Buddy cleared his throat. Harold licked his lips and stared into Libby's eyes, which were beginning to grow slightly dull with waiting. Buddy looked down the aisle for Pastor Chuck, licked his lips, rocked back on his heels. I looked at Lou and Lorraine, who were looking down the aisle for Pastor Chuck, waiting in the silence while Harold and Libby tried to hold their stares. Harold pulled his other hand away to wipe his head, then wiped his hand on his pants and found Libby's hand again. He licked his lips. Libby's eyes grew darker. The corners of her mouth were falling, as if tugged by strings. Her photographer snapped a picture. Buddy cleared his throat. Harold rocked on his heels, broke his stare very briefly to check the ceiling, then stared at her again. The corners of her mouth suddenly reversed themselves and her eyes simultaneously brightened as if to say *don't worry, darling*. She tugged his hands and Pastor Chuck appeared, reclaiming his position. He whispered, loud enough for me to hear, that the rings were *momentarily* missing. He said, "Someone has probably turned them in to the Lost and Found, which we will check later, but for now, it will be just fine to continue the ceremony using these imaginary rings." He held out his palm.

Libby's eyes filled with tears.

"It's okay," Harold said quickly. "We'll find them right afterward. It's just a—"

"Did you look on the backs of all the toilets?" Buddy said. "I think I put them on the back of a toilet."

Libby said, "Do you know how much those rings cost?"

"Did you take out insurance?" Buddy said.

"We'll just proceed," Pastor Chuck said. "With these imaginary rings. Everything will be fine." He smiled again and told Buddy that when the time came, he should pull the imaginary rings from his pocket and hand them over.

Libby's mouth fell open. A crease formed above her nose, her forehead carved with wrinkles. Lou stepped forward. He touched Libby's elbow. He said, "What's wrong, dear?"

"He lost the rings," she said.

Lou gave Harold a disappointed look. Harold pointed his thumb at Buddy.

"I must've left them in the bathroom," Buddy said. "An honest mistake."

Lorraine stepped forward to see what the problem was.

"What's the problem?" she said.

"He lost the rings," Lou told her, voice rising.

Lorraine gave Harold a disappointed look. Harold pointed his thumb at Buddy.

"They were on the back of a toilet," Buddy said.

"Close to a thousand dollars is how much," Libby said.

Harold said, "Let's just proceed with these imaginary rings." He opened his palm.

Pastor Chuck said, "Those rings right there will work just fine."

"We'll get some new ones later," Harold said.

I stepped forward. I said, "I have a suggestion." Everyone looked at me, Libby with squinted eyes. I said, "Maybe Lou and Lorraine could let you borrow their rings, just for the ceremony."

Lorraine said, "We can't take our rings off."

"Oh for Christ's sake," I whispered. "It would just be for a few minutes."

"I mean we can't get them off. They've been on so long, our fingers have grown around them and we can't get them off." She tugged on her ring to show it wouldn't budge, then she gave me a raised eyebrow know-it-all look like my sister gave me when we were children.

Lorraine said, "Even if I could take it off, Libby wouldn't be able to get it on. Her fingers are too fat. She's always had fat fingers."

Libby released a soft sob.

I looked around at other hands, but they were empty—Mercedes, Pastor Chuck, Buddy—my own family—Mary, Carol, Sue, Lois and Linda—no one was wearing rings. And I wasn't wearing my ring. I hadn't worn it since I'd gotten married because it was always clanking things and getting in the way when I worked outside, and I'd decided it was a useless symbol anyway.

I faced Libby's guests. I said, "Is anyone wearing a wedding ring we can borrow for five minutes?"

Libby said, "Oh my God. Let's just—"

Not a single one of Libby's guests was wearing a wedding ring, which I found surprising.

"Let's just get this over with," Libby said.

"It'll be fine," Pastor Chuck said. "I've heard about this sort of thing happening before. One time, this Pastor friend of mine in Buffalo—Reverend Red is what he went by in the online class we took together? Or did he live in Fresno? Yes, come to think of it, Reverend Red lived in Fresno with his mother. Anyway, he told a story of how he had to improvise with imaginary rings once just to get through a ceremony, but it turned out to be quite memorable. Plus, the rings are purely a—"

"Please," Libby whispered. "Please get on with it."

I returned to my seat and Lorraine and Lou returned to theirs. When she turned to face the room, Lorraine offered a giant smile that must have exhausted her.

Pastor Chuck lifted his chins and proceeded with the service, smiling through the remainder of the vows, holding his hand out to receive the imaginary rings from Buddy, who removed them from his coat pocket and placed them in Pastor Chuck's palm. Libby rolled her eyes. She looked tired now, eyes coated with a hazy gloss. All the beauty she'd radiated some minutes ago was replaced now with quiet contempt. The photographer snapped a picture.

Harold wiped his forehead with his sleeve. Then he removed an imaginary ring from Pastor Chuck's palm, lifted Libby's left hand, and slipped the invisible ring on her finger while repeating, too softly, Chuck's words. Libby lifted her eyes to meet his. Her eyes were fully glazed now and the corners of her mouth were turned down again.

Libby picked up Harold's imaginary ring from Chuck's palm and placed it on his finger, repeating, in monotone, Chuck's words. Harold offered a painful smile. His forehead glistened again with sweat. Libby looked at Chuck. She lifted her eyebrows as if to say, can we end this god-forsaken wedding so we can get on with the argument, please?

Chuck said under the authority vested in him, etc., that he could now pronounce them, etc., and that Harold could go ahead and kiss the bride.

Harold's eyes sprang open like he'd crapped himself. Ally struck the first of her fat major chords, but it was too soon. Harold had not kissed the bride. He had not moved. Nor had Libby. Ally kept playing. People's hands were poised for clapping, waiting for the kiss, but neither Harold nor Libby moved toward each other. They released each other's hands, but still, they did not move. And I heard him, even over Ally's loud piano. I heard him say, "I know. You're right." Then Ally caught up with the moment, looked their way and stopped playing, her open-mouthed expression full of fear that *she* was the one who had caused the problem.

In the silence, Harold said, "Sorry." He turned his back on the crowd then and stepped between Pastor Chuck and Buddy and walked, head down, toward the rear white wall, opened the white door in the center of it, stepped through it, and closed it again.

Buddy looked at me and I looked at him and we both looked at Libby, who just that moment turned to Buddy. Something strange and soft came over her face then, a mask of resignation, even as her eyes grew wet, and a kind of poise that clearly suggested she was capable of waiting for a more appropriate time to start killing people. She even managed a glance at me, with a kind of half-smile, before she looked at her parents and the people behind them. She was very pretty in that moment, I thought, and I could see, even then, why Harold might have loved her. Then, very calmly, she started addressing us as if she were holding her own private press conference.

She said, "I'm sorry, but I had to stop it. It was the right—he's too young, I'm afraid, and he has been too damaged for too long. I thought I could help him, but when I looked into his eyes today, I could see that he needs more help than I can give. We have managed to save ourselves a lot of grief today. Thank you all for being here to support me during this difficult time, a time we can learn from." Mercedes went to her, put an arm around her and turned her toward her parents, who ushered her toward the rear wall and through the same white door Harold had gone through. Harold, I knew, was already long gone. He would be hiding out somewhere. He would call us to come and rescue him.

Chapter 11
Harold

I found my way out of the rear of the hotel and walked as quickly as I could down the city sidewalk to the nearest bar, a small, dark, and mostly-empty dive where Merle Haggard greeted me as soon I stepped in, singing "If We Make It Through December." I ordered a shot of bourbon and a beer. One guy shot pool by himself at the back room's only table, one sad-looking older man stared into his beer at one end of the bar, and the bartender, a chain-smoking zombie in his mid-fifties, looked like he hadn't slept in several weeks, probably since his own divorce. After I ordered my second beer, I did what any mature man in my situation would do—I called my mother to come and rescue me.

While I waited, I explained the events to myself like this: it was too long to look into the eyes of someone who was looking too long at someone she didn't seem to like the looks of. What I'd seen, beneath the way she looked at me, was the twisted shape of the voice I'd heard the night before, when she whispered in my ear after Buddy's speech, reminding me of the conditions I'd agreed to when we got back together—that we would never take our children (plural) to visit my family, although my parents could visit *us*, so long as they did so separately, and not more than twice a year, and only if they stayed in a hotel. I'd agreed that we would cease birth control measures once our wedding week rolled around, even though the thought of being responsible for even one child terrified me. Even before she let go, I still feared—while I stared into her cold gaze— that no one else would ever come along to look at me at all. But she was right to let go. The longer I looked into her eyes, the more I thought of letting go too. I thought I should go ahead and take the action that she'd been helping me see that I should take, which was to divorce my DNA, break the cycle of failed love and stand alone as my own strong person. But I don't know if I would have let go, because she let go first.

On my third beer, with Merle on to a new song (the old man at the end clearly had loaded up the Haggard), Jude walked through the front door with Mary on her heels, followed by Carol, Sue, Sarah, Lois and Linda. They each hugged me. They each patted my back. They each said I was better off now than I would have been later. They each looked into my eyes and asked if I was okay. I said no, I wasn't okay. They said I would be eventually.

As soon as I thought to ask if they'd seen my father, he walked in. He came to me at the bar and touched my shoulder. He looked me in the eyes. He said, "You're welcome." He got the bartender's attention, and asked people what they were drinking. "It's on me," he said. "And also Jude."

"No," Jude said. "Let's—"

"Who's hungry?" Mary said.

"I'm hungry," Lois and Linda said in unison.

"Let's go somewhere a little more lively," Carol said.

"But Merle Haggard's on," Buddy said.

"This way," Sue said, and she waved her arm and walked toward the door and back out into the blinding sunlight and down the sidewalk away from the church with everyone following. Buddy and I lagged behind a couple of steps while the women talked and laughed about the people on Libby's side of the aisle. As soon as Buddy put his arm around me, I remembered the time we had walked through a landfill looking for money he'd thought to hide in a trashcan, which I had thrown away. He turned to look at me now, peering over the tops of his glasses, which meant something serious was on the way. He said, "Are you okay?"

The women laughed at something I hadn't heard, and their laughter sounded good. We walked a few more steps. I said, "I think I should go home for the rest of the summer."

"Might be a good idea," he said. "I know a condo that's going to be vacant in a couple days. I'm going to New Jersey to marry that ex-nun I met online who has a sixteen-year-old developmentally disadvantaged son she says I'd be a good influence for."

"New Jersey?"

"We're both very optimistic that we can make each other happy. It just goes to show—life is long and new adventures wait around every corner."

"Can you give me a ride back home?"

"I rode with your mother. I'm sure she'd be happy to give us both a ride."

For two days, I slept on the couch and my grandmother slept in my old room and Captain Phil and his oxygen tank slept in my mother's room. All day for those two days I helped my father pack boxes, then I loaded them into the U-Haul trailer he'd hooked to his truck.

"How in the hell," he kept saying, "does a person accumulate so much shit?"

Repeatedly, he told me to take anything I wanted. "And I mean *any-thing*," he said. "All this will be yours one day anyway."

"Leave the bed," I told him. "And these two books by Viktor Frankl."

"All a man needs," he said. "A bed and Viktor Frankl."

The next day, about noon, when he announced he was ready to begin his journey, Jude and I and Captain Phil stood around his truck to wish him well. I hugged him, then Jude hugged him, then Captain Phil shook his hand.

Jude said, "Good luck. I hope we never see you again."

"Thanks."

"Because if we never see you again, it'll mean you're happy and you don't want to leave the ex-nun."

"Or it could mean she killed me," he said.

"*Or*," I said, "it could mean your truck broke down and left you stranded."

"Or that," Buddy said. "Thanks for the farewell party. Stay in touch."

He got into his truck and pulled away, a thin stream of black smoke leaking from the tailpipe. He waved one arm out his window while we waved from the driveway. We watched the U-Haul disappear.

My mother wiped her eye. She said, "I'm going to miss the old ass-hole."

Captain Phil gave her a puzzled look. He said, "Why would you miss an asshole?"

"I wouldn't miss all assholes," she said.

Captain Phil shook his head and walked away, hands behind his back.

I moved into the condo and stayed until the end of July.

176

I avoided Phil—who kept telling me why I should join the Navy—so I often went a couple of days without seeing my mother too, or anyone at all, though Jude sometimes brought me leftovers my grandmother had given her to share with me. She'd look me over while I was lying in bed with Viktor Frankl and ask how I was doing, and I'd lie and tell her fine, and she'd say, "No, you're not. You should take up running. Or biking, or golf. Or walking. Try walking. You want heartbreak? Try being a parent for awhile when your child is going through heartbreak. Ask your grandmother what that's like. Your grandmother knows." Then she'd shake her head at all the holes Buddy had left in the walls and comment on the peculiar odor (which I could not detect) that she accused him of leaving behind. Then she'd say, "Shape up, Harold. You did the right thing. Stop thinking about it."

I thought of calling Libby. I thought about it almost constantly. I also waited for her to call me. Then I'd turn off my phone and place it outside in the chair with Sister Agnes, the landfill mutt with the soulful eyes who seemed much sadder now that Buddy was gone. I'd put my phone in her chair so I wouldn't be tempted to look at it, then I'd return to Viktor Frankl, who had survived much worse. I could go ten—sometimes *fifteen* minutes without retrieving it to see if I'd missed any calls. I never did.

Every few days around sunset, my grandmother called to say, "Harold? Sparky wants you to take him home." And I'd pick him up in his truck and drive him around and take him back, and we'd chat for awhile like best friends, excited to be headed home together. Sometimes, he'd stumble upon a moment of clarity. His favorite phrase at such times was this: "Don't get old, Harold. Whatever you do, don't get old." It sounded like good advice, and I began to imagine ways I could prevent it.

When Janice, his nightly caretaker, quit—citing her own health problems—I took over for a few days. I helped him with his nightly bath. While I pulled off his pants, which he often soiled, he asked where Roberta was. When I helped him into the tub and handed him his lathered rag, he asked where Roberta was. When I said, yes, I would wash his back for him, he asked where Roberta was. When I helped him wash his hair and helped him rinse it and when I pulled him out of the tub and helped him dry off while he sat naked on the closed toilet-lid, he asked where Roberta was. Each time, I answered patiently with the lie that Jude invented—that Roberta was staying with Carol so she could help with Sarah's children, a lie designed to make him think she wasn't sleeping with another man.

One time, while sitting in the tub, right after asking where Roberta was, he said, "Where's Libby?"

"She's in Atlanta," I told him.

"Gone with the wind?"

"I think so," I said.

"It's never too late to win her back. Send her flowers and sing to her and tell her that you love her. That's how I win Roberta back. Where *is* Roberta?"

And I told him again, patiently, where Roberta was.

Some nights, I'd cook us hotdogs, and we'd eat while we watched the Braves. Occasionally, he'd say, "I can't keep my eye on the ball. I can't tell when it's a commercial and when it's the game." And I would tell him which was which and remind him of the score. And he'd say, "Don't ever get old, Harold. Don't ever get old."

After I helped him to bed, I'd go to the couch and try to sleep in the empty living room, loud with clocks. I kept my phone charged in case Libby called. She didn't. I came closest to calling her between the hours of one a.m. and four a.m. Very often, I was still awake when my grandmother entered at five a.m. Other times, if I dozed off, she'd wake me gently, touch my head with the rosary ring she wore and invite me to stay for breakfast, but I always declined to spare her the work of feeding two men, then I'd walk through the dark morning back to the condo, where I tried again, and failed, to sleep.

One afternoon, my ex-uncle Hammer knocked on my condo door. When I went outside, he pointed to a kayak strapped to the top of his jeep. He said he'd gotten it off of a guy who owed him some money, but it was mine if I wanted it. The following week, after the family found another caretaker, I left my phone with Sister Agnes and pulled my kayak to the river. I'd never been in a kayak, so the thought of tipping over and drowning was a good distraction.

If the tide was right, I went out in the early evening, once dusk had forgiven the cruel heat of the day and the soft light promised to linger for a long while yet and the shadows stretched in distorted shapes beneath the ancient oaks. It was the time of day when I felt caught between the past and the future on a slender moment of time that was achingly beautiful because I knew it would not last. At such times, I started missing people who were dead and not dead. I started talking to myself. Sometimes, when I must have had my grandfather's voice in my head, I'd hear myself say, "Where's Libby?" Then I'd laugh at myself, sound carrying across the marsh.

To catch the tide perfectly meant it was at its highest and most still, when the water had finished coming in and sat motionless for a moment as if it meant to rest and gather its thoughts before deciding to turn and ease back out.

I'd put my kayak in and paddle slowly around the winding bends of the backwaters, marsh grass above my head on both sides. I sank inside the smell of salt and mud and something primordial I could not name. I rowed slowly toward the very end of Burnett creek to the spot where Sparky had warned me, years before, alligators went to breed. I wanted to find them. And I wanted to come upon some of the dolphins we sometimes saw who would follow schools of mullet. I rowed above the stingrays related to the ones I had seen as a child when my grandfather caught them unintentionally. He once pulled a pregnant stingray to the bank and showed me how the babies' tails are covered in a sheath that protects their mothers. I stayed out too late some nights, knowing I'd have to row back in the dark. I went beneath the highway overpass, where bats dropped down and circled me in their clumsy loops of dips and swirls. Above me, tractor-trailers took the pine forests to the papermill.

I rowed around the narrowing bends, ducked beneath the low-lying limbs that leaned over the water, touched the roots that hung from the bank, and continued down the creek as it narrowed past the backs of houses, yards packed with junked cars, broken appliances, a disconnected toilet. Bullfrogs and crickets kept me company. Egrets flew above me, headed to their roosts. In the near-dark one night, I saw a ghost. It zoomed back and forth across the length of a back yard, thin and grey. And even after I saw that it was a long strand of Spanish moss hooked to a dog run that moved as the dog moved, I could not shake my first impression. The dog himself, a pit bull with cropped ears and cropped tail, opened his mouth to bark, but he made no sound. The choker chain attached to him had likely damaged his throat. Farther along, as the creek continued to narrow and dead-end into the marsh, I heard big splashes that must have come from gators who heard me first, but I never saw them.

I adopted imaginary ghosts and carried them home, slivers of moonlight showing the way. The rowing exhausted me, especially when I moved against the tide, and my sore shoulders coaxed me into deeper sleep than I'd known for a long time.

By the end of July, for the first time ever, I looked forward to the classroom.

I had waited too long to find a new place to live, and when I called Richard Jenkins to ask if he knew of anyone who needed a housemate, he said, "No. But stay with me until you find a place."

He rented a 1930's-era brick duplex inside a crowded and treeless neighborhood of people who wandered the streets carrying sticks and bats, coming and going among groups who stood outside the corner liquor store, bars across its windows. He had nine cats, one litter box, no television, no internet, no phone, piles of clothes scattered on the floor, stacks of books spread on the clothes, open notebooks spread around a living room lit by one floor lamp with a crooked shade.

When I arrived for my first night, he pointed to his only furniture, a loveseat. I slumped on one side and he sat on the other. Two black cats lay between us on top of three open notebooks, licking each other's ears. My throat itched instantly, and my eyes began to burn.

Richard said, "I'm pretty sure I'll be moving in with Maya very soon, so it looks like you and the cats could have this place to yourselves."

"Maya, your student?"

"*Former* student. Potato?"

"What?"

He pointed to a fifty-pound bag of potatoes lying on his kitchen counter beneath a 24-roll pack of toilet paper next to a case of Lysol next to an orange cat who sat on top of an open notebook with his foot pointed toward the ceiling, licking between its legs.

I said, "Do you have alcohol?"

"I stopped drinking. Just last week. Maya asked me to quit, so I said I would. Does it smell bad in here?"

"Yes," I said. "It smells bad. And I think I'm allergic to cats."

"If you badly needed a drink in order to take the edge off, however, I would have better manners than to make you drink alone. Maybe one drink would help you take the edge off."

I touched the nearest black cat beside me and decided I could overcome my allergies through a vigorous act of will. If I couldn't overcome them, I could certainly diminish their effects. I closed my eyes to concentrate.

He went to the kitchen, pulled a bottle of vodka out of the freezer and poured some into two glasses.

I said, "I thought I was completely over Libby until I got back to town, but now I have this strong desire to call her, which I know I shouldn't act upon."

He handed me my drink. He said, "You need yoga. Maya is instructing me in Yoga and Buddhism. Guess what else—she's pregnant. We're both very excited. I've decided that being a parent is the most courageous and radical act we can undertake to improve the world."

The black cat bit me. I held my hand and cleared my throat and squinted my burning eyes. I said, "Congratulations. Mind if I lie down? My chest hurts."

I sank to the floor and lay on my back, completely still, hands to my side. I stared at a ceiling stain shaped like a one-armed fetus. A cat vomited in the next room while another scratched in the litter box.

"Breathe deeply," Richard said. "You've got a great corpse pose going there. Becoming a father at fifty seems right to me. That's a good age for male maturity. But there are no guarantees. I have a friend who got a vasectomy at thirty, convinced he'd never want children, especially with his first wife. Then he remarried at forty and got a vasectomy-reversal, a $20,000 procedure with only a 50% success rate. So he did it and it worked, but his son grew up to hate him. They haven't spoken in years. Also—don't worry about Libby. She moved back to New York. Maybe I should have shared that fact earlier. She left a letter in your office mailbox to tell you where you could find your things. Claire, our department assistant, took the letter from Libby, who dropped it off and then told her exactly what the letter said, I'm not sure why."

"What did it say?" I said.

"She didn't say."

One black cat exited the litterbox, shook its front paws, then a new black cat entered, turned around and stared at me while it peed.

"I'm having trouble breathing," I said.

"This is the requisite suffering. Keep your energy focused on emptiness."

One cat sniffed my right ear while another sniffed my left. My eyes and nose were burning, but I didn't blink. I said, "Are you and Maya getting married?"

"Why would we get married?"

My throat was closing up.

Richard said, "Your whole life awaits. New opportunities exist around every failure."

Was he quoting my father to me? I coughed. The two cats backed away from my ears.

Richard said, "Embrace the emptiness and see what emerges around the next corner. As I said at our last department meeting before summer break, I'm planning to resign in December, and the new chair is likely to be an overly-officious bully with unreasonably high standards, and the president has promised layoffs, based on seniority and performance. You might want to keep your eyes open for new opportunities."

"You said this at the last meeting?"

"Yes."

"I wasn't listening." A different cat sniffed my right ear, then licked it with its scratchy tongue. It was a nice sensation. "Libby used to say I was a terrible listener. I remember her saying that."

Richard said, "At the end of this year, Maya and I are leaving the country."

"You're leaving the country?"

"I announced that too. We can't live here if another Bush is elected, as I fear will be the case. We'd prefer not to raise a child in this country regardless. We're thinking Barcelona. Maya will give massages, teach yoga and Buddhism, and I'll be a house-husband, take care of our child, maybe write a novel."

"Do you have more alcohol?"

"Maybe one more drink wouldn't hurt," he said. "Let me say, that's a very accomplished corpse pose you have going there. You're a natural. Yoga and Buddhism could help you, Harold. The first goal is to embrace the suffering. The second goal is to realize the emptiness."

A cat climbed on my chest and sniffed my nose.

"If you need a place after we move to Barcelona, I'll talk to my landlord about you taking this place. Do you like cats? Hemingway said cats will teach you all you need to know about human behavior. He said cats are honest, but humans hide their emotions all the time."

I closed my eyes. Another cat was scratching in the litter, and a fresh wave of shit came sailing across the floor at nose-level. I put my palms on my face and coughed.

"Embrace it," Richard said. "You're doing very well."

The following morning, August 7th, our first day of classes, I went to my campus mailbox, found Libby's letter, took it to my office, and cut it open with a pair of scissors. It was a handwritten note. She'd provided the address of the storage facility where she'd taken my clothes and my few possessions. And she added this: "I paid only through the end of July. It would be nice if you reimbursed me. I hope you're managing your grief in healthy ways. I'm sure you've tried to call, but I changed my number so I could manage my own grief more properly. I've arrived at a point now where I would not be entirely averse to talking (preferably between 7-8 p.m., Mon-Thurs), especially if you are thinking of hurting yourself or someone else. L."

She left her new number. I looked at the pair of scissors I held and thought of hurting myself or someone else. I picked up my office phone to call her and tell her that I had, in fact, just now experienced this thought after reading that she'd been so certain I had tried to call her, an action I had taken great pains to avoid. I dialed the first eight digits of her number. I hung up and stared at the phone. By the time I looked at the clock again, I discovered my first composition class had started without me. I walked down the hall, down three flights of stairs, down another hall and entered the wrong room. I apologized to Ms. Osborne and to her students, all of whom seemed excited by the interruption. I went to the room next door, without a syllabus and without a book. I faced fifty eyes from twenty-five heads. I realized something strange. I was not sweating, nor was I on the verge of sweating.

I said, "Good morning."

I sat on the front table, feet dangling, and I looked across all the blank faces facing me. I said, "I'm happy that you all are here. I congratulate you for getting past the challenges you've already faced, big and small, that conspired against your being here today. I applaud you for enduring the loss and trauma you have already experienced and I respect the courage you will demonstrate as you keep moving toward your goals in the face of inevitable conflict. I'm happy to be here myself, albeit somewhat tardy. I have no syllabus to give you. And no excuses to hand you. I'll probably have a partial syllabus on Wednesday, but I make no promises. Today, we're going to talk about why we're here and how we think about thinking. We're going to talk about who we are and who we can become." I paused. I said, "First, let me tell you the story of how I came, this summer, to meet the work of Viktor Frankl. And then—oh, this will be fun—I'll give you a writing assignment you can bring me on Wednesday that you'll read aloud to your new classmates and confidantes."

The semester moved more quickly than any other. Richard moved in with Maya and left his cats. I opened windows, bought four more litterboxes, a case of Lysol, took daily antihistamines, and learned to live with puffy eyes and inflamed sinuses and a condition that felt like a constant cold. The cats and I started talking. I left Libby's letter on the dresser and looked at the number every time I passed. I asked the cats if I should call her. I asked the cats what would become of us when Richard left the country and I lost my job. They said, "Feed us." They said, "Love us." They said, "Can't it be enough to know that you are needed?"

I spent more time preparing for classes and more time responding to students' writing, which meant the work kept piling up and the likelihood of my finishing it kept decreasing. Still, for the first time ever, I enjoyed being in the classroom, and at the end of the semester, my evaluations improved.

Mr. O is kind of awkward, but he makes you not be afraid to talk. I don't even mind going to his class because it helps me remember I should stop listening to my Daddy, who says I should drop out and get a second job. I wrote some things this semester I never thought I'd share with anybody. I doubt I'll make an A, but at least I got some stuff out of my system that was sitting heavy on my heart, and I'm more determined than ever to keep going till I get a diploma I can use to hit my Daddy on the head with.

Once a week through August and September, I called Jude to ask how she was doing. Each time, she offered the same report: she was fine and happy, my grandparents were fine and healthy, her dogs were fine and healthy, and Captain Phil was still breathing. "Fine," she'd say again. "Everything's fine." If Captain Phil was not in the room, she would ask if I'd heard from Buddy, and each time I said *no.*

At the end of September, he finally called to give me his new number and told me to pass it on to my mother in case she ever needed it. We didn't talk long. "Fine," he said. "Doing fine." In the background, I heard a male voice shout, "Kiss my dick, motherfucker!"

"That's Leonard, son of the nun." Buddy said. "Let me call you back in a little bit."

He never did.

In October, Jude told me she'd rented the condo to a divorced ex-convict she met in church, through Father Cletus. I pressed for details, but all she volunteered was that she enjoyed having someone interesting back there to talk to. "I can't wait for you to meet him," she said. "He's had a difficult life, but he's doing well now, and having a quiet place helps him stay on track with his rehabilitation."

In early November, while watching election results unfold, I dialed the first seven digits of Libby's number, then hung up. I wanted to hear her righteous indignation. I wanted to commiserate. I wanted to see if she wanted to leave the country with me.

In mid-November, I called Jude to tell her I was staying in Atlanta for Thanksgiving. I made excuses about wanting to catch up on rest and grading, and I lied about having somewhere to go. I did not reveal my biggest reason for wanting to stay away, which was to avoid Captain Phil, a loud Bush-backer, who would continue to talk about the merits of a military career and insist that I should join the Navy.

Three days later, Jude called to tell me Captain Phil was gone. She'd asked him to move out because his paranoid jealousy over the ex-con had started to resemble Sparky's periodic insanity, and she was too old, she said, to deal with babies.

So I went home for Thanksgiving. The children and grandchildren cooked the food and took it my grandmother's because—as Jude revealed for the first time—Roberta had talked recently of flagging energy. I drove Sparky around the block and back home again. Once, he said, "Harold, you're starting to look old." I agreed with him. The ex-con wasn't in the condo. He'd driven to Florida to visit his sister, who had just gotten out of prison herself after serving a short sentence for breaking and entering, armed robbery, and aggravated assault; apparently she'd broken into her ex-husband's house, and what she'd stolen was the very steak knife she threatened to kill him with, along with her old toaster. "You'll meet him at Christmas," Jude said. "I've already invited him to Christmas dinner."

On Thanksgiving day, Jude said, "Let's give your asshole-father a call. See how he's doing. You call in case the ex-nun answers, then hand me the phone."

He answered on the fourth ring.

I passed the phone to Jude and stood beside her so we could both hear. "Doing fine," Buddy said. "Great to hear from y'all."

In the background, Leonard shouted, "Lick my balls, Snoopy-fuck!"

Buddy said, "We're watching the parade."

Leonard said, "Suck my ass, dick-cunt!"

"Nice," Jude said. "Happy Thanksgiving." She handed me the phone and walked away.

Buddy said, "Let me call you back. Tell everybody I miss them."

On December 23rd, after working all day to submit my final grades of the semester, I started home at seven p.m., when traffic wasn't terrible. With the exhausting semester behind me and with an uncertain year ahead of me, the night looked darker and lonelier than most, so I listened to all of Gram Parsons and Emmylou Harris and started feeling better.

I'd finished reading one hundred essays from students prematurely old because they worked full-time while going to school while raising families while overcoming their own tortured backgrounds of poverty and violence inside broken families who considered college a luxury. Some students might have been best served by repeating courses, but I didn't have the heart to fail anyone. Every essay reminded me how narrowly I had managed to squeeze through high school *and* college, and how lucky I was to have a job reading incoherent freshmen essays, though that job would likely end soon.

Otis Redding got me to Savannah, where I stopped for a six pack, then I put in Vic Chesnutt, who got me home three beers later, at midnight. The dogs—there were just two of them now—recognized me as soon as I stepped from my car, and their barking turned to tail-wagging. I crouched and closed my eyes, buried my nose in their dirty coats.

I drank my fourth beer on the porch, facing the dark marsh and the dark river, and I remembered a time, ten years earlier, where I sat in the same spot, playing a harmonica I imagined might reach the ears of someone in my future who would be less lonely for having heard it.

On my fifth beer, I thought of writing Libby a letter. I had passionate arguments to make about all the conditions I would insist upon in the event that we ever got back together. But I feared a letter would be a waste. She would only retaliate point by point with a book-length letter of her own meant to rationalize her counter-conditions (if she offered any at all), while documenting, in comprehensive detail, all of my deficiencies for which I should seek therapeutic help, and she would close with a warning that if I failed to adjust my thinking, I would definitely be destined to repeat the lives of my parents and end up exactly like them—alone. A tiny part of my mind conceded that her reasoning *would* reveal something that could prevent me from ending up alone. Toward the end of my sixth beer, I decided that I would, over the next few days, write Libby a letter and welcome her response.

I told the dogs good night and I told the river and the marsh and the night air good night, and I went inside to the foldout couch with a strange sensation of rising hope, some of which had to do with knowing my grandmother would come down the dark hall in a few hours and add me to her morning prayers.

Chapter 12
Harold

December 24, 7:35 a.m.

My mother woke me with a song.

It started from the far end of the house and waltzed down the hall: "Hello my baby, hello my honey, hello my ragtime gal!" It moved down the steps into the living room: "Send me a kiss by wire, baby my *heart's* on fire!" I pictured her doing a little dance, carrying a cane like Michigan J. Frog, kicking each foot high. She stopped at the foot of the couch. "If you refuse me, honey you'll lose me, then you'll be left a-lone, oh baby, tele-*phone*, and tell me I'm your *ooooown*." It sounded like she was turning a circle while she sang—I pictured one fist on her hip, the other hand spread wide: "Everybody loves the—everybody loves the—everybody loves the Michigan *Raaaag.*"

She said, "Harold? Are you awake? Lots to do, Harold, lots to do. No time to lie around and feel sorry for ourselves. Let's go save a lost cause and help the helpless. If you ever want to feel better about your own little bit of suffering, you should help the less fortunate. Let's go. Coffee's on the counter."

Ten minutes later, she was driving us downtown through the grey and chilly morning. We passed a few empty stores with For Sale signs in the windows, including the hardware store that had belonged to her second husband, Johnny Tate, which neither of us commented on. We passed the bar I worked in after graduate school, also for sale, deserted, dark and gloomy, a good home for ghosts. She took us through old neighborhoods of abandoned and foreclosed homes, rotting Victorians split into six or eight apartments, some with plywood-covered windows, one blackened from fire, another leaning badly, knocked off its foundation, supposedly a crack house here and a meth house there. She turned down an alley, pulled behind a concrete building and stopped.

"I'll wait here," I said.

"No. You have to help me load some things, and you have to meet

188

Paulski, my new boyfriend and tenant. He's from Massachusetts."

"Boyfriend?"

"His name's Paul, but I can't pronounce his long last name, so I call him Paulski. You can call him *Mr.* Paulski. When he got out of prison, he slept in the rectory greenhouse for awhile—in a lawn chair! Can you believe that? A *lawn* chair!"

"You never told me—why he was in prison?"

"Oh—this and that. Nothing too serious."

She got out of her car, found the right key, unlocked the back of the thrift store and stepped inside. I followed. There were racks of old clothes, a musty smell from the closets of dead people, shelves crammed with china, trophies, microwaves, toys, paperbacks. Jude pointed to the front counter, where a man stood on a ladder, taping a piece of paper to the wall.

She stepped toward the ladder quietly, almost tip-toeing, then stopped and yelled his name. Her voice would've made most people jump, maybe fall and break a neck, but he didn't flinch. He tore a final piece of tape and applied it to his sign.

He said, "What? You trying to scare the holy fucking hell out of somebody? Huh? You trying to get somebody's fucking neck broke? Is that it?"

"Watch your language, Paulski. I brought my son to meet you. He's liable to think you're a dangerous ex-con."

On the bottom rung, he said, "Holy fucking hell. Your son's here? The professor? Christ-almighty, you should have fucking said something already."

He smiled at me then, moved his Scotch Tape from his right hand to the left, then extended his hand for shaking. We were about the same height and had similar builds, but he made constant little jittery movements, even with his eyes. He set his tape on the counter, pulled his cigarettes from his shirt pocket, looked at Jude, then back to me, shifting from one foot to the other and back to the first.

"Your mother," he said. He lit his cigarette, inhaled, wiped his thumb across his nose and pointed at me. "She's alright, your mother. A little crazy, maybe, but she's alright. Might be the nicest woman I ever met, come to think of it." He pinched his nose and laughed without any sound coming out, then sniffed loudly and shifted his weight from foot to foot.

"Stop it," Jude said. "You're just trying to flatter me so I'll lower your rent. Are my food boxes ready?"

"Didn't I say they'd be ready? I told you they'd be ready and they're ready. I had to do it all by myself too because no-fucking-body else around here's worth a fucking shit, you know, but I got it done. I guess you want me to load them for you too?"

"Harold will help."

He took long strides across the room, raising his cigarette to his lips, and Jude followed. I read the sign he'd taped to the wall, a note written in orange crayon: "*Dear whoever: I know your talking about me so you better cut it out or I'll kill you.*"

In the rear corner of the store, Jude laughed like she'd heard the funniest joke in history. She said, "Stop it, you fool."

By the time I got back there, he passed by me, carrying two boxes filled with canned food and small presents, wrapped, cigarette hanging from his mouth. I loaded one box and Paul loaded two more. He closed Jude's trunk, dropped his cigarette in the alley and stepped on it. Then he opened Jude's car door for her and smiled.

"What a gentleman you are," she said.

"Merry Christmas, Harold," he said. "You keep your mother honest, now. She needs some help sometimes."

"Don't we all, Paulski?" she said. "I'll let you know about Christmas dinner."

"Whatever is fine by me," he said. "Let me know if you need any help with anything."

Jude drove away. She said, "Isn't he charming?"

"Why," I asked again, "was he in prison?"

"Oh, just a minor little domestic altercation of some sort involving an ex-wife where he happened to punch a couple of cops. He confessed to being high on cocaine at the time, which didn't help of course, but he swears he hasn't had any drugs since then. He's a recovering alcoholic too. He says the condo is perfect for him. It helps him stay out of trouble."

I didn't know what to say to this right away, so I didn't say anything.

"Have some more coffee," Jude said.

I did. She drove slowly down an old street full of potholes and crumbling asphalt, and stopped at the back entrance of the government housing units surrounded by a tall black fence. She looked at a note she'd written. She said, "One box goes to 113, and one goes to 146. Ring the doorbell and tell them it's from St. Sebastian. Don't dawdle."

I took the boxes and put them on the peoples' stoops, but I didn't ring their bells. It was still a little early, and I didn't want to wake anyone. I also didn't want people to confuse me with the more powerful giver who is owed endless thanks by the less powerful taker.

When I got back to the car, I said, "So this guy has a violent history? A wife-beater?"

Jude drove deeper into the southside. "He says he never touched her, and I believe him. Apparently, she went a little crazy one night while she was also on cocaine, or maybe she was already crazy, or maybe he drove her crazy, who knows? But they had an argument, things got out of hand, cops were called, cops were punched. Then while he was in prison, she burned down their trailer, and while the trailer was burning, apparently, she sat behind the wheel of his truck and blew her brains out with a shotgun. He still drives the truck, which feels a little creepy inside. At least it did the couple times he drove me to Winn Dixie. Kind of eerie, you know? Gave me the willies being inside of it. I don't think I'll get into his truck again."

She stopped in front of a long row of shotgun shacks and looked at her piece of paper. She pointed to a pink house whose porch was wrapped in Christmas lights. "And for your information, his staying in the condo is not all pity and charity. In exchange for rent, he keeps up my place and Mom and Dad's place and Mary and Carol's place. He's a self-taught horticulturist. You know those azaleas out back? He practically raised them from the dead, and then carved a swan into the middle of them. *He* says it's a swan. It looks more like a duck to me, but I complimented his swan. He has lots of landscaping ideas."

I kept staring at her.

"What?" she said. "I'm not going to *marry* him, for God's sake."

I took the box to the porch and came back. Jude drove through the end of town beneath the long limbs of the live oaks stretching over the streets, dripping with long strands of moss, a beautiful sight in late December. She moved toward Highway 17 and the Jekyll Island bridge.

"He's had a hard life," she said. "His parents are dead. Actually, they've been missing for a long time, though he says they'd never talked much anyway, and he's got no one else in his life except a deadbeat son in Massachusetts who only calls when he needs money. I was thinking I might invite him to our own little Christmas dinner at my house, since we won't have the normal thing this year."

We'd crested on top of the bridge, sun shining softly on all the marsh and water below, then coasted down the other side, past the Jekyll Island entrance and continued down Hwy 17.

"Why wouldn't we have the normal thing this year?" I said.

"Have you had more coffee yet?" She turned down a narrow dirt road and drove between deep ditches and thick woods.

"Tell me," I said. "Is there a family scandal going on?"

"Yes. You're adopted."

I kept staring at her.

"That *would* be funny though, wouldn't it?"

I stared, waiting. The dirt road was long and straight, and she was going slow.

"I didn't want to tell you until you got home, which is what I normally do, as you know, tell you everything at once, plus I'm sure I would've lost my composure on the phone."

"Tell me."

"Both Sparky and Roberta are in the hospital, but they're supposed to both come home today. Sparky went in three days ago, and Roberta went in a day later, which is weird, like she let go and collapsed from exhaustion as soon as he went in. Sparky's heart is failing and Roberta's lungs are gone. What we *are* sure of, is that Roberta wants them both at home. She's lost a lot of strength and she's on oxygen, but yesterday, when the doctor bent down to ask how she was feeling, she grabbed his tie and pulled him down toward her mouth. Her eyes were just little slits, but they were strong, and she told him, she said, 'I'm ready to die now, but I'm going home to do it.' When the doctor stood back up, he had water in his eyes, and all he could do was give her a little nod. Mary and Carol and me were watching, and we all just lost it and started sobbing, but Roberta stayed strong. Sparky, meanwhile, keeps seeing his mother beside his bed. He calls out for her in a whisper and sometimes reaches his hand out for her. Other times, he calls for Roberta."

At the end of the dirt road, she stopped in the driveway of a clapboard tin-roof house, plastic over the windows, tires on the roof, a junked car in the center of the yard surrounded by pink toys.

She said, "They get the last two boxes."

I took the boxes from the trunk and set them on the porch, then hurried back to the car, feeling like a burglar.

Jude turned the car around and started back down the long dirt road. I said, "Why didn't you tell me?"

"I just told you why I didn't tell you."

"What else do you need to tell me?"

"Just three other things."

"*Three* other things."

"I guess you'll see, in your Aunt Carol's yard, a For Sale sign. She's decided she wants to live in an apartment complex in town, close to a grocery store so she'll never have to drive, which I can partly understand. Your Aunt Mary, meanwhile, might move to Texas with a man she met at the Waffle House who claims to own a horse ranch there. I met him, and he *is* nice, but I warned her, I said, fools rush in. People never listen though, when they think they're in love. You ever notice that?"

We got on Hwy. 17 again and headed back toward the Jekyll Island bridge.

"What else?" I said.

"I'm not doing so great myself, money-wise. The property taxes went way up this year because we got rezoned as part of the subdivision, and I haven't worked since July, when Bruce said he would give me one more final chance to divorce Phil and marry him. So I told him no, again, and thought it best to resign immediately, which wasn't a pretty scene at all, poor guy, but I should've ended it a long time ago, way before Captain Phil showed up. So I'm not sure what I'm going to do. I'm not sure what'll happen to Roberta and Sparky's place or Carol and Mary's place or whether I can even hold on to my place. On top of all that—this last thing is really nothing, so don't worry, okay?"

I looked at her and waited. It felt like my chest was taking on water.

"I'm waiting for a few test results. I'd been having some chest pains for awhile, so I finally went in to see Dr. Maggie—you remember Dr. Maggie? You went to school with her daughter at St. Sebastian—what was her name? She was a pretty girl and has turned out to be a pretty woman with two very pretty daughters. Dr. Maggie showed me all the latest pictures while I was getting my tests. She lives on St. Simons in a pretty house with a pretty husband—Maggie's daughter, I mean. What was her name?"

"Melissa," I said quickly, to encourage Jude to get on with it

"Melissa," Jude repeated, happy to know the name. "She owns a dance studio on the island, and is apparently—"

"Please," I said. "What about the tests?"

"The EKG showed some kind of abnormality, but Maggie assures me it's a normal abnormality, and she gave me some medicine and took some other tests and told me to come back in a week. Which might be tomorrow. What's today?"

"Tomorrow's Christmas."

"Day after tomorrow, then. Maybe you could go with me if you want. No big deal."

I told her I would.

"It's probably nothing," she said. "I hope it's nothing, anyway."

She paused while we went up the bridge. I looked at her.

"I think that's all the news I have. That's enough news to dump on you all at once, isn't it, on top of the stuff you're already going through? I'm very sorry. It comes in streaks doesn't it? And things change, don't they? Eventually. It may be a hard stretch, but we'll help each other carry our crosses, which is what this life is all about after all, isn't it? You okay?"

We crested at the top of the bridge and seemed to hover there a second just in front of the long strips of light that were shooting down in a fan-shaped pattern.

Jude said, "Isn't that beautiful, though?"

I agreed it was, though I can't remember whether I said so. I can't remember saying anything for quite awhile. I'd already retreated to my fear-furnished cave of denial and detachment, where I usually curled up with an imaginary blanket and waited for forces to have their way with me, though I was thinking already—just that second—I was thinking of a precise moment in the near future when I would summon the necessary strength to bust free of the cave and storm out with raised arms, super-hero-like, determined to control my own destiny and effect some radical change on behalf of everyone who needed help. That's what I was think-ing. Or imagining. I imagined taking dramatic actions to alter the trajectory of every tragic event determined to collide with a loved one. And to prove people (Libby) wrong for laughing at the thought of me doing so. I imagined myself like this and liked it.

When we got home, Jude called Mary to make sure Roberta and Sparky were still on schedule to be released. Mary said they'd be home in a couple hours, maybe more—after paperwork and discharge instructions—precious hours lost to fluorescent lights and white walls and beeping machines and smiling nurses carrying clipboards and pens.

Jude asked if I'd help carry all her outside potted plants to the glassed-in porch because Josh, her ex-nephew-in-law, had frightened her with a freeze-warning. I insisted I would do it all myself—it was cold and windy and grey, and Jude wore only a Hill's Heating and Air windbreaker, which was not enough. From the shed, I excavated a rusty red wagon and pulled it across the yard, telling her again that I would do it so she would go inside and get warm.

But she hugged herself with one arm and pointed with the other toward a geranium I lifted into the wagon, then I pulled the wagon to another group of potted plants and lifted them.

While we were loading our second wagon-full, we saw the dogs lift their heads and cock their ears toward the road, and when we looked up, we saw an old black truck coming our way with a U-Haul trailer attached to it.

"I wonder who that could be," Jude said.

Sister Agnes, the landfill mutt, barked with Father Cletus, but they were also wagging their tails. Buddy turned off his rattling truck and stepped out, a little wobbly, as if he were stepping off a boat. He squatted to pet Agnes with both hands, then walked toward us, tilting sideways.

He said, "What's for lunch?"

He put his arm around my shoulder and squeezed it. He said, "I came as quickly as I could. I thought you might need some help getting these plants in."

Jude said, "Did the ex-nun kick you out?"

"I was too religious for her." He stepped toward Jude, who was hunched with cold, feet together, knees bent, hands buried in her armpits.

Buddy said, "I'm going to give you a hug now if that's okay."

"Hurry," she said.

After the hug, he cupped his hands on her shoulders. He stared at her as if measuring how she'd coped with the time he'd been away. He said, "Any idea where a homeless fella might find a bed for just one night?"

"Not around here, I don't. The condo's occupied."

He looked toward the marsh, seemingly unsurprised at his luck. "I don't mean to be a burden. I'm fixing to move to Palm Beach anyway. Figure I'll retire there."

"What happened to your mouth?" Jude said.

"I lost my teeth. Left them in a diner, I think, then somebody stole them. I went back to all the diners I'd been to, asking people if they'd seen any teeth lying around or if they'd seen anybody wearing my teeth, but all I got was a bunch of crazy looks."

Jude looked at him.

"Like that one. But I'm here now, even though I spent four hours getting through Philadelphia, got lost in D.C., had a blow out in Richmond, ran out of gas in Fayetteville, drove through a hail storm in Florence and fell asleep at the wheel, for just a second, in Savannah, which is where I figured I better stop for the night—slept in a rest area. But I'm here now, along with my swollen prostate and minor hemorrhoid trouble and a bit of chest pain."

"Such a heroic journey," Jude said.

"Where's Captain Phil?"

"I shipped him off. You can have Roberta's bed and Harold can have the couch. In exchange for your free lodging, you can help Harold move the plants to the porch. I have to go inside now."

"Of course," Buddy said. "I'm an old hand at moving plants."

Jude hurried into the house, and I pulled the wagon toward a dozen more potted plants.

Buddy said, "Son, see if you can finish up while I go pee." He took a step away and turned around again. "I'm sorry about your grandparents. It comes in streaks doesn't it?"

"How'd you know about them?"

"Your mother called me a couple nights ago. She was pretty shaken up about everything. She told me not to come, said she just wanted to talk a minute, but I told her I'd be here as soon as I could. Hey—is that the little red wagon I gave you a long time ago that I used to pull you around in?"

196

"I don't remember you ever pulling me around in a wagon."

"I guess that's not the one, then."

Buddy climbed the porch steps toward the kitchen, stopping to pet Agnes, whose wagging tail thumped against the porch. He said, "I missed you too, ol' girl."

I filled the rest of the wagon, pulled it around the corner to the porch, unloaded it, then made three more trips, by myself. When I finished, I stepped inside and found my mother and father sitting on opposite ends of the couch, facing the television, which was not on.

Buddy said, "You'll have to sit in the middle, son. I just found out that my old recliner has been donated to the charity-case in the condo."

"It smelled," Jude said. "It had that old-man smell soaked into it."

"That was Captain Phil's fault," Buddy said. "He couldn't help it. Men start stinking a little more when they get old. That's what my ex-nun told me."

I sat between them. We faced the blank television. Jude held her phone in her lap, waiting for Mary to call with news that they'd made it home. Buddy reached toward some papers stacked on the corner table.

"Don't touch those," Jude said.

He pulled his hand back.

"Look at the one on top," she said. "It's my annual card from Uncle O, with a poem."

Buddy reached for it and read it. "It's plagiarized." He passed it to me.

"Terrible penmanship," I said. It was signed, "Love always, O." The poem spoke of undying love, loneliness, lost time and missed chances. He'd rhymed December with burning ember. It wasn't awful.

"I sure can pick 'em," Jude said.

"Me too," Buddy said.

We sat in silence a moment, staring at the blank television. My phone rang, an unusual occurrence. I dug it out of my pocket and stared at it while it rang.

"Who is it?" Jude said.

It kept ringing. I said, "It's Libby."

"Answer it," Jude said.

I didn't answer it.

"Let me take it," Buddy said.

It stopped ringing.

"Call her back," Buddy said. "I bet she's calling to wish you a merry Christmas. People get sentimental this time of year. Except for my latest ex, the ex-nun. She doesn't care much about Christmas. She said if she never saw another Christmas, it would be too soon. I don't think she'll be calling."

My phone's voicemail made a sound, but I was in no hurry to listen to the message.

Jude said, "Listen to the message, Harold."

Buddy said, "Guess what a cup of coffee costs in New Jersey. You'll never guess."

"Four dollars?" Jude said.

"Have you been there?"

"It was a guess. Did you find a job there?"

"Where's the remote?" he said.

"Under my thumb," she answered. "You don't want to talk about it? That's fine if you don't want to talk about it. Let's see if something festive is on television like *It's a Wonderful Life*. Check your phone, Harold." Jude turned on the television, lowered the volume, and started changing channels.

I held my phone. I considered deleting the message without listening to it.

"Yes," Buddy said. "I found a couple jobs and I quit a couple jobs. The last one I had was with the Sears Bug Brigade."

"How long did that last?" Jude said.

"Three days. I had to go through a week's worth of training—just to learn how to kill a bug—and on the third day, I saw this group of guys standing with my supervisor in a circle, and they were all laughing, so when I walked up to join them, I discovered they'd been laughing at *me*. They were saying I was strange and didn't fit in. Which I already knew. My ex-nun had already told me I was strange and didn't fit in. So here I am, back in south Georgia, getting ready to start all over again from scratch one more time."

I looked at my screen. I did not listen to the message.

Buddy said, "But don't be thinking I'm going to move in with you and stay here forever."

"Okay," Jude said.

"Don't be getting your hopes up."

"Alrighty."

"I have no intention of moving in."

"Okay."

"Unless you want me to. I will if you insist. But maybe just long enough for me to weigh some options, decide what's next. I've been thinking I might call my former Miss America, give her one more chance to see if she wants to get married."

Jude flipped through the channels. I looked at my phone. I pressed the voicemail button and listened to the message.

Buddy said, "Go back."

Jude said, "What?"

"Go back to that movie you just passed."

Jude turned back to the classic movie channel.

Libby said, "Please give me a call as soon as you can. I'd like to talk." Her voice was soft. It was soft and inviting and vulnerable. She may have had a cold.

"I'm *in* this movie," my father said.

"I'm sure," Jude said.

"It's called *The Swan*, starring Grace Kelly, filmed at the Biltmore Estate in Asheville in 1955. I was fifteen, and they had a big casting call, so I showed up with a few thousand others and the director liked my looks. Right after that, I was in *Days of Thunder* with Robert Mitchum."

"Can I turn it now?"

Buddy said, "My role was to hold the reins of a horse that was attached to the Queen's carriage. That was my role."

Jude said, "Harold, what did Libby's message say?"

"She said to call her."

"Are you going to call her? Maybe you should call her."

"No," I said. "Maybe." The letter I'd thought of writing last night seemed a better idea so I could make more sense of what I wanted to say.

"Let me call her," Buddy said. "I'd like to see if she's forgiven me yet."

Jude said, "Harold, make some popcorn."

Grace Kelly appeared to be playing a princess who was in the process of breaking the heart of a poor professor.

"She loves him," Jude said. "But he's too poor. Same old story."

"I think my big scene is coming up," Buddy said.

Grace Kelly told the poor professor that their union would be impossible.

"Or maybe we've missed it," he said.

"Are you sure this is the right movie?" Jude said. "I don't remember you ever saying anything about co-starring with Grace Kelly."

"It's not my fault you can't keep up with all of my movie roles."

"Harold?" Jude said. "Are you going to make some popcorn?"

"I can't eat popcorn with no teeth," Buddy said. "What's for lunch?"

"There will be food next door. And a lot more coming I suppose. But *I'd* rather have popcorn. Harold, are you going to make popcorn?

Grace Kelly looked the poor professor in the eyes, prepared to break bad news.

"I'm tired," Buddy said. "I haven't slept very well for a few years."

"Me too," Jude said, "Wake me up when you make your grand entrance."

"Harold?" Buddy said. "Wake me up when I make my grand entrance."

Grace Kelly offered a long speech to the poor professor about their doomed love. Buddy started snoring. Jude breathed deeply. The poor professor limped out of the room, wounded, and then The Prince walked in, wearing a thin mustache. Grace Kelly and The Prince went to the balcony and talked of how they knew they were right for each other all along. Jude's head fell off her hand, then she put it back and went to sleep again. Buddy's snoring grew deeper. Grace Kelly and The Prince locked arms and turned to go back in. The orchestra swelled, red curtains came together, and the credits started rolling. I read every name I could, breathing very softly and remaining very still so I wouldn't wake my parents.

I thought of calling Libby. I imagined how a conversation might go. Based on her tone of voice, she might talk of how being alone through the holidays (except for her parents) was making her sad. She might say she had done a lot of thinking over the past six months and had arrived at some conclusions that could, with certain conditions, result in a reunion. She might ask me to come to New York City for New Year's Eve.

Buddy snored. Jude's head fell off her hand, and she righted it again.

Jude's phone rang and made us all jump. It was Mary, saying Roberta and Sparky were home. We walked over, the three of us. I kept my hands in my pockets, one hand on my phone, though I did not look at it. We found Roberta and Sparky arranged in the living room in their hospital beds, side by side. Roberta smiled beneath her oxygen mask when she saw me. She lowered the mask to her neck. She held her hand up for me to take hold of, rattling the rosary wrapped around her wrist, and whispered to me in a raspy voice. She said, "Hello, honey. How do I look?"

I told her she looked beautiful, and I bent to kiss her on the lips.

She said, "Forgive yourself, and you will be forgiven. We must forgive ourselves and each other too." Then she winked at me.

Buddy stepped beside me. He said, "Hello gorgeous. Can I have this bed when you're done with it?"

"I'm glad you're home," she told him. "My people go away sometimes, but they always come back."

"I'm happy to have a place to come to," he said, and he sounded like this was the most sincere thing he would ever say. His voice even quaked a little. Jude stepped beside him and slapped his shoulder.

She said, "Mom, did you know Buddy starred in a movie with Grace Kelly?"

"I always liked Grace Kelly," Roberta said.

I went around to Sparky's bed and looked down at him. His eyes popped open, surprisingly bright and blue and innocent, and with his white hair standing up, he looked like a very serious little boy. He said, "Mama?"

"It's Harold," I said.

"Who are those people climbing in the window?" he said.

"I don't see them," I answered.

"Is it time to go home?"

"Not yet," I told him.

"Tell me when."

I said I would.

Jude and Mary went to the kitchen to talk, and Buddy followed to find a biscuit. Someone else came in the back door, maybe Carol. My cousins followed, carrying food. Their children ran into the living room with devices pointed at their eyes, veering around the hospital beds as if they'd always been there, then plopped themselves on the far couch. Uncle Sludge came in, removed his hat, and said "Hey-here" to no one in particular, head pointed down, voice flat. Uncle Hammer entered five minutes later, removed his hat, and started singing, "How Great Thou Art." Josh, Fuzzy, and Moose sprinkled in through the morning. Bruce Hill came too, and offered Jude a hug. They all bent to kiss Roberta's head and touched her hand, and each time someone stepped around to Sparky, he said, "Mama?"

Paulski came too, bringing a pan of macaroni and cheese, which he told me contained a tablespoon of red pepper, three kinds of cheese, bread crumbs spread on top, browned and crispy. A baby cried from the kitchen.

Sparky said, "Roberta?"

She said, "I'm right here, honey."

Uncle Hammer sang softly, "A Closer Walk with Thee." Uncle Sludge wiped his cheeks. Sparky called for Roberta and Roberta answered him. The children looked up from their games and registered the color of the music. The other men sat with their heads bowed, hands folded between their knees. The women arranged things in the kitchen. Jude told Buddy not to eat all the biscuits. Lois held her baby and said at least it wasn't as hot as it was last Christmas, but Linda disagreed that it was hot last year, and no one else seemed to remember too well for sure.

Sparky called for Roberta and Roberta answered him.

I reached into my pocket and felt my phone.

Uncle Hammer sang and Uncle Sludge wiped his cheeks. Buddy followed the women into the living room, where he sang loudly and deeply the background parts that echoed Uncle Hammer's soft words, which now swelled with the voices of the women joining in, sounding like a well-trained choir whose voices meant to float through the roof and travel the skies, clinging to clouds that carried them across the continent.

I pulled out my phone and stepped outside, thinking I'd call Libby. I walked to the river. A cool breeze blew against my face and the grey sky matched the grey moss that swung from the oaks. I stood in the spot where my grandfather had done so much of his fishing. I looked out at the high water, which had already crested and was just now beginning to move back out. A hundred yards to my right, two ducks followed each other in a circle. Past them, a fish jumped. Past the fish, on the far point in front of my mother's house, eight pink cranes occupied the top of a dead tree.

I stared at my phone. I stared for a solid minute, maybe longer.

I imagined another conversation with Libby. Based on the tone of her message, it sounded like she might be willing to listen for as long as I wanted to talk about how I was managing my grief. She might coax me into elaborating. She might say, very softly, that she was sorry. She might say we could manage our grief more properly together and for some time to come. She might say, under the right conditions, that children could save us.

A cool wind came across the marsh, bringing salt and mud and something primordial I could not name. I turned to look at my grandparents' house. Through the living room window, I saw everyone huddled around my grandparents' beds, mouths moving in unison. Again, I faced the water. I looked at my phone. I turned it off and slid it into my pocket. And then I turned and walked toward the house to join my family, me with no talent for singing, ignorant of the words.

Matthew Deshe Cashion was born in North Wilkesboro, North Carolina, and grew up in Brunswick, Ga. He earned a master of fine arts degree from the University of Oregon. His first novel, *How the Sun Shines on Noise,* was published by Livingston Press, in conjunction with the University of West Alabama. The novel was a finalist, among 400 manuscripts, in the 2003 William Faulkner Creative Writing Competition co-sponsored by The Pirate's Alley Faulkner Society and The Mary Freeman Wisdom Foundation based in New Orleans, La. His story collection, *Last Words of the Holy Ghost*, won the Katherine Anne Porter Prize in Short Fiction in 2015. He has worked (in this order): on a tobacco farm, as a short-order cook, in fast-food, at a video store, in an airport tollbooth, as a door-to-door environmental fundraiser, at a chemical plant (now an EPA super-fund site), in construction, as an AM disc jockey, as a waiter, as a third-shift convenience store clerk, as a blood donor (part-time), and as a bartender. He has also been an AP award-winning journalist, and he has taught literature and fiction writing at the University of North Carolina at Charlotte and Mitchell Community College, in Statesville, North Carolina. He now teaches at The University of Wisconsin, La Crosse, where he is the faculty advisor for *Steam Ticket*, a student-run literary journal.